"Don't you miss having someone special to talk to late at night?"

Nick asked, his thumb brushing across her knuckles. "Or miss just knowing that someone is there for you if you need them? Somebody who cares?"

"What I don't miss is wondering when he'll leave," Marianne said tartly. "My husband walked out on me, but I kept the best part of the marriage—my son, Clay."

Nick's fingers stilled. He must have misunderstood. He'd thought she was a dyed-in-the-wool career woman.

"You have a child?" he repeated.

"A teenager," she corrected, smiling at his surprise. She turned her wrist until their palms touched. "I wasn't being coy the other night, Nick. My schedule is hectic. With Clay around, I'm seldom at loose ends."

Reluctantly, Nick let her remove her hand from his. *A child.* Could he make room in his heart to love another child?

Dear Reader,

Welcome to Silhouette **Special Edition** . . . welcome to romance. Each month, Silhouette **Special Edition** publishes six novels with you in mind—stories of love and life, tales that you can identify with— romance with that little "something special" added in.

This month, Silhouette **Special Edition** has some wonderful stories in store for you, including the finale of the poignant series SONNY'S GIRLS, *Longer Than . . .* by Erica Spindler. I hope you enjoy this tender tale! *Annie in the Morning* by Curtiss Ann Matlock is also waiting for you in September. This warm, gentle, emotional story is chock-full of characters that you may well be seeing in future books. . . .

Rounding out September are winning tales by more of your favorite writers: Jo Ann Algermissen, Christine Flynn, Lisa Jackson and Jennifer Mikels! A good time will be had by all!

In each Silhouette **Special Edition** novel, we're dedicated to bringing you the romances that you dream about—the type of stories that delight as well as bring a tear to the eye. And that's what Silhouette **Special Edition** is all about—special books by special authors for special readers!

I hope you enjoy this book and all of the stories to come.

Sincerely,

Tara Gavin
Senior Editor

JO ANN ALGERMISSEN
Family Friendly

Silhouette Special Edition

Published by Silhouette Books New York

America's Publisher of Contemporary Romance

SILHOUETTE BOOKS
300 East 42nd St., New York, N.Y. 10017

FAMILY FRIENDLY

Copyright © 1991 by Jo Ann Algermissen

ISBN: 0-373-09692-5

First Silhouette Books printing September 1991

JO ANN ALGERMISSEN

lives near the Atlantic Ocean, where she spends hours daydreaming to her heart's content. She remembers that, as a youngster, she always had "daydreams in class" written on every report card. But she also follows the writer's creed: write what you know about. After twenty-five years of marriage, she has experienced love—how it is, how it can be and how it ought to be. Mrs. Algermissen has also written under a romanticized version of her maiden name, Anna Hudson.

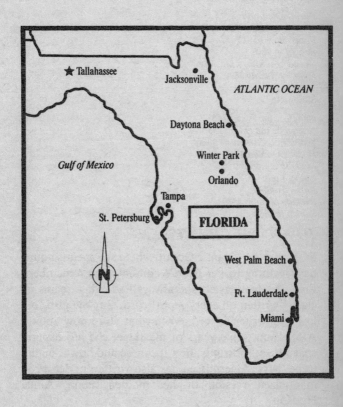

Chapter One

"Talent Plus—temporary employment agency," Gregory Bennigan said, his eyes following the direction of Nick King's steady gaze. He nudged Nick in the ribs, wiggled his shaggy blond eyebrows comically and added in a hushed tone, "Marianne Clark is probably one of the reasons King Enterprises is doing so well in Orlando."

Curious as to what correlation his accountant could possibly see between a temporary employment agency and the success of a company that distributed sports equipment and operated health centers, Nick succinctly asked, "Why?"

"Believe me, the mere thought of Marianne's talented little fingers pecking away on my typewriter is enough to make *this* ninety-pound weakling start pumping iron and buying cases of jogging shoes."

Nick chuckled. "You'd better forget the Nautilus equipment and concentrate on the jogging shoes. You and Beth have only been living together for a week. If she heard what you just said, she'd—"

"Race my skinny butt right down the church aisle?" Gregory supplied, nodding and returning his client's wide grin. "Uh-uh! Beth moved in with me. I didn't move in with her. When she starts humming 'The Wedding March' she can move out. You and I are two birds of a feather—strictly noncommittal when it comes to women."

Nick kept quiet, but silently denied Gregory's claim. Seven years, he thought. Was that how long it took to start getting over tragedy? Had time numbed the anguish he had felt over the loss of his five-year-old daughter and the subsequent breakup of his marriage?

He inhaled sharply as Marianne Clark glanced in his direction. Her vivid green eyes were lit with laughter as she smiled at Gregory. She waved, then turned back to the elderly woman earnestly speaking to her.

"Forget her," Gregory advised. "She's turned down dinner invitations from half the men who attend these chamber of commerce shindigs. Marianne is in love with Talent Plus." Scratching his smooth jaw speculatively, he added, "But then again, her elusiveness may be one of the reasons Marianne is so appealing to confirmed bachelors. I wouldn't mind latching on to a career woman who is not the least bit interested in filing a joint tax return."

Nick's dark eyes strayed from Gregory back to the redheaded woman wearing the forest-green suit and wide-brimmed straw hat. He took Gregory's line of reasoning a step further. A woman who wasn't interested in a joint return wouldn't be interested in filing tax deductions for children, either. He could see himself caring for another woman, but never would he allow himself to love another child.

"Are you one of the men she turned down?" Nick asked, his curiosity growing.

"Nope. She's not my type. I prefer a woman who can't balance a bank statement, much less compile a computerized spreadsheet."

Nick skeptically raised one eyebrow. "For someone who claims to be uninterested, you sure know a hell of a lot about her."

"King Enterprises may be my biggest account, but it's not my only client."

"Talent Plus is your client, too?"

"Yep," Gregory boasted. "That's why I know that particular redheaded ball of fiery ambition isn't the right woman for you. You may have the same C.P.A., but you don't have anything else in common with her. She's cerebral . . . you're physical. All she thinks about is fitting the right person into the right job. All you think about is fit bodies. Just imagining the two of you together brings up an image in my mind of round pegs and square holes." As though to clinch his argument, he leaned close to Nick's ear and whispered, "She's the kind of woman who thinks the Miami Dolphins live at Sea World."

"So you wouldn't recommend that I make her acquaintance?"

"Nope. Not unless your male ego needs deflating."

"I don't suppose you'd care to introduce me to Marianne Clark, would you?"

"You think you can score where every other man here has failed?" Gregory gibed, chuckling at the idea.

"Maybe." Nick's thoughts hadn't gone beyond meeting an attractive woman. "I won't know unless I ask her, will I?"

"Ten push-ups says she'll turn you down quicker than it takes me to do them."

"No bet."

"Twenty push-ups," Gregory bargained as Nick started to move to where Marianne stood. "With one hand tied behind my back."

Nick shook his head.

"C'mon, Nicholas! Be a sport. Just think of it this way... if I win and she turns up her pert little nose at you, I'm giving you an opportunity to relieve your frustration by dropping down to the floor and giving me twenty."

"Thanks, but no thanks. I'll introduce myself. See you later."

"Good luck, buddy." Jovially he slapped Nick on the back. "You're going to need it."

During the few seconds it took him to maneuver through the crowd, Nick gathered his thoughts and began to formulate a plan of action. Appearances were important. He touched the knot of his tie to make certain it rested squarely between the sharp points of his collar, then smoothed his hands over the lapels of his conservative charcoal-gray suit. Satisfied that he looked presentable, he concentrated on what he'd say to her.

Everyone Nick had met at these chamber of commerce functions attended them to network with other businessmen. It seemed logical to him that discussing business would be the best starting place for phase one of a relationship. She couldn't turn on her heel and evade him if he began their discussion by telling her that King Enterprises employed several secretaries, clerks and receptionists, could she? For good measure he'd also throw in the fact that his company staffed eight health spas and gyms located in several major cities in the South. Surely those tidbits of information would pique her interest.

If phase one worked, Nick mused, he'd immediately advance to phase two—getting to know her personally. He glanced toward Gregory and wondered if his accountant knew more than he'd told him. With Gregory's quirky sense of humor, he might think it funny for Nick to approach a woman in love with another man. Gregory might enjoy seeing him get the royal brush-off.

It surprised Nick when he realized he was actually nervous about introducing himself. He took a deep breath to fortify himself. Ms. Clark might not be interested in Nick King, the man, but she should be interested in Nicholas King, owner of King Enterprises.

As ready as he'd ever be, Nick slowly exhaled, and strode purposefully toward Marianne.

"The chamber of commerce just has to do something about that private parking lot behind the restaurant!" Lila Boynton griped.

Marianne listened to Lila's complaint about the lack of parking spaces on Park Avenue as though it were the first time she'd heard it. Other members of the group avoided the elderly lady because Lila had a reputation for meandering all around a topic without reaching the point she meant to make. Marianne didn't mind. Lila was lonely. Many of the women Marianne placed back in the work force had the same problem.

Besides, Marianne thought, it was better to concentrate on Lila's unsolvable problems than to flirt with danger by returning her surreptitious gaze to the man who stood beside her accountant.

Who is he? Marianne wondered, nodding her head in agreement as Lila paused to take a quick breath. Must be fairly new to the area or she'd have met him while out recruiting new business for Talent Plus. Greg kept glancing at her. Why didn't he bring the stranger over to meet her?

"Yesterday, I wanted to shop at Bebe's Children's Shop for my niece—you remember, Sara, don't you?"

Marianne nodded.

He looked familiar, but she couldn't place him. Since she had always prided herself on her ability to instantly remember names and faces, it bothered her that she couldn't identify him. Not even to herself would she admit that not knowing the most attractive man in the room contributed to her vexation. She felt certain that once she put a name to his face she wouldn't give him a second thought.

"I had to park in the lot behind the train station! Oh dear, I can tell by the expression on your face exactly what you're thinking. That's only a couple of blocks from the shop…that I wouldn't have to spend my hard-earned money to go to that fancy new exercise place if I'd walk more often."

Exercise, Marianne mused, picking up the drift of Lila's conversation. Why did that ring a bell? She grinned. Dumbbells! That was it! The stranger has something to do with the new health gym. She'd made a business call on the manager—a blond, blue-eyed Nordic god who looked nothing like the man she tried to identify.

"...but my dear, I was on my lunch hour! I didn't want to miss the special at the Winter Park Grill—the New Orleans salad." She touched Marianne's arm. "You know, the one with blackened shrimp and chicken."

Shaking her head, but not having the vaguest idea how blackened shrimp had gotten into the conversation, Marianne noticed the peculiar look Lila was giving her. She'd missed a cue. Automatically, Marianne changed the direction of her head movement from side to side to up and down.

"It's served with a honey-mustard dressing," Lila explained, obviously bewildered by Marianne's inattentiveness. "Well, never mind, I guess I was digressing from the parking problem. There I was, in a hurry, looking for a place to park. I must have wasted ten gallons of gasoline driving around and around that parking lot! At least ten times, maybe more..."

Inappropriate though her response was, Marianne's grin broadened as she remembered where she'd seen that man's face. Advertising! During the media blitz for the grand opening of the Winter Park King's Gym, he'd been on the television commercials. His face was plastered on billboards all over Orlando! No wonder he look so familiar.

Lila gave her a sharp nudge, and Marianne jumped.

"I said, my dear, I want you to meet Nicholas King," Lila repeated. The man Marianne had been racking her brain over stood less than a foot away. His large hand reached out to greet her. "Mr. King, this is Marianne Clark—Talent Plus. If you ever need temporary help, she's the one to call. She has a *very* good reputation here in Winter Park."

If he'd been a snake, Marianne thought as she placed her hand in his, she'd have been bitten. She realized she was still grinning up at Nicholas King like some star-struck groupie.

"I'm pleased to meet you, Mr. King," she said, recovering her wits quickly, straightening her face and releasing his hand.

"My pleasure, Ms. Clark." He turned to Lila, lifted her frail hand to his lips with old-world courtliness and said, "I'd like to combine business with pleasure by dancing with Ms. Clark while we discuss her agency. Would you excuse us, please?"

Marianne had heard of elderly women twittering, blushing and being tongue-tied, but she'd have given odds that Lila would never indulge in such a display. And yet, Marianne had to believe her own eyes and ears.

Not only is Nicholas King extremely handsome, she thought, he's utterly charming to elderly women.

"You made her day," Marianne complimented when they were out of Lila's hearing range. At the edge of the dance floor, she removed her hat so that the brim wouldn't poke Nicholas in the chin while they danced. She smiled up at Nicholas. "Your television commercials aren't half-bad, either."

"They're only 'half-bad'?" he asked, liking the teasing lilt in her voice. The thick skein of silky hair that had been caught up in the crown of her hat cascaded down her back. The light fragrance of jasmine lured him closer. He fought the urge to caress her hair and discover if it felt as silky as it looked.

Phase one of his original plan was in immediate danger of being blown straight to hell. "Why not half-good?"

Marianne chuckled. "There are only two kinds of commercials, Mr. King—half-bad and awful. Most of them fall into the latter category, which makes remote control push-button maniacs out of us all."

As unexpectedly as a tropical shower falling from a sunny sky, she moved into his open arms as though dancing with him were a normal daily occurrence. That shocked Marianne. She usually tensed when a man invaded the imaginary circle of privacy surrounding her.

Mr. King is nice to lonely, little old ladies, she rationalized silently. Without the tiniest flicker of gratitude she should have felt, Marianne also noticed that he held her at a socially acceptable distance. Like Lila, Marianne felt twittery on the inside. Her face felt hot. She found she was having difficulty keeping her head from dropping to his muscled chest.

There was some unidentifiable force surrounding Nicholas King as he led her through several intricate dance steps that made her feel totally feminine, completely helpless.

An alarm sounded inside Marianne's head. Helpless and useless were words she'd used interchangeably in the diary she'd kept during and after her marriage.

Her ex-husband had a take-charge-of-the-situation personality. At eighteen, he'd led her around more than a dance floor. And when he'd "outgrown" her, he'd demanded a no-fault divorce.

Marianne stiffened as she recalled the crash course she'd gone through to do some "growing up." It hadn't been easy. Not with minimal work skills and a three-year-old son.

"Did I step on your toes?" Nick asked, aware that she was no longer gracefully following his steps.

"No." To avoid letting him get a glimpse of her inner turmoil she focused her eyes on the thin gray stripes on the burgundy background of his tie.

She was ten years beyond feeling helpless. She had no desire to let destructive emotions dominate her life again.

The orchestra switched from one slow tune to another without missing a beat, prolonging their dance. Marianne wished it would end. She had to think of some excuse to get away, far away from Nicholas King's charisma!

"Tell me about Talent Plus," Nick said. He wanted her to melt against him, to let the music work its magic, but he sensed her desire for the dance to end quickly.

"Talent Plus matches women who need work with employers who need workers."

"So you're a matchmaker?" Nick teased, hoping to amuse her. "Like the star of *Hello, Dolly*?"

"The principle of supply and demand is the same," she admitted, swallowing a soft chuckle. "Only the motivation factors are different. The majority of our clients are motivated by a drawer filled with unpaid bills."

"And the others?"

She shrugged. "There are probably as many different reasons for a woman to become a temp as there are jobs available."

"Such as?"

"High school graduates who don't know what occupation they're interested in. Women whose children have left home. Married women who are bored with housework and want part-time work." Single mothers who have to work to supplement their child-support payments and to maintain their sanity, she added si-

lently. Aloud, she finished the list with "And sometimes they work for mad money."

Look up at me, he silently commanded. "What's
your gimmick?"

"Gimmick?" She raised her head. For an instant
their eyes collided. His were black as sin . . . and every
bit as tempting.

"Every successful person in private business that I've
met has something that sets their business apart from
the competition. There must be a multitude of temporary agencies in the Orlando area. Why should King
Enterprises pick Talent Plus?"

Marianne paused. Her usual canned sales pitch depicted what specific services Talent Plus supplied to an
employer, but it didn't explain her "gimmick." Her
green eyes shone with a passionate fervor as she decided to reveal what she considered to be the real reason behind her success.

"We're family friendly. First, Talent Plus focuses on
a woman's priorities, then we try to eliminate stress
factors that she worries about while she's on the job."
Marianne could feel herself stepping up on a soap-
box—a safe place for a woman overly attracted to the
man who held her loosely in his arms. By the end of the
dance Nick would be yawning in her face! "The workplace was conceived by men, for men. It's okay for a
man to give his wife a peck on the cheek and hurry off
to work. Women don't have that luxury, even in the
supposedly enlightened nineties. The wife has the children, the house, even the dog to worry about before she
goes to work. And when she arrives, she has to deal
with guilt feelings for not being at home. The plus in
Talent Plus is providing what the other agencies
don't—a genuine effort to remove the stress elements

that prevent a woman from being productive on the job.''

Marianne grinned as he stumbled over her toe. Her bluntness had obviously caught him off balance.

"Sorry," he said.

"Is your apology for the working conditions at King Enterprises? Or for mashing my big toe?"

"Stepping on your toe. To the best of my knowledge, my employees are satisfied with their pay, working conditions and fringe benefits."

Marianne had heard the same statement made by scores of businessmen. She couldn't fault them for believing what they said. She just had to show them the error of their ways.

"If the workers aren't on strike and job turnover is lower than ten percent per year, they're satisfied. Right?"

Dodging her question, Nick teased, "Since you've taken the lead, would you mind edging us toward one of those tables? I'd like to sit down and hear more about Talent Plus...without getting elbowed in the back."

"Should I apologize?" she countered cheekily. A gentle pressure on his shoulder followed by a light squeeze of his hand and she had him backing toward a vacant table. When he shook his head, she didn't mind telling him, "I've been practicing the box step with a couple of teenage boys in the neighborhood who want to learn how to dance. I guess leading has become a habit."

The twinkle gleaming in his dark eyes told her that he didn't mind following her footsteps—as long as she led him where he'd planned on going.

Nick pulled out a chair. "Can I get you something to drink?"

"White wine would be nice. Thanks."

"Don't go away. I'll be right back."

Marianne watched him pivot on one foot, then agilely move between the tables like a professional race car driver moving through heavy traffic. She should have been mentally compiling solid reasons why Nicholas King should sign a contract with Talent Plus. But like an observer at the Daytona 500 watching a sleek race car, she was fascinated by his leashed power and strength.

Self-consciously her hands skimmed over her waist, hips and upper thighs. She watched her weight, but she would not have objected to waking up some beautiful morning and discovering that the Good Fairy had shifted a few pounds from one place to another. Until that unlikely event occurred, she was satisfied with her appearance.

As a gymnasium owner, Nick probably had to keep physically fit. She smiled at the thought of King's Gyms' advertising campaign. It would have fallen flatter than a pancake if Nick had had jowls drooping below his grin and a paunch rolling over his waistband. Fitness was his signature trademark.

What was hers? Marianne glanced down at her tailored suit. It projected the image she wanted to create. Professional, but not afraid to be feminine—a professional woman.

"Chilled white wine," Nicholas said as he placed a tall glass in front of her. He held a mug of frothy beer in his hand and seated himself. "While I was waiting in line, I thought about the gyms being user friendly for the women who work there. Exercise is a great stress buster. The managers encourage the employees to use the equipment. In my type of business, is that the kind of thing you meant?''

"It can't hurt."

"But does it help?"

Marianne sipped the wine, savoring its fruity flavor on her tongue, then swallowed. The fact that he'd seriously thought about what they'd discussed flattered her. She was tempted to return the flattery by assuring Nick that allowing his employees to lift dumbbells made his gym family friendly. She couldn't. She had to be true to her own beliefs.

Her eyes met his as she said, "But that's like putting a Band-Aid on a compound fracture. Exercise relieves the symptoms of stress, but I doubt that it eliminates the cause of the stress. Your employee still has the kids, house and dog to worry about."

"Are you implying that for me to have satisfied employees I have to provide day care, housekeeping services and a kennel?"

"That's utopia. Your employees would like it, but from experience I know it's financially infeasible."

Nick raised his voice so Marianne could hear him over the orchestra, which had switched from slow music to a syncopated Latin beat. "Then what are you suggesting?"

"Flexible hours. Counseling. Company sponsored day care for children and elders. Job sharing."

"What?"

Marianne cupped her hands beside her mouth to project her voice. "Two people working the hours you usually schedule for one."

"Let's go outside!" Pointing to his ear, Nick shook his head.

"Why don't I call on you tomorrow?" Marianne stood, removed a business card from her jacket pocket and handed it to Nick. Discussing business on Park Avenue would be as futile as talking over the music in the restaurant. "Two o'clock?"

Nick circled her wrist with his hand. "C'mon. It's my turn to lead."

Several of the younger members had formed a human chain and were performing intricate dance steps. Other couples danced, hip to hip, seeming glued together at the waist. Marianne watched in astonishment. Married couples made similar movements, she mused, in the privacy of their bedrooms.

She silently prayed this wasn't the new dance step she'd promised the boys she'd teach them. The image of her thirteen-year-old son bumping and grinding in total abandon wasn't one she could rubber-stamp Mother Approved!

The next thing she knew, Nick had wrapped his arms around her. "I can't dance to that kind of music!" she protested.

"It's easy. Just follow me." He pocketed her business card. "C'mon."

It was easy. Too damned easy for Marianne's peace of mind. She found herself intimately pressed against Nick, his hands rotating her hips to match the circular motion his hips made. One second she was fastened against him, the next he had her spinning in a dizzy circle, then back into his muscular arms.

Silently she thanked her mother for the dance lessons she'd provided when Marianne was younger. Otherwise, she'd have been making a complete fool of herself by stumbling all over Nick.

Maybe it was Nick's expertise, or maybe it was the primitive rhythm, she didn't know which, but she found herself enjoying the dance. The look of admiration she saw on her partner's face was worth the price of admission to Disney World.

Surprisingly, the dance ended abruptly, too soon for Marianne. Laughing, she asked, "Where'd you learn to dance like that?"

"Television. It's the latest dance craze." Nick followed her back to their table. He picked up both drinks. "Why don't we go out on the terrace where it's cooler?"

After such a burst of exertion the room seemed hot and sticky, and it was filled with smoke. Replacing her hat, Marianne walked beside Nick, his hand lightly guiding her. Outside, she inhaled the honeysuckle-scented air deeply as she looked up at a three-quarter moon hung low in the sky.

"How about you?" Nick inquired. He gave her the wineglass. "You picked up on the steps superquick."

"Dancing lessons." Marianne grimaced. "Tap and ballet, kindergarten through high school. Back then I hated them."

In a hushed voice he confided, "Me, too. Let's keep that private, please."

"Why? Ballet and tap are as strenuous as any more macho sport."

"That's what I told the football players in the locker room." Nick laughed, remembering the noses he'd flattened while defending his masculinity. Nobody called him a sissy, not twice.

"And?"

"I'm also a black belt in the martial arts. Few athletes realize it, but ballet and martial arts complement each other. Balance. Agility. Strength. Same ingredients, different approach.''

"Different outcome," Marianne added, grinning up at him.

Her heart did a tiny flip-flop as he shed his jacket, hooked it on one finger and swung it around his shoulder. In that pose he had to be the sexiest man in central Florida.

Be still, my heart, she warned silently. Get your greedy eyes off him and your mind back on business!

"Didn't I read somewhere that King Enterprises' corporate headquarters originated in North Carolina?" she asked, unconsciously bending her neck so that the brim of her hat hid her face. "Why did you move them to Orlando?"

"So I'd meet a delightful redhead and live happily ever after?" he ventured recklessly, determined to see her concealed face. To blazes with phase one, he wanted a phase-two relationship with Marianne. "How about the two of us starting with dinner at La Maison Friday night?"

Marianne's chin involuntarily jerked upward. Their eyes clashed for several seconds. This was a major turning point; they both recognized that fact. Her mouth felt parched.

Should she encourage Nick or discourage him?

Although she found Nicholas King extremely appealing, Marianne was preconditioned to discourage male attention. Since the emotional upheaval of her divorce, she'd gradually built a new life for herself and her son. Clay and Talent Plus had provided her with the happily-ever-after she'd been denied by her ex-husband. Why risk another emotional nosedive? Why tamper with perfection? The life she'd made for herself was . . . safe.

"I'm flattered, but I'm also busy Friday night." That wasn't a polite lie. She had promised Clay he could invite Brad and Peanut over to the house for videos and pizza. They'd also be sleeping over. No way would she leave three thirteen-year-olds alone. They were good kids, but they could unintentionally wreak havoc throughout the house . . . and not even notice!

"Saturday?"

"Sorry." Baseball practice.

"Busy, as in working? Or busy, as in having another man in your life?"

Marianne smiled enigmatically. Her fingertip circled the rim of the glass, making a pleasant hum, while she considered telling Nick about Clay.

She'd already spent half an hour telling him about her pet projects at Talent Plus. He'd think she was as lonely as Lila if she started being a typical proud mama, rattling on and on about her terrific son.

No, she decided, she'd be as glib as Nick had been with his insincere happily-ever-after line.

"Man? Singular? Why not plural . . . as in several men?" More like boys, she thought, grinning at the pensive look on Nick's face. "My social calendar could be filled for the next six months!"

"Is there more than one man? Are you really that busy?"

She ducked his first question and chose to answer only his last. "I am busy this weekend."

"Lunch?" Nick persisted. He'd hurtled from phase one to phase two too quickly and landed flat on his face. But that didn't mean he should give up on Marianne. What he had to do now was dust himself off and go back to the starting line. "Pick a day that's convenient for you."

"For a business lunch?"

"I haven't contracted with any other temporary agency," he replied smoothly. Instantly conscience stricken, he tried to justify dangling his account in front of her. "I *would* like to continue our discussion about Talent Plus."

"I can think of several women who'd be perfect for the health spa. And at your office you're bound to have days where you could use extra clerical or secretarial help." She'd been thinking aloud. She noticed a tiny flicker of triumph lighting Nick's dark eyes. Not being a woman who made a practice of building false hopes, she said, "Why don't I call during business hours and make an appointment with your secretary? Is Monday okay?"

"Great." He'd tell Irene to set her appointment sometime around noon. "I'll look forward to hearing from you."

"From Talent Plus," Marianne corrected, leaving no room for doubt in his mind. She strolled toward the door.

Nick remained in the evening's shadows, which suited her. Part of her wanted to linger, but she knew it would be unwise. She'd been sending mixed signals to him because of her own jumbled feelings. She had to leave him without any doubts as to exactly where she stood. "I don't want to give anyone in the business community, yourself included, the impression that one of the fringe benefits of contacting Talent Plus is Marianne Clark. As Lila said, I have 'a very good reputation.' I plan on keeping it. See you one day next week, Mr. King.''

Nick returned her smile. As the door clicked shut behind her, he whispered, ''Until then, Ms. Clark.''

Chapter Two

"Mom! I don't have time for breakfast!" Clay shouted from his bedroom. "I'm gonna miss the bus."

Dressed and ready for work, Marianne crossed from the dinette table to Clay's closed bedroom door. She rapped twice, sharply. "You have fifteen minutes, son. We're going to eat breakfast together before you leave."

"Okay! Okay! I'm coming." With his backpack slung over his shoulder, Clay opened the door. "I'm gonna miss the fag wagon."

"Fag wagon?" She pretended not to notice he'd slicked back his hair with something meant to tone down its copper color. Grinning, she remembered being his age and wanting to dye her hair black or bleach it blond. "Another derogatory name for the bus?"

"It's what all the kids call it. Chill out, Mom. I can't wait until I'm sixteen and I get a driver's license."

I can, Marianne thought, dreading the day he'd be alone behind the wheel of a car. He'd scared the bejeezus out of her back when he'd ridden a tricycle!

Clay dropped his book bag beside his chair, sat down, then grinned up at Marianne. "I'd have been here sooner if you'd told me you fixed pancakes. Would you pass the syrup?"

"It's hot." She turned the pitcher's handle toward him. "Are you coming to the agency after school?"

"Uh-uh." He circled maple syrup around the pat of butter on his pancakes. His face lit with excitement. "Special ball practice. I think the coach is gonna let me play catcher at the next game."

Just in the past week the coach had moved Clay from the outfield to the infield. "What about the shortstop position?"

"You know that kid, Troy, the one that played first base and dropped the ball at the last game? He's been begging to play shortstop." He rolled his eyes heavenward. "We're never gonna win if he gets it. But his dad is the assistant coach. You know what that means."

"But Clay, I thought you liked playing shortstop."

"I do. But I want to be the catcher. That's where the action is!" He dropped his fork, making hand signals as though his mother were the pitcher. "It'll be awesome!"

"Awesome," Marianne repeated, wishing her son had an equal amount of enthusiasm for what took place in the classroom. For the tenth time in as many days, Marianne asked, "Isn't your science project due at the end of the week?"

"Yep. It's almost done."

"Then take it out of the oven," she teased, correcting his choice of words. "It's almost *finished*."

"Yeah. That, too!" Clay glanced at the digital clock on the oven and made fast work of disposing of the remainder of his pancakes. He gulped down a glass of orange juice, wiped his mouth, grabbed his satchel and made a run for the front door. "I'm outta here! See ya, Mom!"

"Love you. Have a good…day." The door slammed in the middle of her sentence. "So much for the hugs and kisses before departures," she muttered, wishing he'd never entered the teenage don't-embarrass-me-by-showing-affection stage of growing up. She wrapped her arms around her waist. Unlocking her arms, she decided self-administered hugs were damned unsatisfying. "Clay may not need an occasional hug, but I do!"

Her mind wandered down a forbidden path straight to the memory of how she had felt being held in Nicholas King's muscular arms.

Over the weekend it had seemed as though everywhere she turned she saw a billboard or a television ad with his grinning face looking at her. With his dark eyes focused directly into the camera as he said, "Come on in and have some fun," she'd felt he was beaming a personal invitation straight into her living room.

She'd switched off the television when she caught herself raising her arm and flexing her biceps. His charisma wasn't going to lure her into a hot, sweaty gym with half the female population of Orlando.

And she wasn't going to make an appointment with him through his secretary, either!

She had the perfect excuse for not calling him today. Mondays were hellaciously busy. Marianne couldn't argue with the statistics she'd read in the employment section of the newspaper. Absenteeism peaked on Mondays and Fridays. Contagious as any real virus, beach flu played havoc with job production, especially during February.

She could count on Jayne Travares, her assistant, being swamped with calls until noon. To keep everything held down to a dull roar, Marianne always postponed her own administrative tasks to help Jayne answer the telephone and make placements.

Monday afternoons were spent contacting potential customers. Since unscheduled absenteeism threw employers into a tizzy, they welcomed her as though she were an answer to their prayers. She'd acquired the majority of her contracts through contacts made on the first and last workdays of the week.

Taking a final sip of coffee to sustain her for the next few hours, she closed her eyelids.

An image of Nicholas King appeared.

She rubbed her eyes to erase the image.

Laugh lines crinkled the corners of Nick's devilish black eyes as he gave her one of his special megawatt grins. The background behind his tanned face turned hot pink. Damned if he didn't appear to wink at her efforts to be rid of him.

She blinked her eyes until her vivid imagination quit playing tricks on her.

"I will not contact his secretary for an appointment with him," she vowed, her voice firm with conviction.

She pushed her chair away from the table and rose to her feet. With that resolution embedded deeply in her mind, she picked up her purse and hat, then strode toward the garage door.

She might have made it to the offices of Talent Plus keeping faith with her vow, if she hadn't looked in her rearview mirror. Her green eyes lacked conviction. She started the engine, wondering how long she'd been fibbing to herself.

She'd call him. Not today, while she continued to suffer from the effects of his charisma. Maybe not even tomorrow. But as soon as she'd recovered and felt completely immune to his charm, she'd contact him. She had to get in touch with him, for business purposes.

Thinking like the career woman she was, she said aloud, "It's part of my job description."

"Best regards...blah, blah, blah. The usual," Nick instructed his secretary. "That's all the dictation for today, Irene."

He leaned back in his chair, assessing his secretary's looks and demeanor. Irene's appearance hadn't changed in the ten years she'd worked for him—same tailored suits, same hairstyle, same sensible shoes. Her only concession to the casual styles of Florida was the frames of her glasses. Metal ones had given way to red plastic.

He hadn't noticed any alterations in her personality, either. She treated him with an incongruous mix of deference and irreverence. By observing Irene he couldn't tell if she was satisfied or dissatisfied with her job.

There was only one surefire way to find out. "How do you feel about working at King Enterprises as my secretary, Irene?"

"It's better than selling oranges on the highways and byways." Without glancing up at her boss, Irene pushed her fashionable bifocals to the bridge of her nose, licked her thumb and paged through her stenographer's pad. "Why do you ask?"

Chagrined by the idea of his secretary thinking her job was one step above hawking fruit to tourists, Nick propped his elbows on his desk and leaned toward her. She had a dry sense of humor. Often he couldn't tell if she was putting him on or being serious.

He considered telling Irene about meeting Marianne and the discussion they'd had about businesses being family friendly toward women in the workplace, but he instantly nixed the idea. He'd always kept his personal life to himself. He doubted Irene knew any more than what she might have gleaned from the Charlotte newspaper about his daughter Crissy's death or why he'd allowed Velma to divorce him without putting up a fight. And Irene was smart. Two seconds after he mentioned Marianne's name Irene would put two and two together and know he'd spent the weekend daydreaming about Marianne.

"Just curious," he replied with a dismissive wave of his hand.

Irene snapped the pad shut. "You aren't thinking about lowering the retirement age, are you?"

"No." He noticed she hadn't raised her eyes. "Are you concerned about the retirement benefits?"

"I won't be living the lifestyle of the rich and famous ten years from now, but I'll make it. With luck sometime between now and then I'll win the Florida lottery. Then I won't have to worry about my mother and myself living on fixed incomes."

Feeling safer discussing Irene's personal life than his own, he asked, "How is your mother?"

"Fine."

Watching her fiddle with the wire that held the steno pad together suddenly made Nick doubt her stock reply. "Really?"

"At eighty-three she isn't exactly eligible to model in your commercials, but she's spry." Irene shifted uncomfortably. "She says she's going to live forever."

Nick probed deeper into the sensitive issue. "What does she do while you're at work?"

Irene's head jerked up. "Why the sudden interest in my mother? I take care of her...good care of her. Has somebody been telling you that I don't take care of my mother?"

"No, Irene, of course not." Guilt? he wondered. She'd reacted as though she were a child's jack-in-the-box with him pushing her button. Or, he mused, as though he were threatening to open Pandora's box, filled with woes and miseries. What had Marianne gotten him into? "I am interested, though. What does your mother do while you are at work?"

"Watches television. Looks out the apartment window." Her dictation pad threatened to slip off her lap as she raised both hands palms upward. She stopped the pad's downward slide with one hand. "Sits in the courtyard with a couple of her cronies. Nothing exciting."

Finally he was getting beneath Irene's crusty exterior. "Do you worry about her being home alone?"

"Sometimes," she admitted cautiously. "What are you getting at with all these personal questions? I thought we had an understanding—live and let live. You don't feel sorry for me being saddled with my mother, and I don't feel sorry for you about your daughter and wife."

Nick felt as though she'd lambasted him with the metal coil spiraled along the edge of her steno pad. He'd touched a sensitive spot; she'd retaliated, going for his jugular vein.

"Maybe it's time we did talk about them," he suggested, raking his hand through his dark hair. "We've worked together ten . . . no, almost eleven years. You kept King Enterprises going while I was beside myself with grief. Did you ever think that maybe I would be willing to do something to help you and your mother?"

"What can you do for her?" Irene questioned with derision. "Shuffle her off into an old folks' home? Hide her? Forget her?" Irene rose to her full five feet of height. "I appreciate your belated concern, but I'm perfectly capable of—"

"Sit down, Irene. And calm down." They'd had a couple of differences of opinions over the years, but Irene's current defensiveness tore at him. "What can I do to help the situation?"

Irene refused to resume her seat. "Nothing," she replied stubbornly.

"C'mon. There must be something I can do." He watched her eyes dart from corner to corner of the room, then settle on his face. "Tell me."

"A longer lunch hour?" she replied hesitantly. "Just knowing Mother wasn't futzing around the stove would relieve my mind. I'd be willing to stay later to make up the time. Mother prefers a late dinner."

Flexible hours, Nick thought, hearing the first item on Marianne's lengthy list. "No problem. Anything else?"

"There is one more thing." Irene paused, unsure of whether or not to push her good fortune. "I've hated to ask because I knew it would cause you problems, but . . ."

"Ask."

"My niece, Mom's only granddaughter, is getting married Saturday. The wedding is in Charlotte. My sister has invited us to stay a week, but my vacation isn't scheduled until July.'' Irene fidgeted with the corner of the pad. ''I don't suppose I could move my vacation forward, could I?''

Nick grinned, reaching into his pocket and pulling out Marianne's business card. ''I think you and your mother should go. In fact, I *insist* that you both go. It isn't every day your only niece and your mother's only granddaughter gets married, now is it?''

''No, but it's the end of the month. We're always so busy then.''

''I'll make do.'' He extended his hand with the business card. There were definitely some pluses on the side of taking an interest in his employees' private life. Irene had given him the perfect excuse for making contact with Marianne! ''Why don't you call Talent Plus and see if they can get somebody to fill in for you?''

''I'd have to leave Friday. I could get most of the payroll ready ahead of time.'' Irene sniffed as the realization that she'd being going back home hit her. ''Darn you, Nicholas King! Thirty years ago I swore I'd spit in my boss's eyes rather than let him see me cry. Look what you've gone and done! Broken a perfect record.''

She swiped at her eyes ineffectively with the back of her hand. Nick plucked a tissue from the box on his desk. Irene took the tissue and the card.

Perching her glasses on the top of her brow, she mopped her eyes, then read aloud, ''Talent Plus. It's a local temporary agency, isn't it? Yeah, I've heard of them. Actually, my mother heard of them.''

''What's the grimace for?'' Nick asked, wondering if Irene's frown meant Marianne's reputation wasn't quite as immaculate as Lila would have had him believe.

"Mother wanted me to quit working for you and start working for Talent Plus."

Nick was shocked that Irene's mother thought her daughter ought to leave a perfectly good permanent job, with excellent wages and fringe benefits, for a temporary position. He stared at Irene. "Why?"

"A couple of acquaintances she's made in the apartment building go to some kind of center sponsored by Talent Plus, and she'd like to go, too." Giving Nick the warmest, wettest smile he'd seen from her, she said, "But you're stuck with me. How could I quit now? Longer lunches and an early vacation. What can I say? You're the best. Thanks, boss."

Nick shook his head. He'd honestly thought he'd been a exemplary boss, but in actuality, he'd been insensitive. Marianne was the one who deserved Irene's thanks. She was the one who'd opened his eyes.

"The next time you need something, Irene, why don't you mention it? I flunked mind reading back in college."

When he heard Irene laugh, a rusty sound at best, he felt good all over. "You might want to talk to Marianne Clark about the place your mother would like to attend. Whatever it is that's going on, I'm certain she's the one who started it."

"I'll call her, then I'll get right on these letters," Irene promised. "I'll save the good news for my mother until lunchtime."

Smiling inside and out, Nick laced his fingers behind his head and leaned backward in his chair as he watched Irene hustle from his office. He could quit worrying about faking a reason for contacting Marianne. He had a legitimate one. Arrangements would have to be made for him to sign a contract between Talent Plus and King Enterprises. And, since Ms. Clark was in charge of the agency, that had to be in her domain.

"New client on line three," Jayne mouthed so as not to interrupt Marianne's conversation on another call. "King Enterprises."

Marianne nodded. Her finger moved to the blinking light. She had to take care of this customer first.

For the past ten minutes she'd been haggling with the personnel manager at the bank to set up a dummy account for the temp who evaluated the services at the drive-up windows. Arlene had no idea how difficult it was to locate someone who was willing to drive from one end of Orange County to the other, much less use her own bank account for the deposits and withdrawals.

"We pay mileage and travel time, plus wages," Arlene repeated, unwilling to budge from her tightfisted position.

Mario Andretti doesn't work here, Marianne silently countered. It would take a professional race car driver to make the circuit that fast. She'd tried it herself and hadn't been able to get the job completed on schedule. Only the fact that the hourly pay was on the high end of the agency's scale balanced out the discrepancy in time.

"Let's not quibble over how long it takes a temp to go from one bank to the next. The point is that you expect the temp to use her personal checking account to make these transactions. On the monthly bank statement, she is charged for those deposits and withdrawals, not to mention the charge for printing the checks. A dummy account would solve the problem.''

''I can't authorize funds into an account that every Tom, Dick and Harry can access. What happens if she writes a check and keeps the cash?''

A light bleeping noise indicating the person on hold had been waiting for a full minute distracted Marianne. She rubbed the plastic square covering the pulsating light as though the gesture would soothe Nick King's impatience.

''I trust my employees.'' Marianne heard the skeptical noise Arlene made and added, ''Why don't we try the dummy account for this next evaluation period? If the account comes up short, Talent Plus will make up the difference.''

''I'll have to get approval on this,'' Arlene stated. ''And you'll probably have to make an addendum to our contract guaranteeing payment for any deficits.''

''Call me when you've worked out the details, Arlene. I'll start lining someone up to handle the job. It's been good talking to you.''

''Same here. Bye.''

Marianne paused before switching lines. She felt her heartbeat accelerating to match the fast rhythmic beat of the flashing light. Nick hadn't waited for her to contact his office. He'd taken the initiative. She wasn't certain if that was a plus or a minus. One thing she was certain of, she couldn't keep him waiting any longer.

''Talent Plus. Marianne Clark. I'm sorry to have kept you on hold. How may I help you?''

''This is Irene Zane at King Enterprises. I need an executive secretary starting Friday of this week through all of the following week.''

Marianne had expected to hear Nick's masculine voice. She glared down at the mouthpiece as though the inanimate object had played a nasty trick on her. Not in a million years would she have admitted that hearing a female's voice instead of Nick's was a disappointment.

"That should be no problem, Irene. I'll need some specific information . . . qualifications, hours, pay."

Pencil in hand, Marianne prepared to fill in a standard form. The sharpened point snapped before she'd completed the first letter of the company name. Hastily she replaced the pencil with a pen, jotting down the skill qualifications on the appropriate blanks.

Listening to Irene's requirements made identifying the right person simple. All Marianne had to do was look for a secretary with fire shooting from her fingertips!

"As for the hours," Irene said, "eight to five-thirty, with a half an hour for lunch."

"Would Mr. King consider having two people fill your position?" She'd thought of two women who'd meet the requirements, but both worked half days to accommodate their schoolchildren's schedule.

"I like the idea of it taking two people to do my work, but I'll have to check with the boss. I didn't ask him what the hourly rate would be, either. Would you mind if I put you on hold while I ask him?"

"You could . . ." What the heck, Marianne thought. She'd kept Irene waiting for several minutes. Turn about was fair play.

Music created to soothe the savage breast interrupted Marianne's half-voiced suggestion to call back. She glanced at the light indicators on the phone. Two lines were busy. One line was available for incoming calls. She could wait until that line started blinking.

The hold button had to be the most irritating invention in technological history, Marianne thought, impatiently strumming her fingernails on the sleek fruitwood finish of her desk.

"Ms. Clark?"

"Yes."

"If you're available, Mr. King would like to meet with you at one o'clock to finalize the details. He mentioned something about signing a contract, too."

Perched on the edge of her swivel chair, Irene glanced up at Nick. He'd followed her out of his office and taken the liberty of resting his hip on the desk's corner while he openly eavesdropped on the conversation.

Silently coaching from the sidelines, Nick mouthed, "More jobs."

"More jobs," Irene repeated.

Nick gestured toward the ceiling.

"Could you hold on just a second?" Irene clamped her hand on the receiver. "You need a roofer?"

"Not a roofer!" Nick whispered. "High-paying jobs! Tell her we'll be interested in hiring scads of women sometime in the near future."

"I've always been lousy at charades," Irene grumbled. "Why don't you go back in your office and talk to Ms. Clark? You can get everything settled over the phone."

Nick shook his head, signaling an emphatic "No!" The last thing he wanted to do was settle up on the telephone. His backside slid off Irene's desktop as though it had suddenly scorched the seat of his pants.

Giving her an unmistakable message, he tapped his wristwatch and held up one finger.

"I'm back," Irene said, removing her hand from the mouthpiece. "Is one o'clock acceptable?"

While Marianne waited, she'd tried to think of a valid excuse for being unavailable. She wanted her next meeting with Nicholas King to be on her terms, when she felt completely in control, ready for any situation. This afternoon was altogether too soon for any of those conditions to exist.

"Mondays are busy at Talent Plus," Marianne hedged. As though on cue, both light indicators on the phone made a liar out of her. The Monday morning rush was over.

How could she justify not pursuing a new account? Wasn't she the one who'd told Jayne that the day a business stopped growing was the day it started dying?

Unable to think of one sound business reason for not making the appointment, Marianne added, "But I'll be there if you'll give me the address."

Irene circled her thumb and forefinger and held it up for Nick to see. She hadn't the vaguest idea why her boss was acting peculiar, but who was she to argue? After all, as of this morning Nick King was the sweetest boss in the sunshine state!

Chapter Three

"Lunch?" Nick offered, gesturing toward a small table in the corner of his office. He'd instructed Irene to hold his calls. "You mentioned to Irene how busy Mondays are for Talent Plus, so I assumed you probably skipped lunch to make your appointment. If it looks as though I ordered everything on the menu, it's because I did."

Marianne gave the table a cursory glance. She attributed her loss of appetite and jangling nerves to the splendid specimen of the male species within touching distance. His charisma radiated well within the boundaries of her privacy circle. He was dressed casually in a trendsetting bright cherry-red workout suit that accentuated his bronze skin tones, and she had difficulty focusing on anything else in the room.

"You aren't one of those career women who skip lunch so that you don't have to exercise, are you?" Nick teased.

"No." She forced her eyes to leave his face and stare blindly at the cornucopia of food. She felt a chair nudge the back of her knees. She placed her briefcase on the floor. "Thank you."

Nick placed a paper plate on the table in front of her. "Don't stand on ceremony. Help yourself."

Marianne heard only the last two words—help yourself. On both occasions she'd been with him, her brain cells refused to issue that simple command!

"Let's see what we have here." He uncovered one platter and bowl after another. "Sliced roast beef, ham, chicken, assorted cheeses, seafood salad, garden salad, macaroni salad, assorted breads, a selection of desserts . . . fresh fruit. I'd say the deli hit all five food groups." His eyes met hers. "It all looks tempting."

Tempting? Marianne echoed silently. This man personified the word. With each shallow breath she inhaled she fought temptation. She'd cut off the blood circulation to her fingers by clenching them tightly on her lap to avoid the temptation of grazing them across his closely shaved jawline. She'd ignored the odor of fresh rolls, tempted only by the fragrance of his aftershave cologne. She'd heard romantic love words substituted for his recitation of the gustatory delights. Five minutes with Nick King and she was a certifiable expert on avoiding temptation.

She ripped her eyes away from his persuasive gaze. At random she selected a kaiser roll. It could have been made of sawdust or pixie dust, she wouldn't have noticed.

Holding up a bottle, Nick asked, "Wine?"

"No, thanks." Just slicing the kaiser roll taxed her powers of concentration. Alcohol was completely out of the question. Her eyes kept finding their way back to his profile. She'd never felt this drawn to a man, not even Ed—and she'd had Ed's child.

"Can I help?" Nick offered.

"What?"

Nick removed the roll from her hand. One neat stroke of his knife and the bun appeared to separate magically into halves. "Your knife doesn't have a serrated edge."

"Remind me never to apply for a job at a bakery. I'd be fired before the end of the first shift."

Her attempt to cover her ineptness with humor brought a devastating flash of Nick's white teeth as he smiled.

Did he have to be handsome and nice, too? Why hadn't some cheerleader-type back in his college days latched on to this man? For that matter, why hadn't he attended the chamber of commerce social gathering with some gorgeous aerobics instructor draped on his arm? But most important, why was he looking at her as though she'd recently won a beauty contest?

Without paying attention to where her fork landed, she speared a couple of slices of meat, placed them on the roll, spread mustard on them and took a bite.

Marianne had no self-delusions. She wasn't a beauty queen. As a child, she'd always been described as the skinny, redheaded kid with long legs and knobby knees. She might have improved some with age, but the only man who'd ever seemed to find her attractive was her high school sweetheart and onetime husband. And even he'd "outgrown" her.

Nick clicked his fingers in front of Marianne's face.

Startled, she jumped. Squashed between her tightly clenched fingers, half of her sandwich fell to the paper plate. A sweep of hot blood washed beneath her pale skin.

"Sorry. It's been a rough morning," she said, using the first excuse that popped into her mind. To divert attention from her breach of manners, she nodded toward the row of engraved plaques on the wall. "Are these all yours?"

"No, only a few are mine. Sporting equipment distributors sponsor dozens of teams in dozens of sports. Irene thinks bare walls are a waste of space so she had the plaques framed and the trophy cases built."

On Marianne's way in to Nick's office Irene had introduced herself. From speaking to her on the phone Marianne had formed a mental picture of an attractive woman, extremely competent, around thirty in age. But in person Irene looked as though she'd stepped off a recruitment poster for the United States Marines.

"Irene isn't what I expected."

"What did you expect?"

Marianne slowly began to relax, feeling at ease discussing his personnel situation rather than anything personal.

"From the skills level Irene expects of a temporary replacement, to be that fast herself, I suspected she had fire shooting from her fingertips. But I didn't expect her to look like..." She paused, searching for a polite description for a woman who looked capable of breathing fire from her nostrils, too.

"A dragon lady?" Nick supplied, amused by Marianne's astuteness. "Irene often refers to her secretarial position as 'Executive Dragon Lady in charge of defending King Enterprises'."

Marianne grinned. "Does a dragon lady work set hours or does she roam free?"

"Until today, Irene worked from eight to five-thirty." Wanting Marianne to realize their discussion on Friday had been more than idle chitchat, he added, "I made Irene's hours flexible so as to accommodate her need to care for her elderly mother."

His first step to make King Enterprises family friendly pleased Marianne. "Pardon the pun, but you don't waste time once you're on the right track, do you?"

"Your idea made good sense. When Irene gets back we'll see how it works, then I'll try one of the other suggestions you mentioned."

Marianne's hope that she'd be able to schedule some job sharing grew faint. Once she had Nick's signature on the dotted line, she'd have to recheck the files and find someone who did meet the criteria.

"What are the chances of you temporarily taking over the position of official dragon lady?"

"No soot," Marianne said, holding up her fingers. "I'm unqualified. And I have my own business to manage."

Reluctant to let the pleasurable thought of seeing Marianne every day for the next week pass from the realm of possibility, he said, "Sometimes I have to roll up my sleeves and deliver a shipment of equipment. Doesn't that sort of thing happen in your business?"

"Once in a blue moon I get a client who is difficult. Then I have to make a choice. Do I want to refund the client's money and drop the account, or do I fill in for a couple of days to find out exactly what the problem is?"

"Speaking of accounts," Nick said, steering her away from the loophole she'd revealed, "did you bring a contract for me to sign?"

"Yes. It's in my briefcase." She wiped her fingers on her paper napkin, opened her briefcase and handed an envelope and brochure to him. "I'll be happy to go over it with you."

"That won't be necessary." Nick glanced over the contract as he crossed to his desk and wrote his name on the dotted line. He felt as though he'd signed a multimillion-dollar deal as he returned the contract to the envelope and sealed it for good measure. He placed the envelope on the table. "Signed, sealed and hand-delivered."

"Thank you." Elated, she tucked the envelope in her briefcase. "I'll be checking back with you periodically for evaluation purposes."

Nick took the liberty of pouring her the glass of wine she'd refused earlier. "Would you propose a toast?"

To refuse the wine after completing the deal would be churlish, Marianne decided. Her fingers brushed against his. His casual touch breached the walls of confinement where she'd suppressed her awareness of him. "To—to King Enterprises."

"Talent Plus." A pure bell tone rang as the crystal rims of their goblets touched.

Ladylike or not, Marianne drank the wine thirstily, hoping it would extinguish the flames licking her insides, turning her blood hot. It only succeeded in making her slightly dizzy as she heard him ask, "Marianne, would you go out with me?"

Carefully, she placed the goblet on the table to give herself a moment to think. She watched Nick refill her wineglass without stopping him. Each moment it took him to pour gave her another second of contemplation.

She wanted to accept. But it was the very intensity of the yearning she felt that made her cautious. Nick had an unsettling effect on her. He stirred her curiosity and her imagination. Not to mention her hormones, she added dryly. Up until the moment she'd seen him across the width of a crowded room, she'd been relatively content with the life she'd made for herself. She had a career she enjoyed, a son she adored and money in her bank account.

Why take a chance on mucking it up?

Nick neatly rotated the bottle to stop the flow of wine. He'd have preferred an instant response to his invitation, but he respected her thoughtful deliberation. An optimist, he took her deliberation as a good sign. If she wasn't attracted to him, she'd have blurted out an excuse and rushed out the door.

From what Gregory had told him he knew she focused her energies on her business. He knew from experience how demanding operating a business could be. But he also knew it could leave the owner in an emotional vacuum, as if he or she were a modern version of Sleeping Beauty. He wasn't a prince, and yet he wanted to be the man who kissed her lips to awaken her. His eyes moved to her lips as he placed the bottle on the table.

"I would like to, Nick," she replied honestly. "I really would, but I can't."

"Would you mind telling me why?" Her eyes wavered, but Nick refused to release them by glancing away from her. Whatever her reason, he wanted to hear it. "Don't tell me you don't date clients, either."

"I haven't dated clients," she quipped, cheekily disobeying his direct command without giving him a straight answer.

"I can understand why business ethics might prevent you from socializing with a *prospective* client, but business associates have mingled socially since the women's liberation movement. Your professional reputation isn't at stake. We are equals, aren't we?"

"Yes."

"Then what's the problem?"

"I don't want to get involved with you or any other man."

"Why?"

Persistence thy last name is Nick King, Marianne thought. "My life is simple. Uncomplicated." When the expression on his face told her to skip the excuses and get down to the real reasons, she said, "Because I don't believe in the happily-ever-afters that you joked about the other night. I bought that line when I was young and gullible. I paid the price for my stupidity."

Nick reached for her hand. "I was married, too," he confided quietly. "And yes, I did joke about moving to Florida in hopes of finding a lovely redhead and a happy ending. But tell me, Marianne, what happens when you give up hope of finding a happy ending? How do you keep putting one foot in front of the other when you know you'll never get any place that really counts? Is that living or existing?" Shadows darkened his eyes. "Hell, Marianne, if there's no hope for happiness what is there?"

"Contentment," she replied, stubbornly clinging to the lessons she'd learned. "I am content."

"Are you, Marianne? Can you honestly tell me there aren't times when you'd sell your soul to have someone put their arms around you and hug you?"

Like this morning, when Clay left for school? Marianne shook her head in denial, both to Nick's question and her own thoughts.

"Don't you miss having someone special to talk to you late at night?" His thumb brushed across her knuckles. "Or miss just knowing someone is there for you if you need them? Somebody that cares?"

"What I don't miss is wondering when he'll leave or when and if he'll return. My husband walked out on me, but I kept the best part of the marriage—Clay, my son."

His fingers grew still on her hand. He must have misunderstood. Gregory had said she was a dyed-in-the-wool career woman! "You have a child?" he repeated.

"A teenager," she corrected, smiling at the note of surprise in his voice. "Clay would be thoroughly insulted if I called him a child. He's only thirteen, but he takes his role as 'man of the house' seriously." She turned her wrist until their palms touched. "I wasn't being coy the other night, Nick. My schedule is hectic. Between Talent Plus, Clay and his friends—who spend more time at my house than they do their own—I'm seldom at loose ends."

Reluctantly, Nick let her remove her hand from his. By all rights the knowledge that she had a child should have made a difference in how he felt toward her. The evening he met her he'd realized he needed to start putting the pieces of his life back together. But a child?

Could he make room in his heart to love a child other than Crissy? And if he did, would he survive if tragedy struck again? It was something he'd have to consider seriously before he became involved with Marianne.

Marianne studied Nick's thoughtful expression. She could only conclude from his pensive silence that her mention of her son had quelled his enthusiasm to be with her. She felt an odd mixture of disappointment and relief.

Be glad, she coached. Whatever complications Nick thought dating a woman with a child entailed, it wasn't her problem. It was his. Better to have found out now than when Clay answered the doorbell!

Cutting off the uncomfortable silence stretching between them, she rose to her feet and said, ''I need to go over a couple of items with Irene and then I have to get back to work, Nick. Thanks for lunch.''

Nick stood. He hadn't responded well to the bombshell she'd dropped, but he didn't know how to tell her about Velma and Crissy. Much as he wanted to see Marianne again, it was better to wait until he had sorted through his feelings. And yet he hated the idea of saying nothing.

Her hand was on the doorknob before he said, ''Marianne, would you mind if I called you at home in a couple of days?''

She turned, unable to resist the beseeching tone of his voice. Something was troubling him. She could see it in his eyes, in the way his shoulders sagged. The compulsion to walk over, put her arms around him and give him a hug was overpowering.

No, she corrected, stiffening her spine. He's trouble. Play it smart, lady. Keep everything strictly on a business level. Don't rock the boat.

Softly she turned the handle and opened the door. ''No, Nick. I'd rather you didn't.''

The next three days in February were the coldest on record in central Florida. The Arctic jet stream dipped into the sunshine state causing freezing rain, hail and occasional snow flurries. Newspapers and the electronic media called it the worst freeze in modern history.

Thursday morning, Marianne shivered as she sat in her car in the Talent Plus parking lot, watching people scurrying to get inside their offices. Like many Floridians, she had a wardrobe suitable for a subtropical climate. No coat. She'd never needed one. What made the below-freezing temperatures worse for her was that they made it clear that the hot flashes she'd been having couldn't be blamed on Mother Nature. They only occurred when she thought of Nick King.

Late at night, long after Clay had gone to bed, she'd lower the thermostat to conserve electricity, bundle up beneath the covers and try to answer the questions he'd posed.

What happens when you give up hope of finding a happy ending? How do you keep putting one foot in front of the other when you know you'll never get any place that really counts? Can you honestly tell me there aren't times when you'd sell your soul to have someone put their arms around you and hug you?

Like a looped tape on an answering machine, his questions circled around in her mind, never changing, never giving her clues to the answers, only causing more questions to arise.

Since she left Nick's office she'd begun to notice how her days and nights revolved around meeting the needs of others—Clay, her employees, her clients. She rarely thought of her own needs.

What had happened to *her* private dreams? Had the struggle to provide for her son by building a successful business taken precedence over those dreams? Why had she given up on finding a happily-ever-after ending?

Day-to-day survival accounted for putting her own needs on hold immediately after her divorce. She'd put on a brave front, but she remembered being scared, too scared to dream for fear of her romantic dreams turning into another nightmare. She knew of other women who'd divorced and remarried, and remarried, and remarried, making the same mistakes over and over again. She'd vowed not to let that happen to her.

She'd avoided that trap as carefully as Florida's Seminole Indians had avoided signing treaties with the white man. And like the Indians, she'd eluded being caught.

Now, she wondered if she'd been running so hard and fast that she'd never stopped to realize that she wasn't a frightened young woman. She'd matured. She had confidence in her judgment. She could stand on her own two feet without leaning on a man for support. There was no longer a reason for her to be afraid.

She could thank Nick for this new sense of awareness. At the same time, she felt like cursing him. He'd turned her skin inside out, leaving the sensitive nerve endings exposed to the frigid air. He'd made her feel alive, aware…alone. At night hot flashes made her kick aside her blankets. She'd awaken cold and lonely, wondering what she'd missed. As she stared at the alarm waiting for it to ring, she almost hated Nick King for penetrating her circle of privacy and stirring up feelings she had thought dead, but that must in truth have been buried alive.

Insomnia had made her irritable. She'd started this morning off by snapping at Clay for booby-trapping the kitchen doorway by leaving his baseball cleats there for her to trip over. Yeah, yeah, she'd been the one who'd suggested he put them where it would be impossible for him to get out of the house without them, but couldn't he pick a less irksome spot? Bleary-eyed, she'd almost broken her fool neck!

She wasn't winning any popularity contests at work, either. Business had been slow all week, which increased her irritability. It was as though the entire permanent work force had taken a vote and decided to cut down on absenteeism. Or perhaps with the weather unseasonably cold, they'd decided to cut down on electrical usage at home by soaking up the free heat at work. Whatever the reason, Marianne wanted the cold snap to end. And the hot flashes, too!

"Aren't you freezing to death?" Jayne Travares asked, knocking on Marianne's window to get her attention. A transplant from Michigan, Jayne was wrapped from head to toe in wool. "You'd better get inside before you catch pneumonia!"

Marianne forced a bright smile on her mouth and nodded. "Woolgathering must have been keeping me warm."

Jayne chuckled and opened the car door. Marianne noticed Jayne was looking at her oddly.

"Did I say something funny?"

"No. Up in Yankee land we call what you were doing staring off into space. I like woolgathering better. Sounds like something everybody should do on a cold winter morning—before they clock in at work, of course."

As they hustled across the parking lot to the front door, Marianne wondered if she'd snapped at Jayne, too. While she unlocked the door, Jayne did a little jig to keep warm.

"Brrrr," Jayne complained, shivering while she began removing her outer layer of clothing. "The sunshine must have thinned my blood. This is shirtsleeve weather back home."

"I'll have the coffeepot percolating in a minute," Marianne said, shedding her coat and hanging it in the front closet. "I need something to thaw out my bones."

A blinking light indicated an incoming call. Both Jayne and Marianne jumped for the phone.

"Got it," Marianne said, picking up the receiver. "Talent Plus. Ms. Clark speaking. How can I help you?"

"Hello, Marianne. Dragon lady here. Do you have someone lined up to protect the moat and slay the evildoers while I'm gone?"

Marianne grinned. "As a matter of fact I do. Her name is Lou Mackintosh. I'm certain Mr. King will be pleased with her."

"I doubt it," Irene groaned. "Just between you and me, it's a good thing I am going to my niece's wedding. Otherwise, I'd be tempted to throw Mr. King headfirst off the castle wall, straight down into the moat."

"What seems to be his problem?" Only women have hot flashes, she thought.

"I don't know what his problem is. Could be the cold is bothering his knee injuries. Could be he's got castle fever from being cooped up inside 'cause of the weather. Whatever it is, he's acting worse than King Henry the Eighth when his gout flared up. He's being so ornery I thought I'd better warn you. It's going to take a tough old bird to put up with him.''

Marianne chuckled for the first time in three days. ''I'm a little short on tough old birds, but I'll issue the temp a suit of armor.''

''I just don't want to get an emergency call from him while I'm at the church listening to 'Here Comes the Bride.' The mood he's been in, that might happen.''

''Irene, I promise it won't. I'll throw him in the moat myself if he gets too difficult.''

''Ha! You'll never qualify as a tough old bird. From what my neighbor ladies say about you, you'd probably fix chicken noodle soup and sing him lullabies.''

''Neighbor ladies?'' She blocked the thought of spooning hot soup between Nick's lips. It conjured up a cozy picture of the two of them in his bedroom. Marianne unbuttoned her bulky cardigan sweater as her skin warmed instantly. ''Do they work for Talent Plus?''

''Nope. They're my mother's age. They have family who work for Talent Plus, so they know you from the Youngsters' Place.''

Marianne nodded. She'd converted a small home into a day-care center for children and senior citizens.

''Mother wanted me to quit King Enterprises and start working for you so she could go there twice a week. It's amazing how being around children rejuvenates the old folks.''

''And the children love their 'adopted' grandparents, too.'' Marianne smiled. The agency's employees went to work relatively worry free. ''Perhaps I can help out even if you aren't working for me. Why don't you give me a call when you get back and I'll see if I can make some arrangements for your mother."

"We'd appreciate that. Mother gets real lonely with me gone all day. Uh-oh, that's the other line ringing. Thanks again, Marianne."

Hanging up the receiver, Marianne asked Jayne, "Lou is still scheduled for King Enterprises, isn't she?"

"Yes." Teeth chattering, Jayne huddled in front of her computer screen, rubbing her hands on her arms to get her circulation going. "I don't suppose you'd let me take that assignment. It's not as though we're swamped around here."

"I'll need you here when the weather breaks. I'm counting on the beach flu to strike in epidemic proportions." Marianne poured both of them a cup of coffee. "Here. This should make your thermostat climb."

Jayne took quick sips as she said, "That guy on the billboards...Nicholas King...he's the only reason the temperature didn't drop another ten degrees in Winter Park. Does he look that good in real life?"

Better! Marianne replied silently. But not wanting to encourage Jayne, she joked, "No beefcake discussions are allowed within these four walls. Have you forgotten about your pet peeve?"

"That men believe women who grow long blond hair have depleted their brain cells?" Jayne sighed, drank from her cup, then sighed again. "It's different for men. They can be drop-dead good-looking *and* still be considered smart. I know you want to make a good impression on Mr. King with the first temp we furnish. Don't you think Lou is older than a woman he'd hire?

"Lou is younger than Irene."

Smiling, she added silently, Lou is also capable of standing up to King Henry the Eighth with gout. Nick deserved to have to deal with a genuine battleax. If he wasn't pleased with her choice, she'd have the perfect reason to eliminate him from her files. That might be the only way she'd get him out of her dreams.

"Oh," Jayne said, disappointed. "Would you let me do the follow-up report on Lou?"

Marianne remembered telling Nick she'd be doing the evaluation report. She opened her mouth to relay that information to Jayne, but when she saw the wistful look on Jayne's face she couldn't refuse her.

Perhaps, in the long run, Jayne would be doing her a tremendous favor. Marianne had an ample supply of unanswerable questions keeping her awake at night without being near him.

"Suits me." In a teasing voice she added, "Just try not to drool on the evaluation form. It makes the pages stick together."

Jayne giggled. "I'll try, but I won't make any promises. Frankly, I think you're a fool for handing him over to me on a silver platter."

"From what I've seen of him, Nick is too much his own man to be served up on a silver platter."

"Nick?" Jayne repeated. "Did you just call a client by his first name?"

Marianne had slipped and Jayne had caught her. She'd have to be careful not to make that mistake again. She picked up the King Enterprises file she'd placed in the Out box.

"You take Mr. King's file. It will be one less thing for me to worry about."

As she passed the file to Jayne, she hoped that getting rid of the paperwork would also help rid her of the nagging doubts Nick—Mr. King had caused.

Chapter Four

"Lou!" Marianne shot to her feet. "You're supposed to be at King Enterprises. What are you doing here?"

"I quit!" Lou spit. The angry look in her eyes dared Marianne or Jayne to coax her into changing her decision. "I am not going back there. Now or ever! Wild horses couldn't drag me back to that job."

Although Marianne had chosen Lou as Irene's temporary replacement, she'd given Jayne the account. She didn't want to step on Jayne's toes by asking for Nick's file. She said to Jayne, "Would you like to take Lou to the consultation room to discuss the problem?"

Wide-eyed, clearly terrified by the thought of dealing with Lou in such a mood, Jayne shook her head. She quickly pulled out her center drawer and extracted the King file. Jayne obviously felt she couldn't dump it on Marianne's desk too soon. "No. You talk to Lou. I'll answer the phones."

"Fine." Marianne tried to defuse Lou's anger with a warm understanding smile. Lou compressed her lips into a stubborn straight line. She wasn't about to be pacified so easily. "Come with me, Lou. We'll have this problem taken care of in no time flat."

"You can't pay me enough to make me go back this afternoon," Lou stated with finality, following closely on Marianne's heels. Once inside the smaller office, Lou slammed the door and pointed her finger at Marianne. "I told you when I signed up with this agency that I refuse to work for a boss who expects me to kowtow to him. I am an executive secretary, not a waitress! Not a delivery boy!"

"I'm certain whatever happened can be straightened out to everyone's satisfaction." When Marianne had made her selection, she'd completely forgotten Lou Mackintosh was a militant feminist. But had she remembered, she was honest enough to admit she would still have given Lou the assignment. "Have a seat and calm down."

"Calm down? Calm down! If I go back there, I'm liable to have a stroke! Not only did Mr. King want coffee, he expected me to know His Majesty's imported coffee was brewed with bottled springwater. And that he wanted exactly one and a half tablespoons of cream stirred into it . . . gently! God forbid I should bruise the cow juice!" Her jowls quivering with indignation, she held up three fingers and sputtered, "I had to make three pots of coffee."

"Three?" That was excessive, Marianne agreed, and completely unlike the Nick King she knew. But then again, Irene had warned her Nick was being difficult.

Lou nodded. "I threw out the first pot because I used tap water. It took seven cups out of the next pot for me to get the cream just right because I kept measuring it wrong or, and I quote, 'I bruised the butterfat'!"

Marianne cupped her fingers over her mouth to stifle her smile. Lou had mimicked perfectly Nick's horrified tones, including his slow, North Carolina drawl.

"That left one cup," Lou continued. "I drank it...straight, like a shot of red-eye whiskey. When His Majesty the King wanted a second cup, I had to make another pot!"

The finger Lou had been waggling in Marianne's face became clenched into a fist that she planted on her hip. "But that isn't the worst part. By then, I had used up the bottle of springwater, so he sent me to the grocery store to buy another bottle."

Marianne clicked her tongue sympathetically, wondering what had gotten into the pleasant, generous man she had met.

Lou began pacing in front of Marianne's desk. Absentmindedly, she thumped the paper sack she held in one hand against her thigh, drawing Marianne's attention to it.

"I was determined not to be unreasonable, though. I figured Mr. King's regular secretary spoiled the man rotten, so I bit my tongue as I served him his second cup of coffee and asked him if he had any letters to dictate." She paused, glancing at Marianne. "You know I'm proud of the fact that I take shorthand at 120 words per minute. Well! Mr. King doubled my rate! He sounded like a tape recorder set on fast forward!"

A bubble of laughter lodged in Marianne's throat. Her eyes must have given her away though, because

Lou shot her a dirty look and sharply said, "It is not funny."

"No, it isn't," Marianne agreed wholeheartedly. She began to suspect Nick's behavior must have been intentional. "I'll have a talk with Mr. King."

Lou raised the brown paper bag she'd been clutching in her left hand. She turned up her nose as she dropped it in the center of Marianne's desk. "While you're straightening him out, you can return these to him. I am not going back there! Don't open the sack or you'll be sorry."

Smaller than a bread box, but larger than a toaster. Marianne tried to guess what the sack contained. From the tilt of Lou's nose, her first guess was rated X.

"It's his stinky running shoes!" With a heavy dose of righteous indignation, Lou revealed Nick King's blackest of sins committed against a secretary. "On my lunch hour, he expected me to drop them off at the shoe repair to have the Odor-Eaters replaced!"

"Unforgivable," Marianne said, her chest heaving with suppressed laughter. She didn't know why Nick had behaved so outrageously, but now there was no doubt he'd done it purposely. "I'm glad you returned to the office, Lou."

Having expended her wrath, Lou sank into a chair. "He's impossible to work for."

"Absolutely."

"If I were you, I'd just mail him his stinky shoes and drop his account! Of course, that might be the end of getting your mail delivered here. One whiff and the postman will go on strike!"

"I think you're being too lenient. Don't you think Mr. King deserves . . . equal treatment?"

A mischievous glint lit Marianne's green eyes. Unless the unseasonable weather changed, Talent Plus wouldn't be busy Monday. She wouldn't send an unsuspecting replacement for Lou. She'd take care of Mr. Nick King's problem. Jayne wouldn't mind in the least making coffee and running Nick's errands.

"What are you going to do?" Lou straightened, leaning forward in her chair. "Something ghastly, I hope."

Marianne recalled Irene's threat to throw Nick King into the castle moat. A delightful idea, but considering she couldn't lift him with a pulley and hoist, that would be impossible.

"I'm not sure... yet," Marianne answered thoughtfully. "But I'll think of something appropriate before Monday."

Nick licked the envelope he'd addressed to Lou Mackintosh in care of Talent Plus. The letter of apology and bonus check he'd stuffed inside it helped salve his guilty conscience. He'd been a ring-tailed polecat. Irene would have beheaded him if he'd pulled one of those stunts on her.

But, being a difficult client was the only means he had of seeing Marianne again.

Monday, she'd thrown two lightning-fast punches capable of knocking out a professional heavyweight boxer. She'd told him first that there was no room in her schedule for him, and second that she had a son. Stunned by her verbal blows, he'd been too winded to detain her. Victorious, she'd walked right out of his office before he could get his brains unscrambled.

An odds-maker would have given ten to one against Nick becoming a significant part of Marianne's life.

Those odds would have doubled if his fear of loving a child was factored in.

Nick reared back in his chair and propped his heels on his desk, waiting for Marianne to call him. He steepled his fingers across his chest as he thought of Marianne's son, Clay. Other than the boy's name and Marianne's devotion to him, he knew little.

Could it be that Clay, not Talent Plus, was the main reason behind her lack of interest in men?

Marianne's professional ethics were beyond reproach. It would naturally follow that her morals would be, too. It would be safe to bet she did not parade men through her son's home.

The more he learned about Marianne Clark, the more his admiration for her grew by leaps and bounds.

His fingers collapsed on his chest. He hoped it was the element of surprise that had caught him ill-prepared to cope with the idea of Marianne being a mother. He'd been dumbfounded.

"Thirteen," Nick murmured. "A teenage boy." Had Crissy lived she'd be the same age. His stomach twisted into a familiar knot. God help him, he didn't think he'd ever get over Crissy's death. It was a sadness he would always carry with him.

Divorce had left its mark, too, but the passage of time and a meeting with the right woman had made him reconsider the possibility of his finding happiness. But thoughts of caring for, perhaps learning to love, another child had thrown him into a tailspin.

After several days of thinking about Marianne and Clay, he'd decided that comparing Crissy and Clay was like comparing apples and oranges. Clay wasn't *his* child. The bond between Crissy and himself had been forged before she was born.

He'd never feel the same way about another child, therefore, he wouldn't be emotionally ravaged if some tragedy befell Clay. He could be friendly toward Marianne's son, but remain slightly aloof. He wouldn't let his heart become involved with her child.

Once he logically thought through the knotty problem and came to a viable solution, he'd started the wheels in motion to get together with Marianne. Irene's departure and the arrival of Lou had provided an ideal opportunity to test the loophole in Marianne's policy of personally guaranteeing her client was satisfied with the temporary help's performance. Unaccustomed to deliberately being a royal pain in the posterior, he'd had to improvise as he went along.

Nick grinned. Lou had not returned from lunch. He glanced at his watch. Unless he was way off his mark, Lou was chewing on Marianne's ear. Any minute he expected her to call him. All he had to do was stay on the offense, without being offensive!

The ring of the telephone broadened his smile. His feet dropped to the floor as he reached for it.

"King Enterprises."

"Mr. King, this is Marianne Clark. We have a problem."

"We certainly do. I know I agreed to flexible work hours for Irene, but the lady you sent has been out to lunch for more than two hours. Isn't that taking advantage of a good thing?"

Marianne's eyes rounded, then narrowed into slits. "Lou won't be returning to your office."

"She won't?" Nick injected a note of surprise in his voice.

"No. She won't."

"In that case, we do have a serious problem. Not only did she leave a mountain of work on Irene's desk, I entrusted Lou with one of my most prized possessions. You really should screen your employees more carefully, Marianne. You sent me a thief."

Marianne eyed the sack she'd shoved to the corner of her desk. "Your running shoes are your prized possession?"

"Those aren't just your plain old garden-variety running shoes. They're my *lucky* running shoes. I've had them for years."

Marianne sniffed. "I believe you," she replied.

"I need them by tomorrow morning for a race." Nick grinned, glancing at the envelope with Lou's name on it. Once Marianne saw how contrite he was, she'd forgive him. Optimistically, he hoped she'd be flattered. How many men would go to this much forethought and trouble to be with her? "Shall I come by Talent Plus and get them? Say around five o'clock?"

"I'll leave your shoes in the front office." Testing her theory that Lou's problem had nothing to do with competence and everything to do with Nick wanting Marianne in his office, under his thumb, she added, "Business is slow, so I'm leaving early to watch Clay at baseball practice."

"Baseball? What position does he play?"

"Shortstop last week. Catcher starting today."

"He must be quite an athlete for his age. I'd like to meet Clay. I played ball when I was a kid. Why don't I...?"

"Volunteer to help with the team?" Marianne suggested, tongue in cheek. "The coaching staff for Clay's team is filled. But at the organizational meeting they did mention a dire need for field-maintenance workers. I could put you in contact with the league's manager if you're interested in mowing grass, lining the bases before each game, picking up the trash under the bleachers...that sort of help.''

Lou, you'd be proud of me, Marianne crowed silently. She'd invite Lou to Clay's next game. The two of them could sit in the bleachers and drop a dozen candy wrappers for each cup of coffee Lou had fixed for Nick.

Nick's grin faded to a grimace. The maintenance crews undoubtedly worked before the games, when Marianne wouldn't be at the ballpark, and after the games, when Marianne would be gone. He'd be working his butt off and still wouldn't be with her.

"Nick, are you there?" Marianne asked after a lengthy pause.

"Yeah. I'm still here." He loudly rustled the pages of the calendar on his desk. "I'm checking my schedule."

"Too busy?"

"Other than the race tomorrow morning, I'm free this weekend." What am I getting myself into? Marianne's good graces, he replied silently. "Why don't I pick you up at Talent Plus? We'll go to the ballpark, and I'll talk to the field manager while you watch Clay practice?"

Marianne grinned. Since Nick didn't show a moment's remorse for upsetting Lou's day, she'd upset his. She had absolutely no intention of being anywhere in the vicinity when he arrived. Turn about was fair play, wasn't it? She didn't give herself a chance a reply. She knew what she was doing was unprofessional, but she owed him for several sleepless nights and his cavalier treatment of Lou! "Three-thirty?"

"I'll be there. Bye." Hanging up the phone, Nick raised two fingers for victory and shouted, "All right!"

Marianne dropped the receiver in its cradle and dragged one finger through the air. "Score one for the good guys . . . and the bases are loaded with the home-run hitter coming up to the plate!"

Her eyes fell on the sack containing Nick's "lucky" running shoes. Nick was a competitive sportsman. Winning a race was probably of utmost importance to him. Although he'd denied winning the trophies in his office, when she read the inscriptions to avoiding gawking at him, she'd discovered the majority of the plaques and awards hung on the wall had his name on them. What would happen if something unfortunate happened to Nick's precious running shoes?

She opened the sack, turning her head slightly to avoid getting a strong whiff of them.

"'I've had them for years,'" she quoted, pulling the brand-new shoes from the bag. "You're a dirty scoundrel, Nick King! Odor-Eaters, my foot!"

Talk about the power of suggestion, she thought. She'd actually imagined the smell of stinky shoes!

So why had Nick instructed Lou to take them to the shoe repair? Mentally she stepped into Nick's shoes. He must have taken one look at Lou and thought of Irene. Unless Marianne was badly mistaken, Irene didn't make coffee or run errands for Nick, either.

Marianne went back to her basic premise: Nick wanted her to take Irene's place temporarily.

Suddenly, his devious reasoning became crystal clear. Nick had figured Lou would quit. Lou would either toss the shoes in the trash or take them to Talent Plus. Then, if Marianne didn't contact him, he'd call the office to complain about Lou and ask for his shoes.

"He probably expected me to rush right over with them," Marianne muttered. Congratulating herself for foiling that part of his plan, she opened her middle desk drawer and pulled out a pair of scissors. "So, Mr. King, winning by fair means or foul is how you play the game, huh?"

Snip! Beneath the shoelace hole, she cut the lace three quarters of the way through. If Nick King wanted to play games with her, she'd make the game interesting. Snip! Another shoelace adjustment. She was careful the cuts were hidden and the strings remained strong enough to hold for one hard jerk when Nick tied the laces. By the time Irene returned, he'd wish he'd treated Lou as though she were a princess!

Winning that race ought to be a real challenge, Mr. King, she gloated silently. Her toes curled as she imagined him trying to hold his "lucky" shoes on his feet.

She shoved the shoes back in the sack. And now, for Lou's replacement. She'd send Jayne over to finish Lou's work. And since the cold snap had slowed business to a grinding halt, she'd contact the answering service to take any incoming calls. When Mr. Nick King arrived at her doorstep he'd find only a box containing his shoes waiting for him.

"Jayne?" she called. "Would you come in here, please? I have a special favor to ask of you. One I think you'll thoroughly enjoy!"

Promptly at three-twenty-five, Nick jogged from where he'd parked his car in the empty parking lot to the front door of Talent Plus. He grabbed the door handle. Expecting it to swing open, he tugged lightly. He pulled harder, thinking it was stuck. And then he yanked it with all his strength.

It was locked.

He cupped his hands to block the glare from the sun and peered through the plate-glass door. The lights were off. The desks were empty.

He rapped on the glass with his knuckles. Marianne must be in one of the back rooms working, he decided. He waited a few seconds, glancing up and down the street, then pounded on the door. He glanced at his watch to make certain he was on time.

A sinking sensation hit him in the pit of his stomach when he looked down at the sidewalk and saw a brown sack with a note stapled to it. He stooped and picked up the package.

"Mr. King," he read aloud. "Good luck at the race tomorrow. I've made arrangements for Lou's replacement. Marianne."

He ripped off the square, flipping it over to see if there was a postscript telling him where Clay's practice was held.

Silently he read, "P.S. You are a royal stinker!"

"Damn!" Nick muttered, irritated with himself for egotistically believing that his spreading lime on Clay's baseball field would make Marianne forget Lou. Remembering Lou's envelope, he pulled it from his jacket pocket. He'd planned on giving it to Marianne as a peace offering. He jammed the envelope through the mail slot in the door.

Now what? Go home and wait until Monday to contact Marianne? He disliked that idea. Unless he reasoned with her, in two days there was no telling how angry she'd be. He had to talk to her. Now.

He tucked the sack of shoes under his arm and strode rapidly back to his car. Finding Marianne shouldn't be too difficult. How many Little League fields could there be in Winter Park?

Five fields later, when he was close to giving up hope of locating the right one, he drove by the Winter Park High School athletic field. Boys who appeared to be in their early teens were playing a practice game.

Nick breathed a sigh of relief as he saw a woman wearing a broad-brimmed hat seated alone in the bleachers. He parked his car, content to just watch her while he came up with a foolproof plan. So far, his plans had proved him a fool. He had to do better this time or she might not give him another chance.

"Good catch, Clay," Marianne shouted, proud of her son for flipping his mask off his face and catching a high pop-up fly. She covered her mouth with her hand as Clay's face turned beet-red.

What a bundle of contradictions, she thought, plopping down on the bleachers. He's disgruntled when I don't cheer and embarrassed when I do. He considered it perfectly normal to ignore her during the entire practice, but God forgive her if she missed a game. That was a cardinal sin.

Maybe contradictory behavior is a male trait, Marianne thought, caused by their missing chromosome.

Nick's behavior certainly fluctuated. Just when she'd almost decided he had to be one of the nicest men she'd met in a coon's age, he revealed his true colors—black with a wide white stripe running from his head to the tip of his tail.

A piece of white cloth waving at the end of the bleachers caught her attention.

"Peace talks," Nick called softly, waving the T-shirt he'd tied to the end of a tennis racket. "Truce?"

"No mercy," Marianne decreed, but his ridiculous flag earned him a smile. When she felt her heart skip a beat, she turned her face back toward the field. She sternly reminded herself how angry she was with him. "I'm loyal to my employees, Mr. King."

"I'm willing to make reparations," Nick offered, daring to advance slowly toward her.

"Stop waving that silly truce flag, please. Clay just glanced over his shoulder to see what the infielders are giggling about. He's watching you."

The look she gave Nick stopped him from coming any closer. He sat down on the bleacher a step beneath hers. "Is that Clay playing catcher?"

"Yes. But before you get involved in watching the game, let's take care of business, Nick. What about the 'mountain of work' Lou left piled on Irene's desk?"

"I exaggerated a little."

"A little?"

"Okay, a lot," Nick admitted. "For the sake of fairness, I'm willing to give Lou another try."

That's big of you, Marianne thought silently.

With a strong hint of sarcasm she said, "Lou requested her next assignment be at the coffee shop on Park Avenue. The one near the shoe repair store. She felt her secretarial skills were below the standards of Talent Plus. As a direct result of your diligent training, she felt she'd be a whiz at brewing springwater coffee."

Nick groaned aloud. "My plan wasn't as clever as I thought it was, huh?"

"You intentionally planned on making Lou's day miserable?"

"There was no malice intended. I just wanted her to quit."

"Why?"

Scooting closer until the hem of Marianne's skirt brushed his knees, Nick said softly, "You wouldn't squeeze me into your schedule, so I squeezed you into my workday. You've been on my mind. I wanted to see you. Is that so wrong?"

"Why didn't you pick up the phone and call me?"

"Because you'd have made excuses to avoid me. Wouldn't you?"

"Probably," Marianne admitted.

"Absolutely." He lightly trekked his forefinger across the back of her hand. "You had a perfectly legitimate work-related excuse to call me any day this week. You didn't. You haven't given me a second thought, have you?"

A delicious shiver traveled up her arm. If she told him that she'd thought of little else, he would get so bigheaded she'd have to squeeze his head to get it between the goalposts on the other side of the field!

"You've crossed my mind once or twice," she replied.

She could feel her resolve to get even for Lou's sake weakening with each hop, skip and jump his finger made over her knuckles. Knowing he'd gone to this amount of trouble to see her did flatter her ego.

"Mom!" Clay shouted, jangling the chain-link fence behind the batter's box. Who's that guy playing pat-a-cake with her hand? he wondered. He'd just made a fantastic play to first base and she hadn't been watching. "Mom!"

Marianne snatched her hand away from Nick. "Yes?"

"I'm gonna ask a couple of guys over to watch movies tonight. Okay?"

"Okay. It's pizza night. They're welcome for dinner if it's okay with their mothers."

"We could all go out for pizza and to the movies," Nick suggested quietly. "My treat."

Although Nick's invitation appealed to Marianne, her son had taken off to run the bases with his buddies, which she knew was the last ritual of the daily practice. It was too late to change the plans so radically.

"Why don't you join us?" she suggested. "Clay won't mind."

Nick grinned, glad she was no longer furious with him, but aware of the hostile glare Clay had pitched at him when his mother wasn't watching. "You're sure I wouldn't be intruding?"

"I'm sure. Clay's attitude is the more the merrier. He'll probably get a kick out of meeting the man responsible for keeping Orlando supplied with sporting equipment."

Clay slid into home plate, kicking up a cloud of dust. Jumping to his feet, he expected to hear his mother scold him for grinding dirt into his white shorts. He hated it when she made a fuss in front of his friends. When he didn't hear anything, he looked toward the bleachers.

His eyes narrowed, turning dark green with jealousy as he watched the stranger who was cozying up to his mother. With a look of pure disgust, he pounded the dirt off the seat of his pants. She'd completely missed his awesome slide into home plate!

Chapter Five

"Clay, I'd like you to meet Nick King." Marianne beamed with motherly pride as Clay firmly shook Nick's hand. "And these other baseball heroes are Brad Aspen, pitcher, and Ryan Brittle—Peanut to his friends—the second baseman. Does Mr. King look familiar to you guys?"

"Yeah. Kind of," Peanut said, pumping Nick's hand. His face scrunched up as he tried to place the man's face. "Hey, I know who you are. You're the guy on the King Gym billboards, aren't you?"

"Yeah," Brad said, impressed. "You must be as strong as Arnold Schwarzenegger!"

"Stronger," Peanut bragged. "Atlas."

"Phooey. Just because he owns a gym, that doesn't make him a muscle man," Clay scoffed, thumping Brad on the arm. "My mom could lift weights if she wanted to."

"Yeah, and I'm only a ninety-pound weakling according to my son," Marianne teased. She looped her arm around Clay's slouched shoulders. "I've invited Mr. King to share a pizza with us. How about that?"

"Great . . . neat," Brad and Peanut chorused enthusiastically.

Nick winced inwardly at the glare he received from Marianne's son. "Is it okay with you, Clay?" he asked.

Glancing at his mother, knowing she'd be annoyed if he gave a smart-aleck reply, Clay muttered. "I guess so, if the other guys don't mind. C'mon, guys, Mom doesn't have room in her car for all of us. Let's start walking."

"Brad, Peanut, why don't you ride with me," Nick offered. "We'll follow Clay and his mother home."

Marianne gave Clay's shoulders a hug. "Sounds better than the shoe sole express. Right, boys?" Peanut and Brad chuckled, nodding their approval. She waited for a positive response from Clay, but he opened the passenger's door, tossed his catcher's glove in the back, flopped into the seat and slammed the door. "We'll see you at the house," Marianne said to the others as she got in the car.

Staring out the windshield, Clay waited impatiently for his mother to circle to the driver's side of the car. Silently he mimicked Nick. Why don't you ride with me? Clay can go with his mother. Big shot! That's what he thinks he is. Just because he owns a couple of gyms that doesn't mean he can boss me around!

Marianne settled into the driver's seat and started the car. One glance at Clay and she knew something had upset him. If he stuck out his bottom lip any farther she could plant a dozen rows of corn on it!

"Buckle up, son."

"We're only going a couple of blocks. You plan on wrecking the car?"

"No, but car accidents aren't usually planned." Marianne snapped her seat belt in place. "That's why they're called accidents."

"Funny, Mom. Ha-ha."

She waited until he'd buckled up before starting the engine. Then she asked, "What's wrong?"

"Nothing."

"Did the coach do something that upset you?"

"No." Clay turned his head toward the side window. *Peanut and Brad are sucking up to Mr. King, big time,* Clay thought as he watched his buddies giggling. "I get to be catcher at opening game next Saturday."

"Congratulations!" Putting the car in reverse, she backed up, then slowly drove toward the parking lot exit. Smiling, she waved as they passed by Nick's car. Thinking out loud, she said, "I guess we'd better wait at the exit."

"Why? The guys know where we live. Let's go."

Searching for another possible reason for Clay's peculiar behavior, Marianne asked, "Hungry?"

"Starved." Clay's stomach felt as if it were touching his backbone. *Mr. King wasn't going to get so much as one thin slice of his pizza. He'd probably order one with weird stuff on it—like anchovies, mushrooms and green peppers.* "Can we get three large pizzas, with sausage and extra cheese? Brad and Peanut are starved, too."

"You're going to eat a large one? By yourself? Are you sure your eyes aren't bigger than your stomach?" Marianne teased. "Usually you can only pack away half a pizza. I don't mind buying it, but don't waste it."

"I'll eat the whole thing." Clay glanced over his shoulder. He saw Brad leaning between the seats yammering at Mr. King. "He's tailgating, Mom, and Brad isn't wearing his seat belt."

"We're almost home."

Marianne glanced in the rearview mirror. Nick's car tailed at least four car lengths behind them. Since she was driving below the speed limit of twenty-five, Nick was hardly tailgating.

"They're yukking it up like laughing hyenas." Clay turned around, slumping low in his seat, muttering, "We should've walked home."

Impractical and unreasonable, Marianne thought, but now she understood why Clay was being such a grump. At thirteen, practicality ran a poor second against being in the company of his friends.

"I'm glad you rode along with me," she said, letting Clay know she appreciated his company.

"Yeah, Mom. Me, too." No point in all of them getting splattered on the road in a car accident. He closed his eyes, visualizing Nick's car on a hairpin road, like in the movie he'd watched at Brad's house. His brakes go out. A tractor-trailer rounds a curve—on the wrong side of the road. Smash! Clay saw himself running to the rescue, pulling his buddies out of the burning wreckage.

Marianne patted Clay's knee. "Have I told you lately that you're a good kid?"

"Yeah." He'd try to save Mr. King, he thought, visualizing the bursting flames as the gas tank exploded.

"And that I love you?"

"I love you, too," Clay muttered, feeling good about saving his friends. They'll probably spotlight me on the evening news. Yeah, I'd be a real hero.

Marianne watched Clay smile. Just a little tender, loving care, she thought. That was all her son needed to make him feel better. Next time she'd remember not to split the boys up.

"Punch the garage door opener, would you?" she requested as she drove into the driveway.

"You order the pizzas, Mom." Clay pressed the remote control. "I'm gonna see if Brad and Peanut want to play my new computer game, Kung Fu Kid."

Before Marianne could get the back door unlocked, the teenagers had disappeared behind the gate leading into the backyard. Seconds later, she heard skateboard wheels rolling across the wooden skateboard ramp. Oh, for one-tenth of their energy, she thought.

"I wish I had their energy," Nick commented from behind her.

Amused by the boys' wild baseball stories he'd listened to, Nick found his fear that Marianne's son would remind him of Crissy had begun to subside. Clay and his buddies were typical teenage boys—rowdy, physical, always trying to best one another. In comparison, Crissy had been ladylike and refined. Apples and oranges. Definitely.

"I was thinking the same thought. Frankly, there are times when Clay runs me ragged." Marianne led the way into the kitchen. Removing her hat and tossing it on the counter, she added, "I wasn't fibbing when I told you I was busy this weekend. There are times when I think my main duty as a mother is chauffeuring my son and his friends hither and yon."

Nick watched her thick braid fall to the center of her back, exposing her fragile neck. An irresistible impulse urged him to reach out, lift the braid and use the tip of her hair to paint silken strokes along her nape.

He shoved his wayward hands into the pockets of his sweat suit.

"And here I thought you just weren't interested in going out with me." Pleased by her open response, he asked, "Why didn't you tell me that you had a teenage son the first night we met?"

"I thought about it when you asked if there was a man in my life, but I'd already bent your ear about my second love—Talent Plus. I didn't think you'd care to listen to me brag about my boy. Proud mothers tend to get carried away when asked about their kids." She picked up the telephone receiver. "What do you like on your pizza?"

"Whatever the boys are having is fine with me."

"Sausage with extra cheese?"

"Fine. Unless you'd like to share one."

Marianne grinned as she poked the telephone's buttons. She was on the verge of deciding she wanted to share more than a pizza with Nick. "With the works? Everything? Including anchovies?"

"You can have my anchovies."

"Mercy, a real grown-up deluxe pizza?" She felt her mouth water in anticipation. "I can't remember the last time I ordered one. Make yourself at home while— Uh, yes, I'd like to order..."

Nick unzipped his jacket, letting it fall open but not removing it. His glance roamed around the kitchen. Judging from the number of cookbooks and the conglomeration of utensils sticking from a crockery pot labeled This Is An Equal Opportunity Kitchen, Marianne liked to cook. And he enjoyed eating a home-cooked meal.

A winning combination, Nick thought silently, his gaze returning to Marianne. She'd kicked off her high heels. Her toes wiggled as though glad to be free from her shoes' confinement. Watching her gracefully balance on one foot while she massaged the ball of the other, Nick contemplated the pleasure he'd get from stroking her feet, ankles and calves. Without the silk stockings.

Marianne put down the phone. Lowering her foot, she spun around and asked, "Nick, what would you like to drink with your anchovy-less pizza? A soft drink? Wine? Beer?"

She caught his eyes leisurely traveling from her ankles upward until their eyes met.

"Have I told you what an attractive woman you are, Marianne?" He moved closer to her, giving in to his urge. He coiled her flame-colored hair around his wrist.

"No," she hiccuped, suddenly aware they were alone in her kitchen. She could hear the boys whooping and hollering outside. They'd stay outside until she called them in for dinner.

She could hear her breath coming in shallow gasps, and felt her face tilting up toward Nick's like a flower glorying in the warmth of the winter's sun. Her skin tingled with awareness at his touch on her hair. Her eyes closed. Not thinking, only feeling, she lifted her hands to his chest.

It would be easy, so easy, to get involved with Nick King, she thought, allowing a pleasant weakness to invade her. He stirred up memories of being held closely in a lover's arms, the joy of a man's touch. For all that had gone wrong in her marriage, the physical side of it had been good. The bedroom had been the one place she'd dared to be bold and adventuresome. If sex were the glue that held marriages together, hers would have remained whole.

Sex? Marianne opened her eyes and stepped backward. Her fantasy world had been spinning far faster than the real world. She had to slow down. Nick had accepted an invitation to share a pizza, not her bed.

But she could tell from the burning intensity she saw in his dark eyes that his imagination had been as fertile as her own. You're both adults, she admonished. Talk about it. Don't avoid it.

"It's been a long time since I've been this...close to a man."

"Or wanted to be?"

"Yes." She turned and walked to the refrigerator. Each fraction of an inch she moved away from Nick helped her to regain her clear head. "Sex wasn't the reason for my marriage landing in the divorce courts. I'm not ashamed to admit that my first year of celibacy was difficult."

She opened the door and removed two cans of cola, then put them on the counter while she filled two glasses with ice. Nick waited patiently for her to finish her thought, which she did as she put their drinks on the table.

"But I didn't think it was fair to drag a string of men through Clay's life just to satisfy my sex drive. I wanted my son's respect. I still do."

There, she thought, I've laid it on the line. I've let him know I'm interested in him, but not at my son's expense.

"Sex isn't why I'm here, Marianne." He lifted the tab on her can, picked up her glass of ice, tilted it and poured the fizzy liquid down the inside. "Not that I don't think you're sexy as sin. You are."

"It's different for you. You don't have a child you're responsible for," Marianne said. Then, realizing she'd jumped to a conclusion, she added, "Do you?"

"No. I don't have a child to care for."

Nick made a ritual out of pouring his cola into the glass while he considered telling her why his marriage had ended. What could he say to a woman who'd devoted her life to her child? "I killed my daughter. She'd be Clay's age if it weren't for me." Marianne would neither understand nor be able to forgive him. How could she? He'd never been able to forgive himself. He wanted to open up to her, but he couldn't. Not yet.

He looked up. His eyes met and locked with Marianne's. He felt the tension of the half-truth he had told standing between them.

Seeking safer territory, Marianne said, "I'd better call the boys. The pizza should be here any minute."

"I'll get them." Nick rose and crossed to the sliding door that led to a screen-covered pool. "Are they out back?"

"Yeah. Go out the screened door at the far right of the pool." She smiled. "Your ears will lead you to them."

"Did you see that one?" Peanut crowed, rocking to the back of his skateboard to stop it. "I must've gone twenty feet into the air before I turned."

Brad nudged Clay. "He almost splatted, huh, Clay?"

"No, I didn't," Peanut denied. "I just overbalanced for a second."

"That's what I said, pea brain," Brad said, taking the sting out of his criticism and name-calling by grabbing Peanut around the neck and wrestling him to the ground. "You almost splatted. Admit it."

"Get off of me, you hairless moose."

Clay joined in the ruckus, singing, "I am the champion. I am the champion!"

"Go show him how it's done, Clay. I'll sit on his head if he doesn't pay attention."

Nick heard the boyish heckling. He grinned, remembering the days when he had been the same. He reached for the door handle. His hand stayed suspended in midair as he watched Clay skate back and forth on the bowed ramp, picking up speed, coming closer and closer to the lip. His mouth opened to shout a warning. Fear stole his voice.

In less than two seconds Clay shot up the incline into empty space. The sun setting on the horizon silhouetted him as he flew above it. He twisted, and with the precision of a ballerina, he skimmed back down the ramp.

"Im-press-ive!" Brad shouted, jumping to his feet and pulling Peanut with him. "Cool skatin', dude!"

Clay slowed his board to a halt. He saw Mr. King standing like the Statue of Liberty inside the screen. Guess I impressed him, too, Clay thought as he puffed out his chest. Nobody, but nobody, could've done it better. With a quick maneuver that had taken him weeks to perfect, he stomp-kicked the skateboard into his hand.

"Wanna try it, Mr. King?" Clay challenged. "C'mon and show us what you can do."

Nick seriously doubted he could compete with Clay's stunt, not that he wanted to. Clay's recklessness had scared the hell out of him. His heart was still clogging his vocal cords. Didn't Clay realize he could have broken his neck? And Nick would have been helpless to stop the accident from happening.

Inwardly cringing, he wondered if Marianne would have blamed him. Velma had. Crissy's death had been the beginning of the end of their marriage. Nick raked his hands through his hair, trying to calm his fear, as he wondered if lightning could strike the same man twice.

"Hey! You can use my board if you want to, Mr. King," Brad offered.

Nick shook his head. "Time for pizza," he said.

The boys cheered. "Last one in is a rotten egg!" Brad shouted. They pushed and shoved, each trying to be first into the pool area.

"There's plenty to eat," Nick said, his voice scratchy. He held the door open as the threesome scuffled through the opening. He needed a minute to sort through his reactions. "Tell Ms. Clark I'll be there in a second."

Nick ambled toward the skateboard ramp. In the few minutes that had passed the sun had sunk beneath the horizon. Scared, he thought, analyzing his emotions. Petrified scared. Immobilized. But it had been fear, not gut-wrenching agony. Not the bone-chilling anguish he'd felt when he saw Crissy's limp body. Not the heart-stopping pain that had haunted him for months.

Only one child, his child, had the power to destroy him with grief.

Was that the difference? He barely knew Clay. Was love what made the difference?

He had to be careful, very careful, not to learn to love the boy.

"Nick! Your pizza is getting cold," Marianne called from the edge of the pool's deck. She'd waited a few seconds before calling to him. He appeared to be studying the ramp as though it held the answer to the mysteries of the universe. "What do you think of it?"

"It's...scary," he replied bluntly.

"My sentiments exactly. Clay and his dad built it last summer while I was at a small businessmen's conference. I could have cheerfully throttled Ed." She raised her hands to stop Nick when he opened his mouth to speak. "Don't say it. I know I'm overly protective."

"I'd be the same if Clay were my child." There, he'd said it aloud.

But as long as Clay *wasn't* his child, flesh of his flesh, blood of his blood, he was all right. If anything happened to the boy he'd be deeply sorry, but it wouldn't take him to the brink of losing his sanity.

He followed Marianne back inside the house. The aroma of onions and green peppers permeated the air. Marianne sniffed deeply as she slowly opened the pizza box.

"The boys are taking turns playing computer games while they inhale their pizzas."

"Inhale?"

Nodding, Marianne grinned. "I only inhale the aroma. They inhale the food. I swear my boy has lost the ability to chew his food. I used to think it was only Clay until I started watching his buddies. None of them chew. Sniff, sniff, and it's gone!"

"Since you mentioned it, I seem to recall my mother telling me I must have an extra set of teeth in my stomach because I only used the ones in my mouth to smile with."

Laughing, Marianne said, "Why don't we watch the movies I rented? When the boys get tired of the computer games they can join us. You get the sodas. I'll carry the pizza and set up the VCR.''

Minutes later, she gave Nick his choice of films. ''Comedy, mystery, action film or sci-fi. What will it be?''

''No romance?'' he teased.

''Clay picked them. His taste doesn't run toward the mushy stuff.'' Which is probably for the best, she silently tacked on. Sitting next to Nick while watching hot love scenes would have had a disastrous effect on her nervous system.

''In that case, I'll vote for the comedy.''

''It's slapstick.''

''That's the best kind.''

''Are you sure you wouldn't rather watch the action film? It's supposed to make grown men cry.''

''That wouldn't make a great impression on your son, would it? He walks in and I'm sobbing on your shoulder. What would that do to my macho image?''

Marianne slipped the comedy into the machine. She pushed the fast forward button to skip the upcoming attractions. ''Nothing. It's okay for men to cry when they're hurt or feel compassion for another human being.''

''Clay is going to grow into a fine young man,'' Nick said, meaning it.

''Thanks.'' As she moved beside him she wondered if he had any concept of how good it made her feel to have someone say, ''Good job, Marianne.''

Sprawled on Clay's bed, Brad asked, ''What do you think is going on in there, Clay? Sounds like he's tickling her funny bone.''

Clay shot Brad a dirty look between his computer man's karate chops to Peanut's man. He'd do the same to Mr. Macho King if he laid a grubby finger on his mother. "They're watching a dumb movie."

"My eyes are bonking together." Peanut dropped the joystick. "Let's go in with your mother and Mr. King for a while. I don't care what they're watching. It has to be better than getting kicked in the face."

"I'll play if you'll switch disks." Brad imitated the sound of tank's shells exploding in midair. "How about some tank warfare. I can beat you at that one. I've been practicing on my own computer."

"Okay. Load it up." Clay glanced at Peanut as his friend started toward the bedroom door. "It's a crummy movie, Brittle. I fell asleep watching it."

Peanut shrugged. "I'll be permanently cross-eyed if I stay in here."

"We could go out in the garage and play Ping-Pong," Clay suggested, wanting the three of them to stick together.

"Naw. It's no fun with three people." Brad's face brightened. "Hey, I know what. Let's ask Mr. King if he wants to play doubles. I'll bet he can beat you, Clay."

"What makes you think he can?" Clay demanded.

"Well, he owns a gymnasium. He's probably an expert at all sports, including Ping-Pong." Peanut grabbed Brad by the arm. "C'mon. Let's go see how good he is."

Not a bad idea, Clay thought, switching off the power. He'd been waiting for his mother to ask the guys if they wanted dessert, but she hadn't bothered. She was too busy in there laughing her guts out.

Clay was getting sick and tired of hearing Mr. King laugh, too. Well, if he went out and beat the socks off *her* company maybe his Mom would pay a little attention to *his* company!

Chapter Six

The Ping-Pong ball spun, barely clearing the net on Nick's side of the table. Prepared to have it slammed down his throat again, he had backed up. He made a dive for it and missed.

"My game," Clay gloated. He'd used every trick in the book—spinners, slams, change of pace, alternating corners—and he'd won three games. "Want to go for five out of seven?"

Nick stayed bent over the table. Sweat dripped off the end of his nose. He had forgotten how rigorous Ping-Pong could be. He admired Clay's skill, but the boy's cockiness left something to be desired.

"I think that's enough for one night," Marianne said, handing Nick a towel. "Busy day tomorrow. Nick has a race early in the morning and you have a lawn to mow before baseball practice. Your buddies have already fallen asleep watching the movie."

"Just one more game," Clay pleaded. "You're the one who told me it's rude to quit when I'm winning. I'm supposed to give the underdog a chance!"

"The underdog's tongue is dragging on the table," Nick replied, chuckling. At Clay's age, he'd have been gloating, too. There was nothing better than beating a man twice your size, weight and age. "Let's make it another night, champ."

Marianne gave Clay a motherly glare that clearly said, "Mind your manners and don't make a fuss."

"Okay, okay already. I'm going." Feeling benevolent toward his opponent, he said, "G'night, Mr. King. It was nice meeting you."

"Nice meeting you, Clay," Nick responded. "Maybe next time I'll be more of a challenge."

After Clay shut the door Nick turned to Marianne. "That boy is going to be one fine athlete. Excellent eye to hand coordination."

"Practice is what it took—hours and hours of diligent practice."

"That's what it takes to be good in any sport." Bracing his hands in the small of his back, Nick slowly straightened. "Youth helps, too. Right now I'm feeling every minute of my thirty-seven years."

"Need some help to your car, Grandpa?" Marianne teased.

"From you? I need all the help I can get."

Nick looped his arm across her shoulders. She wrapped her arm around his waist. To prolong the closeness, Nick shuffled slowly to his car.

"My sides are achy from laughing so hard." Nick ran his hand across his rib cage. "Those old silent movies are great. But I think it must take two people watching to really appreciate a good comedy."

"It must." She'd enjoyed their evening. Nick had a charming boyish quality about him that offset the sexual tension being near him caused. She'd felt... comfortable with him. Relaxed. "Those movies weren't as funny the last time I saw them."

Outside the garage, Marianne looked up at the stars through the branches of century-old oaks. "The wind must have changed direction. It's warmer tonight than it was at noon today."

Nick grinned. No way was he going to remind her of how hot under the collar she must have been when Lou returned to Talent Plus. He liked having her tucked neatly under his arm.

With more than one meaning he replied, "I'm glad the cold snap is over."

"Me, too."

Despite his baby-sized steps, they covered the short distance to his vehicle too quickly for his liking. Reluctant to leave, but unable to think of a legitimate excuse to stay, Nick leaned against the bumper. He turned Marianne until she was facing him.

"What is on your busy agenda for tomorrow? I'm free after I run in my race."

"The yard. Clay mows. I trim and weed the beds."

Her palms were resting on the soft fleece lining where his jacket had fallen open at the shoulders. She burrowed her fingertips until she felt the muscular wall of his chest. He felt hot, damp from exertion.

"Does yard work take the entire day?" He wanted to volunteer just so he could spend the day with her. Mowing the baseball field wasn't his idea of a delightful task, but working in Marianne's yard had definite appeal.

"I promised to take Clay and his friends to Wet 'n Wild in the afternoon. We won't get back until late in the evening."

His look of disappointment tugged at her heartstrings. What could she do? Dump her son? Uh-uh. Clay came first. He'd have every right to be furious with her if she started switching his plans around. She'd been straightforward with Nick. To put it in kids' vernacular, Nick could like it or lump it.

"Saturday is booked solid." He'd seen her chin jut forward with defiance and forsook the idea of offering to take everybody in his car. "Dare I inquire about your plans for Sunday?"

"Church in the morning. Clay goes to youth group in the evening." Suddenly conscious of her fingers lingering on his shoulders, she dropped her hand to her side. While she'd been verbally pushing him away, she'd been clinging to his jacket. "Big Sunday dinner at noon, then I usually catch up on the wash, clean house and get our clothes ready for the next week."

"Any chance you could make room for me somewhere between the mop and the chauffeuring?"

"That depends on what you have in mind?"

"Something less strenuous than table tennis, that's for certain," Nick replied, chuckling. "On second thought, I need the practice. As you said, that's what it takes to improve my game."

"What?" she teased. "No Ping-Pong champions employed in your gyms?"

"None. No tables, no paddles, no champs."

"In that case, I guess I'll have to take pity on you." Her eyes smiled up at him by crinkling at the corners. "Say Sunday afternoon? Around five? A friendly practice game of Ping-Pong?"

"You're on." Nick brushed a platonic kiss on her brow. Surprisingly, he found it intensely satisfying. "Are you as tough to beat as your son?"

"Who do you think taught him how to play?" she replied with the same cocky tone Clay had had in his voice when he won.

She had taught Clay the basics of the game when he was seven years old. Within a week her pint-size offspring had trounced her. Marianne's hands slid down the length of Nick's jacket until only the tips of their fingers touched as she stepped backward.

Nick groaned. "I can see I'm going to have to start inventorying different equipment."

"See you Sunday?"

"Mark it on your calendar." Nick broke their fragile contact. "Don't forget. Nick on Sunday. Big, capital letters, please. Preferably in red."

Marianne waited until Nick had reversed down the drive, then she strolled into the house. Forget? Her facial muscles ached as she grinned, which served as another pleasant reminder of how much fun she'd had with Nick. She wouldn't forget. She'd be looking forward to being with him again.

She closed the garage, locked the back door and crossed to the cabinet filled with glasses.

"Mom! We're thirsty," Clay shouted, right on cue. "Could you bring us some glasses of ice water, please?"

"I'm on my way."

Softly Marianne chuckled aloud. Inside Clay's gangly teenage body lived a little boy's heart. Clay was too old to ask to be tucked in, especially when his buddies were sleeping over. He wasn't too big to be dying of thirst every night, though. A drink of water carried to

Clay in her loving hands gave him the same security as enveloping him a warm, snuggly blanket for the night.

"Only a mother would understand," she whispered. "It's a family thing."

Marianne giggled in her sleep. Like a movie star in a silent movie, Nick made a dramatic grimace as he tied a series of knots in his shoelaces. Dressed in neon-blue-striped running shorts and a tuxedo jacket with tails that swept the ground, he limbered up for the big race. Each time he took a step his shoelaces appeared to disintegrate.

In the bleachers a woman with long, flowing red hair covered by a silly polka-dot hat and sporting a paste-on black handlebar mustache, waved a gigantic pair of scissors at the hero.

Snip! Snip! Snip! the caption read.

The hero slapped his face, grinned comically and stopped to tie another knot. The starting gun fired.

Marianne's eyelids shot open. Instantly alert, she listened for another loud cracking noise, one similar to the firing pistol in her dream.

Katydids and the neighbor's lawn mower were the only sounds she heard over the pounding of her heart.

Rolling to her side, she pulled up the coverlet over her ears. She wanted the silent movie to pick up where it had left off—with Nick at the starting line wearing his lucky running shoes.

"The starting line?" She shot up in bed. Her eyes opened wide as she flipped back the covers. Caught between her dreamworld and reality, she swiped the back of her hand against her dry lips. She could almost feel the villain's mustache tickling her upper lip and hear the sound of scissor's blades rasping against Nick's shoelaces. "Nick's shoes!"

She had to get hold of Nick and tell him what she'd done! He would trip and make a fool of himself if they broke at the wrong moment.

She glanced at the clock. Almost seven, she read, grabbing the phone. Her finger punched the buttons to reach the information operator.

"Information. What city, please?"

Winter Park? She didn't know where he lived! "Orlando vicinity. Nicholas King."

"One moment, please. I'm sorry. That number is unlisted."

"Operator, this is an important call."

"An emergency?"

"Yes!"

"I'll have to connect you with my supervisor. What is the nature of the emergency."

"Never mind, operator. Thanks." Frustrated, Marianne dropped the receiver.

Okay, Ms. Cutup, settle down and think! There had to be some way she could get hold of Nick. She couldn't remember him mentioning where the race was being held. How many races could there be? She hadn't the vaguest idea. Clay might know. The school often sent fliers home about sports activities.

She bounced off the bed, stripped her nightgown over her head and dashed to her dresser. In ten seconds flat she had pulled on a pair of green denim shorts, a white top and sneakers and was racing down the hallway to her son's room.

The bed was empty; the floor was full of sleeping bags. Spotting Clay's bright-colored hair, she carefully tiptoed between outflung arms and legs until she stood beside him.

"Clay!" She squatted and shook his shoulder. "Clay, wake up, sweetheart."

"Go 'way, Mom. It's Saturday." He rolled on his side toward her. "Let the grass grow another hour. I wanna sleep in."

"Do you know where a track meet is being held today? Did the school pass out fliers?"

Marianne watched Clay struggle to open one eyelid. It drifted shut before he mumbled something that she couldn't decipher. She shook him again.

"Go 'way. I don't want to run."

"No, sleepyhead. You don't have to run. Just wake up and tell me—"

"Mrs. Clark," Brad whispered. "My dad entered the Magic Race. The starting post is down at Central Park."

"What time does it start?"

"Eight o'clock, I think."

"Bless you, Brad." Marianne glanced at her wristwatch. She had plenty of time, if she hurried. "You boys go back to sleep. If I'm not here by the time you wake up, you can fix yourselves bowls of cereal."

"Biscuits and honey," Clay mumbled. "Bacon and eggs. It's Saturday."

"I don't have time to make them before I leave. I'll fix a big breakfast tomorrow, Clay. Promise." Her knees popped as she straightened. "You boys be good."

Marianne sympathized with Lila's parking problem as she circled through the public parking lot for the fifth time. Was everybody and his brother running in this race? She kept a close look out for Nick. From the cluster of people she could see gathering near the train station, she deduced that had to be the starting point of the race.

To heck with the restaurant owner and his private parking lot, she fumed silently. At the next chamber of commerce meeting she was going to protest right along with Lila! Loudly!

She pulled off the side street into the private lot. The guard, who was standing near the back of the building, waved his arms over his head for her to stop.

Marianne did—in the parking space closest to the street,

"Sorry, lady," the guard shouted as he lumbered toward her car. "You can't park here."

Smiling and nodding, Marianne turned off the engine and tossed her keys into her purse. She *had* parked. The guard simply hadn't realized it, yet.

"Hey!" he shouted. "Are you deaf or just dumb? This is a tow-away zone! Get your car out of here."

"I'll be back when the restaurant opens!" she called over her shoulder. "Reserve me a table, would you?"

She sprinted toward the train station, weaving recklessly in and out of the gathering crowd. She had to get to the starting line. Fast! Before Nick tripped on his broken shoelaces and fell flat on his face!

One leg stretched behind him, Nick elongated his calf muscle by bending his other knee and leaning forward. He closed his eyes so as to mentally prepare for the race by visualizing a map of the racecourse.

Instead, his imagination pictured Marianne's face— laughing, her green eyes bright with contained mirth.

Concentrate, he scolded silently.

Shifting his weight to his front leg, he slowly moved his back leg forward until he stood upright. He jogged in place, shaking his shoulders, limbering his muscles.

"Ten miles," he heard the announcer call.

Ten miles. Twice the distance to the Clark home. He lifted his knees higher. The racecourse came within a mile of Marianne's house. Legs high! Would a one-mile detour cost him the race? Probably. He could tell her he was in the neighborhood, which would be true. Breathe through your nose!

"Nick!" Marianne shouted, spotting him running but going nowhere. "Wait!"

A voice over the megaphone blared, "Runners, get in place!"

"Excuse me," Marianne said, slipping between men and women racers, oblivious to the dirty looks she received. "Nick!"

Focused on the upcoming run, Nick blocked out the sounds and sights surrounding him. He heard only the internal music his mind played that he used to set his pace.

"Ready! Set!"

"No!"

A blank fired through the starting pistol as the announcer shouted, "Go!"

Run or be trampled were Marianne's only two choices. She ran.

While most of the runners set a steady jogging pace, she made a wild dash to catch up with Nick. At any second she expected his head and shoulders to disappear from sight as his shoelaces started to pop.

"Nick," she puffed. She ran hard and fast, drawing closer and closer to Nick's leisurely stride. She reached forward and touched his arm. "Nick!"

Utterly surprised and equally pleased, Nick laughed joyfully. He slowed his pace to accommodate Marianne's shorter stride. Who cared if he came in last? With her by his side he certainly didn't.

Pointing down while she used her body to crowd him toward the side of the street, she huffed, "Your shoes. I...cut...." She looked down at his feet, expecting to see the laces unraveling. What she saw slowed her down to a snail's pace. His shoes weren't clean and spanking-white. These were grubby as hell! "*Not*...your... shoes!"

He let her push him to the side of the pavement. "What's wrong? These are mine. My lucky shoes that I wore in my first winning race."

"Damn you, Nick King. You'd better get out of here fast!"

Marianne muscled through the rows of spectators and headed straight for a vacant park bench. She collapsed on it, then bent over at the waist. Her labored breathing resembled a blacksmith's bellows. She could not believe what she'd gone through to save a man who didn't need saving!

"Breathe through your nose," Nick said, afraid she might hyperventilate. "That's it. In and out. In and out. Slower. Slower."

Marianne tried to obey his instructions, but she was red-faced from more than trying to catch up with a man who didn't even have the common decency to be out of breath!

"You look angry." Nick sat next to her, then scooted a safe distance away when green fireworks seemed to shoot from her eyes. "Furious?"

Speechless, still catching her breath, she bobbed her head up and down.

"Because I dropped out of the race? Don't be. It doesn't bother me that you couldn't keep pace. There will be other races. A little training and you'll be running right up there with the best women athletes in Florida."

The green fires burning in her eyes intensified. If she'd had the strength she would have flattened Nick King! Near exhaustion, she did make a feeble attempt to stomp her heel on the toe of his "lucky" shoes.

"I'm on the wrong track?" Nick guessed.

"Yes!" On the verge of completely losing her temper, she spoke slowly and distinctly. "The boys are at home, alone—destroying the house while they are starving to death. My car has probably been towed away to jail, or wherever they take illegally parked cars. And it's your fault!"

Mystified, Nick asked, "How'd I do that?"

"You told Lou you had given her your lucky shoes! She gave them to me."

"That makes sense? I gave Lou a pair of shoes hoping you would be the one to return them . . . so your child is starving, your house is being demolished, and the cops have your car. I seem to be missing the connection."

"No, you . . ." She bit the tip of her tongue to keep from calling Nick one of Clay's rude names. "Don't you understand? I *cut* your shoelaces! I had to get here and stop you . . . or you'd be in the middle of the street using your face as a concrete plow!"

The nonsensical pieces fell into place. Nick glanced down at his feet and then back up at Marianne. Her face had changed color from vivid red to porcelain white. She wasn't wearing makeup, and he could see tiny golden freckles sprinkled across her nose like gold dust.

The joy he'd felt when he first saw her quadrupled as he realized what Marianne had gone through to keep him from taking a nasty fall.

He wrapped his arms around her, rocking her stiff body against his chest. Lordy, lordy, she was one adorable woman.

"I hear you, Nicholas King. You are laughing. Don't you dare compound what you did by laughing at me!"

"I'm not laughing at you, sweetheart."

"And don't call me sweetheart." She squirmed to be released from his arms. "Let go."

Nick opened his arms, then had to grab her to stop her from toppling off the bench. He released her instantly once she had regained her balance.

"What do you want me to say, Marianne?"

"You could start with an apology."

"Okay." His dark eyes sparkled with pure devilry as he said, "I'm sorry you cut my shoelaces."

Marianne jumped to her feet. "Isn't that just like a man? I try to save him from permanent disfigurement, public disgrace, *defeat,* and that's the thanks I get."

She had pushed both her hands against his shoulders when she heard the first bubbles of laughter coming from deep inside him. She might as well have been a gnat bumping into the Rock of Gibraltar. Exasperated at how little effect she had had on him, she turned on her heel and started trudging toward the parking lot.

"Where are you going?" Nick asked, jogging beside her.

"Home."

"Want me to come with you to help rebuild your house?" he joked. "I have a hammer and some nails in my toolbox. Did I tell you about the cabin I restored?"

"No. And I don't want to hear about it. Why don't you just run along with the other weekend sports fans?" She tapped her forehead. "That's spelled w-e-a-k-e-n-e-d because only somebody weak in the brain department would run ten miles...unless they were being chased by a madman, or madwoman."

Nick gave a shout of laughter that drew the attention of several elderly ladies strolling down Park Avenue. Marianne ducked her head as she recognized one of the women as the personnel director of a large corporation.

"How lóng do you stay angry?" Nick asked, stifling his laughter.

"Forever!"

She couldn't talk and breathe at the same time, not at the rate she was going. She either had to open her mouth or grow a bigger nose. She'd be damned if she'd let Nick King know she was winded, again.

"Is that negotiable?"

Marianne shot him a dirty look. "No."

"Never?"

"Never!"

Nick grinned at her, then swerved off the sidewalk. Turning around and running backward, he shouted, "Hey, Ms. Clark!"

"What?" Grateful for an excuse to stop, she planted her hands on her hips and glared at Nick.

"I wouldn't mind falling for you, lady. When you've cooled off, think about that."

She watched him spin around and turn on the speed, in hot pursuit of the pack of runners, who had by now disappeared from sight. Just what did he mean by that cryptic remark? she wondered silently. That he literally wouldn't mind splatting on the pavement in front of five hundred spectators? Or figuratively, that he wouldn't mind falling for her, as in falling in love?

Chapter Seven

"Get him! Get him!" Clay shouted, tossing the baseball over the runner's head to the third baseman.

Boxed between Clay on home plate and Peanut on third, Brad ran in one direction, pivoted and ran in the opposite direction. "Hey, Clay! Your fly is open!" he shouted suddenly.

Clay's eyes dropped; he missed the ball. Brad darted around him to score a run.

"He went outside the baseline, coach," Peanut shouted. "He's out!"

"You're out!" the coach shouted. "I heard what you said to the catcher. The umpire isn't going to let a practical joke win the game!"

Clay shucked his catcher's mask off his face. "Let 'em have the run, coach. We're gonna beat 'em fair and square," he said as he strutted back to the batter's box. "Cheaters never win."

"You heard me. He's out!" The coach clamped his hand on Brad's shoulder. "Winning isn't every-thing—especially not at a practice game."

"Way to go, son," Marianne said, but not loudly enough to embarrass him. He really is a good kid, she added silently. Not perfect, just a good, normal kid with decent values.

Her lips tilted upward at the corners when she thought about paying the price for pulling a prank. Brad wasn't the only one. Now that she was thinking with a clear head instead of going off half-cocked, she realized she was to blame for her whirlwind race around Winter Park. She glanced at her purse, where she'd shoved the parking ticket. She would have to pay the price with hard-earned cash.

She propped her elbows on the bleachers bench be-hind her, stretched out her legs and crossed them at the ankle. Face tilted upward, she closed her eyes and conjured up a picture of Nick wearing his disreputable "lucky" running shoes. A soft chuckle escaped her. He'd laughed. Not at her, she realized, but at the funny set of circumstances.

I wouldn't mind falling for you. He must have meant literally falling on the ground, she decided. They barely knew each other. Whirlwind courtships only hap-pened on the wide-screen cinemas. Movie producers were smart. They ended their films with the hero and heroine riding off into the sunset together. The hero didn't have a chance to outgrow the heroine. In real life only half the happy endings extended into the twilight years of old age. A couple had to know each other, in-side and out, to make a relationship last.

Marianne blinked. She'd known Ed since middle school, but their marriage was still a divorce statistic.

Maybe whirlwind relationships do have something going for them, she mused, smiling at the thought.

She'd only known Nick for a week, but he'd already revealed his basic character traits to her. Smart. Competitive. Funny. Good with kids. Successful. Attractive. How would knowing him for years and years change those innate traits?

"Watch out, Mom!" Clay screamed, jerking his catcher's mask off his head. "The ball is coming at you!"

Marianne focused her attention on the spinning hardball dropping from overhead. Reflexively, she jerked up her knees and folded her arms protectively over her face.

Catch it! You can! she told herself.

She cupped her hands. It wasn't going to hit her. She kept her eye on the ball. Sliding sideways, she lined up her hands with the ball. She'd been the worst fielder in the history of Winter Park High. What did she think she was doing?

A second later she felt the sting of leather and heard the players cheer. Amazed to find the ball in her hands, she rubbed her fingers over the scuffed hide and laces.

"Great catch, Mom. Throw it over the fence to the pitcher."

Praise from her son? In front of the whole team? Taking her magnificent catch and praise from her son as good omens of things to come, she drew back her arm and hurled the ball toward the field.

"Here it comes!" she yelled. The ball arched beautifully, just as she'd planned, then fell short of her mark. She shrugged. "Well, you win some, you lose some, and some get rained out."

"Can't win 'em all," Gregory said, grinning like a Cheshire cat at Nick. He held up his second place plaque. "I can't believe I beat my own coach."

Nick could. He'd diligently trained to win. But when he remembered why the other runners had nearly a mile's head start, he didn't mind coming in in last place one damned bit. Of course, it would have been great to present Marianne with a trophy. And it would have been good publicity for King Enterprises. "Your time has improved considerably, Greg." Nick grinned. "Remember what you said when I first suggested running a ten-mile race?"

"Yeah." Greg glanced around to make certain his girlfriend wasn't within hearing range. "Unless there was a gorgeous woman running two feet in front of me I'd never make one mile, much less ten. Speaking of gorgeous women, didn't I see a certain red-haired vixen pass me at the starting line?"

"Yes. Marianne was here. She dropped out."

Greg's curiosity grew when he saw Nick grin. "You didn't tell me if Marianne went out with you."

"No, I didn't."

"That toothy grin on your face makes you look like the tomcat that just cornered the market on dairy cows."

Nick laughed. "That's about how I feel."

"You mean she actually went out with you?" Awed, Greg raised his voice. "Heck, man, a date with Marianne Clark is better than winning the trophy today! You broke a long-standing world-class record!"

"Pipe down, Greg." The last thing he needed was to have Greg blaring out misinformation about Marianne's private life. "I didn't say we're dating. In fact, she left the race furious with me."

"I've heard about redheads and their temper. I thought Marianne was the exception. She's the calmest, most sensible woman in Winter Park." His hand made a horizontal line. "You must have done something awful."

"She hates my lucky shoes."

Perplexed, Greg glanced down at Nick's feet. "Those rags on your feet don't exactly enhance your image. Didn't I see athletic shoes on your inventory list?"

"Yes."

"Why don't you get on her good side by wearing a fancy pair of pump-up shoes?" Greg looked at his new running shoes. "On second thought, don't bother. My shoes never seemed to impress her."

Laughing, Nick slapped Greg on the back. "Maybe it's the shoelaces. Some women just go wild when they get them in their hands."

"You two have a private joke. Right?"

"Yep. One I wouldn't even trust with my accountant."

"Listen, ol' buddy, I have an appointment with a warm spa and a tall glass of beer. Want to join me?"

"Thanks, but I have to drop by the warehouse to check out some weight-lifting equipment that the warehouse crew assembled yesterday."

"On Saturday?"

"It's supposed to be a hot item. According to the manufacturer's advertising campaign it'll revolutionize weight lifting. At any rate, the retail stores are anxious to get it stocked. But you know me. I'm a skeptic until I've tried it myself. See you later, Greg. Congratulations!"

Nick ambled toward the public parking lot. As he unlocked his door he wondered if Marianne's car had been towed away. On his way home he could drive by her house to see...no, he couldn't. Once there, he'd find another excuse to drop in and then he'd invent an excuse to stay.

He had to refrain from what the superstar body-builders call straining to the point of failure. At Marianne's home the point of failure would be reached by trying to build their relationship too quickly and wearing out his welcome.

Besides, he did need to go by the warehouse. Resigned to spending the remainder of the day alone, he climbed into his car. While he was there, he could pick up a Ping-Pong table.

Late Sunday afternoon Nick pulled into Marianne's drive, beeped his horn and shouted, "Clay! How 'bout coming out here and giving me a hand?"

Clay turned his cards faceup, three at a time. "You go help him. You're winning. You always win at double solitaire!"

"Uh-uh. He called for you." Marianne pointed to the queen of hearts. "Play that one."

"No way. I'm blocking your king. It's the only card you have left."

Over waffles that morning, she'd nonchalantly told Clay that she'd invited Nick over for Ping-Pong lessons. Clay had razzed her about her ineptness at the game, but otherwise had acted as though Nick showing up was the same as one of his friends coming over to the house—no big deal.

Marianne smiled. Her son would have reconsidered had he seen the way she'd picked through her closet,

searching for the perfect outfit. She'd settled on a tur-
quoise blue jumpsuit she'd been saving for a special
occasion. He'd have known for certain his mother was
taking extra pains with her appearance had he watched
her ransack through her jewelry box to find a pair of
dangling silver-and-turquoise earrings.

A smart child, he'd have quickly realized Nick King's
arrival was a big deal to his mother.

"You can't win, Clay. Your ten of clubs is buried
under that string of cards."

Clay grinned mischievously. "Mr. King can lift a tow
truck. He doesn't need my help." He flicked the corner of the buried card. "On second thought, you
should go help him since he's your company. While
you're gone, I think I might figure out a way to un-
cover it."

"On the count of three we'll both go out."

"You know the rule, Mom. He who quits loses."

"We can't leave company standing out in the driveway, Clay. Nick will think we aren't home and leave.
We'll finish the game later. One . . . two . . . three."

Marianne pushed her chair away from the table,
stood and leisurely walked toward the door leading to
the garage.

She wanted to run to him.

"I win!" Clay chortled. "You quit! Quitters never
win! You've told me that a zillion times."

And I've said be still my heart the same number of
times—just in the past hour, Marianne thought silently. It was a miracle that she'd been able to remember the sequence of the cards.

"Outside, you merciless little cardsharp."

Laughing, she opened the door. Seeing Nick lift a
huge flat box to his shoulder, balance it, then grace-

fully pivot on the ball of his foot reminded her of watching the male star of a ballet. Only there was absolutely nothing sissified about the muscles straining in Nick's shoulders and legs.

"What's he doing?" Clay asked coldly. "Moving in?"

"Of course not, silly," she whispered, her translucent skin turning pink. Louder, she said, "Hi, Nick. Pardon the pun, but is that you're idea of a King-size box of chocolates?"

Nick lowered the box and turned around. His abdominal muscles clenched in response to her beauty.

Are you still angry? his eyes asked as he raised one eyebrow, slightly frowning.

Shaking her head, Marianne grinned at him.

"Is that what I think it is?" Clay asked as he recognized the brand name printed on the sides of the boxes.

"It ain't truffles," Nick drawled, pleased by Clay's enthusiasm.

"Mom! It's that super, fantastic weight-lifting set that's guaranteed to build biceps like Ferrigno... Coe... Mentzer!"

Marianne pushed up her sleeve and flexed her arm. With exaggerated reverence, she gushed, "Gosh. I'll look like..."

"Combes, Dunlap and McLish," Nick said, supplying her with the names of prominent women bodybuilders.

Marianne grinned. "How did you know I put that whatever-it-is on my Christmas wish list?"

Nick winked at her. "Well, I hate to break your heart, but this equipment is for Clay."

"For me? Honest?" Jumping up and down, then running from box to box, Clay could hardly contain his excitement. "Can we put it together now?"

"Not we. You. One of the selling points is supposed to be its easy assembly. There's a demonstration videotape on the front seat of my car that shows how to put it together." Clay dashed out of the garage before he finished. Advancing toward Marianne, he said quietly, "I hope you don't object. It isn't exactly a gift, because Clay will have to earn the equipment. And he'll be doing me a big favor."

"A favor? How?"

"The equipment is designed for the early-teen market. Aside from assembling it, Clay and his friends will have to fill out evaluation forms designed by the manufacturer each time they use the equipment. Nothing difficult. Just a checklist."

Nick felt like a salesman who'd successfully squeezed his foot in the front door with his fast talk. Now the difficult part of his sales pitch confronted him. He had to convince Marianne to make room for him in her tight schedule. "I'll have to work with him on a regular basis to keep close tabs on his progress. I'd be over here three, maybe four times a week. Do you mind?"

"You don't happen to have an ulterior motive tucked away in one of those boxes, do you?" she teased, constantly amazed by the lengths Nick went to in order to spend time with her. His persistence flattered her. His thoughtfulness toward her son completely charmed her. He was making it difficult to keep him at arm's distance. "Hmm?"

Nick grinned. Putting something over on Marianne was impossible. "Yeah, there is. But you have to admit, bringing the weight-lifting equipment for Clay is less risky than antagonizing Lou. That lady had murder and mayhem shooting from her eyes when I handed her my lucky—'' Uh-oh, he thought, his mouth had outraced his brain. He backtracked and amended "Coffeepot?"

"Hey, Mr. King!" Clay dashed into the garage with his arms loaded with small boxes. "I found the videotape and the rest of the pieces to the set. Did you want me to bring in this foil-wrapped box, too?"

"Chocolates," Nick mouthed before putting a respectable distance between himself and Marianne. "Thanks, Clay. That's a little something for your mother."

Clay shoved the box of candy into his mother's hands. "Why don't you give Mr. King a Ping-Pong lesson while I watch the video? I want to get started putting it together while he's still here."

"Don't slam the—"

The back door banged shut.

"The doors will fall off their hinges if your equipment makes him stronger," Marianne said.

"I'm very good at hanging doors," Nick replied.

Is there anything he isn't good at? Her fingers toyed with the frilly bow tied around the box of candy. For every reason she came up with not to shake up her status quo, Nick invented an excuse to tempt her into weakness.

"Thanks."

"You're welcome." His dark eyes beckoned her to come closer. "My pleasure."

Marianne's mind sent an incoherent signal to her insatiable eyes to stop looking at Nick. He'd surely see the place she'd made for him in her heart if she didn't drop her eyes. Without so much as blinking, she continued to stare at him.

"You really don't mind about the equipment, do you?" he asked.

The realization that she could break the tension growing between them by merely lowering her eyes gave Marianne a heady sense of power.

"I don't mind," she said. Her reply was as much to the yearning she saw in the black velvet depth of his eyes as to his question.

She wanted him to hold her, kiss her. Her longing was as great as his yearning.

He removed the candy box from her hands, placing it on an empty carton. He wanted nothing between them when he finally held her in his arms.

He gently pulled her toward him. "Marianne, I've wanted to kiss you since the moment I saw you being kind to Lila. I knew then that you were a very, very special lady."

She heard his soft groan as he elevated her hand to his lips. Somewhere in the recesses of her mind she heard the videotape playing loudly and Clay cheering with enthusiasm. But her senses honed in on the sensations rippling through her as Nick brushed the sweetest of kisses into the palm of her hand.

He raised her hand to the side of his face as his arm circled her slender waist. "Very special," he whispered, lowering his lips to hers.

His cautious kiss, one meant to allay any fears she had, changed to a reckless one when her arms twined around his neck. He parted her lips, wanting to share the heat from the fires she'd caused by pressing herself against him.

A passion Marianne had hoarded, denying its existence, burst from deep within her. She gave him the sweet intimacy of her mouth without hesitation. She could not deny him access any more than parched grass could refuse the summer's rains. Each of his kisses brought her dormant desire bubbling closer and closer to the surface.

Her knees weakened. Nick used his strength to lift her higher into his arms, until her toes no longer touched the ground. Marianne didn't care. She'd lost touch with reality and clung tightly to Nick.

"Sweetheart..."

Nick peppered kisses along her cheek, across her gold-dust freckles, fighting to keep some semblance of awareness as to where they were and who was in the family room. Marianne would never forgive him if Clay came bursting through the door. He wished their passion could magically transport them to his home where they'd be alone in the privacy of his bedroom.

"We've got to stop, sweetheart."

"We've only just begun," Marianne murmured, reluctant to suppress the delectable sensations Nick had awakened in her.

Nick heard the video's music crescendo in volume. At any second the teenage bodybuilders would finish their demonstration. He whispered the one word guaranteed to bring Marianne back to her senses. "Clay."

Instantly her arms unlocked from around his neck and she squirmed in his arms. Nick kissed the tip of her nose, then set her free.

Blushing at the thought of Clay seeing his mother kissing Nick with such wild abandon, Marianne straightened her clothing with one hand and made certain her hair wasn't in disarray with the other. One kiss and Nick had shuffled her long-standing priority list. She'd acted like an irresponsible, self-centered teenager!

To relieve her acute embarrassment Nick said, "We weren't doing anything wrong, Marianne. Just kissing. That's nothing to be ashamed of."

"You don't understand."

He did understand. That was why he'd been the one to end the kiss. A clandestine relationship, sneaking around behind Clay's back, would only lead to future problems.

"Make me understand," he urged.

Her hands fluttered aimlessly. "Clay was a toddler when his father and I separated."

"So?"

"Clay has never seen me kissing a man!" Her voice was low, intense. "He'd be shocked."

"Your son is thirteen. You're how old?"

"Thirty-two."

"Old enough to be kissed without the consent of a third party? You're the adult in this household, the person in charge. Do you think Clay expects you to ask his permission to kiss a man?"

"No, of course not. Clay has probably never thought of it. We've certainly never discussed it. Kissing hasn't exactly been anywhere on my priority list until now."

"Until now?" Nick repeated, relieved to hear her admit that he at least qualified to be on her list. He framed her face with his large hands. "I don't want to shock Clay, either. But I do plan on kissing you. I want everything between us to be open and aboveboard with Clay. Otherwise, we'll be defeated before we begin."

Suddenly, it dawned on Marianne that Nick had been one step ahead of her. He'd been the one who'd made certain Clay didn't unexpectedly catch them kissing. His sensitivity and consideration impressed her.

"Unless Clay rewinds the videotape he's going to be out here within thirty seconds," Nick said, smiling down at Marianne. He realized she needed time to prepare Clay to accept him into their lives. Being a patient man, he could wait. "What say we start uncrating this equipment? I'll need a screwdriver and a hammer."

"The toolbox is in the corner." She brushed a kiss on the heel of his hand. "Thanks, Nick."

"For what?"

"Being considerate of Clay. And of me."

Their thirty seconds was up. Clay charged into the garage.

"I'm gonna have to go next door and get Brad. It takes two to put it together. I'll be back in a minute."

"Why don't you use the telephone?" Marianne asked.

"He's grounded 'cause he sassed his mom." Clay glanced at Nick. "But I think she'll let him come over here if I go beg and plead. I'll be back in a flash!"

Marianne watched Clay cutting across the side yard as Nick selected a screwdriver and started prying copper staples from the end of one carton.

She winked back at him and grinned, then crossed to her car, opened the glove compartment and said, "On the way home from church today, I bought you a little present."

"You did?"

"Nothing extravagant." She handed him a small, gaily wrapped package, holding on to the card she'd also purchased. "It's the thought that counts."

Both curious and impatient, Nick stripped off the paper. Inside he found a pair of shoelaces—with neon-pink hearts on them. Tossing back his head he gave a hoot of laughter. "These are great! I'll be the envy of every runner in the next marathon!"

"There's a card, too." It pleased her immensely that he'd accepted her gift in the same lighthearted spirit she'd been in when she bought it.

Nick made quick work of getting the card from the envelope. On the front a cartoon character stood beside a cliff. Marianne had drawn big shoelaces on the man's shoes, both of which were untied. Inside the character had taken a flying leap. She'd crossed out the printed message and written his enigmatic words, "I wouldn't mind falling for you . . . either."

Sweeping her high into his arms, Nick spun her around and around, laughing joyously as her arms clung to his shoulders. He couldn't have been happier with her gift if the shoestrings had been made of pure gold.

"Stop," she said, giggling. Her fingertips dug into the fabric of his shirt, holding tightly. She felt light-headed and carefree, like a sixteen-year-old instead of a thirty-two-year-old mother of a teenage boy. "You're making me dizzy!"

Neither of them saw Clay standing outside the garage watching them.

"What are you doing to my mother?" Clay asked, unnerved, his voice breaking midsentence. "You put her down before you drop her!"

"She's safe, man." Brad's eyes rounded with awe as they witnessed the bulge of Nick's biceps. "Would you look at those muscles!"

Nick set Marianne on her feet, holding her at the waist for a second until she regained her balance.

Looking hard at them, and not liking what he saw, Clay said, "Brad, *you* could lift her. My mom doesn't weigh much. She's a featherweight."

Marianne, pretending to be miffed, sashayed up to her son and put her arm across his narrow shoulders. "Is that right? A featherweight, huh? Last night when you were sitting in my chair and I sat on you, you said I weighed a ton. That I was squishing you. Who got the chair?"

"You did." Clay shrugged her arm off his shoulders, then picked up a screwdriver and handed it to Brad. He picked up the one Nick had used and muttered, "You guys would have had this unpacked if you hadn't been goofing off."

Choosing to misunderstand, Nick said, "Taking it out of the boxes isn't part of the hour it's supposed to take to assemble it. Want some help?"

"Uh-uh," Clay answered, deciding he didn't want to stand around looking like a dumb kid while Mr. King showed off his muscles. "Brad and I can do it."

Marianne felt guilty. She'd been wrong to distract Nick from getting the equipment unpacked. Clay had rushed back, eager to get started on setting up his new toy and been sorely disappointed to find it still in the boxes. She could understand why he'd be miffed.

"Why don't I go inside and make you and Brad a big pitcher of lemonade?" she offered, to make amends.

"Since Clay doesn't want my help, I'll help you," Nick volunteered. He twirled the shoelaces she'd given him in a wide circle, like an executive's gold key chain. "I'd better put these in my car so I won't forget them."

Clay jammed the tip of the screwdriver under a staple. So that's why we had to stop at K mart, he thought silently. Pink hearts on white laces! I'm glad she didn't give them to me.

He pushed on the handle and had the satisfaction of seeing the staple pop out of the box.

"Do you think he's really gonna wear them in his shoes?" Brad whispered to Clay after the grown-ups had gone in opposite directions.

Clay tapped his temple with his forefinger. "He's crazy if he does."

"Yeah," Brad agreed. "My sister has a pair just like 'em. Weird, huh?"

"Yeah. *Real* weird." The side of the carton fell to the garage floor as Clay removed the last staple. "This is the main part of the frame. Grab hold of the box while I pull it out."

"It looks kind of heavy, dude. Maybe we ought to ask Mr. King to help."

"In the videotape a kid half my size lifted it. Just hold the box like I said." Clay tugged the steel frame forward a couple of inches. Stooping, he grabbed it at the base and tilted it against his shoulder. "It's all a matter of balance."

"Watch out!" Brad cried with his eyes bugging from his head. "It's gonna whack you in the head!"

Nick, who'd been watching from outside the garage, darted forward. He'd wanted the boys to manage on their own, but not if it meant causing an accident!

"Got it," Nick said, catching the top bar before it landed against Clay's shoulder. "You're doing fine,

Clay. Just swing the butt end around while I set it up-right.''

"Let go, would you? Can't you see that I've got it." Clay staggered under the weight, recovered his foot-ing, then straightened. Slick as a whistle, the frame stood erect. He hadn't needed any help. A gleam of triumph lit his eyes. "You said that we're supposed to do it!"

"Okay, fellas." Nick backed off, attributing Clay's snappishness to the his not wanting to look bad in front of his friend. At thirteen, he'd have reacted similarly. "The tough part is over. You're doing great. I'll go in-side and help your mother carry the lemonade out here."

Clay glanced at Brad, who was looking at Mr. King as though he'd done something magnificent. Why? He'd done the hard work. Brad should've been pat-ting him on the back.

"C'mon, Brad." Clay lightly punched Brad on the arm. "We've only got one hour to get it together."

Inside, Marianne put the can of frozen lemonade in the microwave to thaw it. She wasn't ashamed or em-barrassed that Clay had arrived while Nick was play-fully swinging her around. But her son's reaction did bother her. He'd been happy as a lark when he left for Brad's house, and downright disgruntled when he re-turned. She'd thought that teasing him about their nightly battle over who got to sit in the leather chair would lighten his mood. She'd only made his mood sink from disgruntled to surly.

He's starting into those difficult teenage years, Marianne reminded herself as she began filling a plas-tic pitcher with ice cubes. She closed the freezer, thinking Clay's mood swings were enough to test a saint's patience.

"How is the lemonade coming along?" Nick asked from the doorway. He looked forward to the day when he could slip up behind her while she was deep in thought, nibble a path along her nape with his lips and ask if she was thinking about him.

"It's cooking...thawing in the microwave," she corrected when she noticed his dark brows raise. "How is everything going out in the garage?"

He was tempted to tease her by saying the boys had given her car a few dents and scratches, but then she'd dash out there and he'd be stuck making lemonade. Nick seldom victimized himself through poor planning.

"They're busy. Very busy." Without exaggerating, he added, "Clay doesn't want any help."

"I encourage him to be independent."

"He is that." Nick leaned his backside against the cabinet, crossing his legs at the ankle. "We'd better not distract them by using the Ping-Pong table."

The microwave's timer pinged. Marianne circled around the center counter and removed the can. "Afraid I'll beat you, too?" she teased.

"Terrified."

"You don't look terrified, Mr. King." He looked terrific, as if he belonged in her kitchen. She poured the concentrate over the ice cubes, then crossed to the sink, passing right by Nick.

Unable to resist, he reached out and touched her hair. Knowing the boys could burst into the kitchen at any moment added a hint of danger. "Should I tell you how you look, Ms. Clark?"

His dark eyes spoke eloquently for him, making her feel exquisite. She smiled. "Would you reach up on the top shelf of the cabinet behind you and get the tray for me?"

"I take it that means no." He retrieved the tray. Placing it in front of her, he asked, "Has someone told you that your blue-green outfit makes your eyes look as mysterious as the ocean depths?"

No one, she answered silently. Clay certainly hadn't. Compliments were generally in short supply at her house. She was lucky if she got a "you look okay, Mom," which would automatically be followed with "hurry up."

Her heart quickened. Being treated like an attractive woman made her insides feel warm and achy. She gave voice to her silent reply. "No one."

"Your eyes fascinate me. They subtly change color with your clothes, your mood. When I first saw you at the chamber of commerce party, peekabooing from under the brim of your hat, they intrigued me."

Silently, he wondered what hue of blue-green they'd be in the early morning when she first awakened.

"Mrs. Clark," Brad yelled from the garage doorway. "We're dying of thirst out here!"

As startled as though she had jumped from Nick's warm tropical seas straight into Clay's pitcher of iced lemonade, Marianne clenched her jaw to quell a shiver running up her spine.

She sidestepped around Nick and shouted, "I'll be right there, Brad!"

"Thanks!"

Marianne waited to hear the door slam. Instead, she heard the boys' hushed voices.

"Go on in and get him," Clay urged.

"He's talking to your mom."

"So?"

"You said we're supposed to do it ourselves!"

"But you didn't watch the video! We'll never make it in an hour with me stopping every five seconds to tell you what to do. Just get him to come out here to make sure we've done it right."

"It's your equipment. You ask!"

"Never mind, Brad. Since you won't ask for help, we'll stop and *both* go watch the video!"

Marianne heard a tool clang against the concrete. "Brad? Why don't I bring the portable television and VCR out there? That way you can watch the directions while you're working."

"Brilliant idea, Mrs. Clark. We can stop, fast forward and rewind the videotape so we won't get confused."

Nick chuckled and whispered to Marianne, "Yeah, with all those buttons to choose from on the VCR, maybe they'll stop punching ours."

Chapter Eight

"Take it easy, Clay. Atlas didn't hoist the world on his shoulders in one day. I don't want you to hurt yourself." Nick reduced the number of weights Clay had placed on the pulley. "The object of bodybuilding training is to increase the strain on the muscles by gradually increasing the number of repetitions, then going on to heavier weights. It takes patience."

Seated on the bench, Clay pulled the bar that raised the weights on the pulley. "No pain, no gain—isn't that what the pros say?"

"The ones nursing sprains say that," Nick replied. "Breathe naturally."

Nick was having difficulty breathing at all as he watched Marianne bite into one of the chocolate-covered fresh strawberries he'd brought her. There was something deliciously sinful about the way she closed her eyes and concentrated solely on the blend of bittersweet chocolate and nature's sugar. He found himself holding his breath, waiting for her to swallow, then waiting to see if the tip of her tongue flicked the thin trace of chocolate off her lower lip.

Seeing black spots dancing in front of his eyes, he said to Clay, "When you hold it the blood stops flowing to your brain. You'll black out."

"Can I have another one?" Brad asked Marianne, his hand already inside the candy box.

"You're going to spoil your dinner."

Brad grinned and pleaded, "Just one for the road? Please? Lifting weights works up a whale of an appetite."

"One more, if you promise to eat your green vegetables," Marianne said, aware that Brad's mother practically had to spoon-feed anything other than meat and potatoes down the boy's throat.

Nodding, Brad swiped a chocolate, popped it in his mouth, then held up the crossed fingers he'd been hiding behind his back. Mouth full, he garbled, "I gotta run!"

"You'd better run, you little stinker."

"See ya, Clay. Thanks, Mr. King. Training on Tuesday, Thursday and Sunday evenings, right?"

"Yeah. See ya," Clay grunted. He let the weights clang together as he dropped the bar. Sitting up, he shouted at Brad, "Don't forget to fill out the form Mr. King gave you." To Nick he said, "That's six of everything like you told me to do."

"You aren't sore, are you?"

"Uh-uh." He flexed his arm and grinned at his mother. "I feel stronger already."

"Strong enough to polish off a couple of these chocolates?" Marianne asked.

"You bet! They'll give me energy to fill out Mr. King's forms."

"And do your homework, too," she prompted.

Clay groaned as he plucked several candies from the box. "I was hoping you'd forget that dumb limerick assignment."

"Not likely, son. The rules haven't changed. Schoolwork still comes first around here."

"Only a sissy writes poetry, huh, Mr. King?" He gave Mr. King an us-guys-have-to-stick-together look. "Tell her."

Nick held up his hands. "Whoa! Leave me out of this."

He thought he'd given a diplomatic reply until he received Clay's dirty look and watched Marianne raise an eyebrow. He'd lost favor with both of them.

Stymied as to what the appropriate response should have been, he picked up the tray of glasses and gestured for both of them to precede him into the house.

What should he have done? he wondered. What would he have done if Crissy had been the one with the poetry assignment? Simple, he thought. He'd have helped her with it.

But he wasn't Clay's father.

Be careful, he silently coached. You're about to get overly involved with the boy. He watched as Clay disappeared in the direction of his bedroom. It's okay to be friends, but don't start caring too much. He can do his homework without you.

He turned toward the kitchen, where Marianne had begun loading the glassware into the dishwasher. Before they'd shared a pizza he'd decided the timing was wrong to tell Marianne about Crissy. Although he felt she could become a woman with whom he'd share his innermost secrets, it was still too soon. Without baring his soul he had to persuade her a hands-off policy between himself and Clay was for the best.

"What would you have said if you'd been in my shoes?" he asked.

"Go do your homework."

"I didn't think it was my place to give your son a direct order."

Marianne shoved the top rack in the machine and looked up at Nick. "I gave him the order. It would have been nice if you'd backed me up. I can tell he looks up to you."

"But I'd be lying to him if I said writing limericks is my favorite recreation."

"Okay, so you don't write limericks. I'm certain you can think of a man Clay would look up to who does write limericks."

"Not off the top of my head I can't. Can you?"

Marianne paused, trying to come up with the name of a famous male writer of limericks. The sight of Nick, bending over to load a plate in the dishwasher, didn't help her concentration.

"Can't think of one, can you?" He grinned at her.

The naughty limericks Marianne thought of as her eyes were drawn to Nick's smile weren't suitable for a teenager to submit to his English teacher.

Chuckling, Nick brushed his lips across hers. "Something tells me the raunchy limericks I learned at the fraternity house while I was in college would get me in hot water. They were anonymous—for a reason."

His kiss had been fleeting, a friendly kiss, but it must have served its purpose. Marianne couldn't give him the cold treatment when she felt as though she were the one standing in hot water.

"Let's forget about limericks," he suggested, loving how she looked at him. "The evening is young. Let's concentrate on you and me."

"Any suggestions?"

"You could thank me properly for those chocolates you devoured," he hinted brazenly.

She stretched up and gave him a quick peck on the corner of his mouth. "Thanks. Next suggestion?"

"You certainly spurred my imagination." He waited until she'd closed the dishwasher, then folded her into his arms. His lips teased hers by brushing lightly across them. "I guess indulging in long, lazy, wet kisses on the sofa is out?"

She nibbled on his bottom lip. "Way out."

"How about out . . . as going to a late movie?" He'd paused to taste the place where chocolate had clung to her lip. "Most of the theaters have ten o'clock shows."

"It's too late for Clay to go."

"Yes, it is," Nick agreed readily. He enjoyed Clay's company, but he wanted to be alone with Marianne.

"I don't leave him home alone at night. He's too young. When I walked out the front door I'd be inviting trouble in the back door." Torn between wanting to go and knowing it would be irresponsible, she eased away from Nick.

"What about a baby-sitter?"

"Most of the sitters are his age. Usually, if I'm planning on going out on Friday or Saturday night, I make arrangements one or two days in advance with Brad's folks. They have the same problem so we scratch each other's backs. But it's Sunday, and too late to call them tonight." She worried the inside of her lip. "I guess dating a single parent has a multitude of drawbacks. Clay is staying with his dad next weekend. Maybe we could go to the movies then.''

''No maybes.'' Nick grinned. ''A definite yes. You put my name down on your busy calendar for next Friday and Saturday. That is, unless you've made other plans.''

''Along with Tuesdays, Thursdays and Sundays?'' She returned her smile. ''You think you're very clever, don't you, Mr. Nicholas King?''

''You have to admit, it's cleverer than mowing grass and spreading lime at the baseball field—with you here and me there. I wasn't exactly overjoyed with your idea.''

''But you did consider it?''

''Yes.''

Taking his hand, she led him into the family room. ''You know, Nick, aside from your minor character flaws—mistreating temporary employees, being stubbornly persistent and being completely domineering— you are—'' she sat on the sofa and patted the cushion next to her ''—charming, irresistible and quite adorable.''

On the other side of the wall, Clay accidentally on purpose pressed his ear against it as he picked his English book off his desk. Charming? Irresistible? Adorable? She's in there bragging about what a wonderful kid she has. Again. At least this time she'd waited until he wasn't in the same room.

Mothers could be so embarrassing!

Scowling, he wished he'd heard what Nick had said while they were in the kitchen. Thanks to Brad not being much help, they hadn't finished putting the weight-lifting equipment together within the hour time limit, but doing the sets had been a snap.

He sprawled facedown across his bed. He wanted to turn his stereo on, but his mother had a fit when he studied with the volume turned up.

"English. What a groaner!"

Sighing, he flipped his grammar book open and thumbed through the pages until he found the blank page of notebook paper. Jeez, like a grown man really cared about poetry! He'd rather wear shoelaces with little pink hearts on them.

Clay glanced at the wall. His mother could be a big help, but no, she couldn't help him do his homework because her company didn't know when to go home. They were in the family room, probably watching one of his favorite television shows.

He liked things the way they had been before Mr. Lift-Two-Tons-With-One-Finger had arrived on the scene. Not that he'd want to give back the weight-lifting equipment—that was cool. What he didn't like was his mother not paying attention to him.

"Like now," Clay grumbled, flopping over on his back.

He stared at the white ceiling, uninspired. He heard his mother laugh softly.

She probably told a joke I didn't get to hear, Clay griped silently. She should be in here writing a funny limerick that would guarantee him a good grade.

Didn't his own mother care if he flunked English? If she didn't care, why should he? It must not be important, he reasoned, otherwise she would be in here. That made sense to him.

"I'd better go." Nick stood, then offered his hand to Marianne. "We both have to work tomorrow and it's almost midnight. My car turns into a pumpkin on the final stroke of twelve.''

Sliding her hands up Nick's arms until they flattened on his broad chest, she smiled, saying, ''You don't look or feel like Cinderfella. Are you sure you have to go? You'll miss the end of the movie.''

He was sure, all right, but not for the reason he'd given Marianne. The past ten minutes of sitting next to her, only casually touching from shoulder to knee, had tested the boundaries of his self-control. The steamy love story they'd been watching on television had almost caused him to fall from Marianne's good graces. He wasn't going to stick around for the climax of the film.

His large hands spanned her narrow waist, his thumbs restlessly tracing the curve of her ribs, dangerously close to the curve of her breasts.

He'd gone beyond the stage of lighthearted kissing. His moist breath misted over her lips, then whispered a hot caress across her forehead, eyes, cheeks. He hesitated a bare second before taking her mouth, afraid his craving for her wouldn't be satisfied with a kiss.

Sweetly, gently, his lips covered hers as he drew upon the last vestiges of his steely self-control. But steel melts at extremely high temperatures. So did his control when Marianne's lips parted, her tongue enticing his with sensual, erotic flicks.

His hips rocked against her, matching the rhythm to the advance-and-retreat movement of her tongue. No longer did he lightly hold her. He pressed against her willing softness, stoking the fires she'd lit to a fevered pitch. As his hands glided down the feminine curve of her buttocks, an uncontrollable shaft of desire racked every bone in his sturdy frame.

"Marianne...Marianne," he breathed heavily as he slanted his mouth across hers in the opposite direction.

Marianne returned to her senses with a start. It could have been Clay calling her! At any moment Clay could barge into the room.

"What am I doing?" she mouthed against the heat of Nick's skin.

She couldn't blame him; she'd been the one who'd ravished his mouth, dueling with his tongue for dominance. She'd started this. She had to stop it. Though she knew it would take every ounce of her willpower to say no to him, she had to do it or there would be no turning back.

"No."

Weak and feeble though her voice sounded, Nick heard her. Although reluctant to rein in this explosive passion that had ignited between them, he instantly dropped his hands to his sides.

"I should have left," he gasped, trying to master the art of breathing without it sounding like a windstorm.

Knees weak, Marianne struggled to support her own weight, to break physical contact with Nick. It took considerable effort to move scant inches. Giving in to her wild desire would have been far easier.

Unwilling to let Nick take responsibility for her wanton actions, she said, "You aren't to blame, Nick."

"Neither are you." His fingers plowed through his hair. One hand settled on his hip. His body language clearly spoke of frustration. He could no longer go on as they had been, with him making up pretenses to be with her. "You're the first woman I've wanted to be with in a long, long while."

"And you're the first man I've wanted to be with. We're both on unfamiliar territory, aren't we?"

Nick bobbed his head. His breathing had decelerated and he'd begun to think clearly. "You stopped because of Clay, didn't you?"

"Partially." Awareness of her son's proximity was only one of her reasons for not rushing blindly into intimacy with Nick. She had to go slowly, carefully, to avoid repeating the mistakes she'd made with Ed. She'd had firsthand experience then of how it felt to lean on a man and have him suddenly walk. It had been a difficult struggle to get off her knees and stand on her own two feet. Now, with her pride and self-confidence intact, she had avoided becoming dependent upon another man. To be fair to both of them she needed to explain how she felt. "Would you excuse me while I check on Clay? I'm fairly certain he's sound asleep, but sometimes he's unpredictable. I wouldn't want him to overhear us talking."

"I wouldn't, either. Do you mind if I go out in the pool area?"

"No. You go ahead. I'll join you in a minute."

She needed to think this through. Nick did, too. Neither of them could change their past. Clay wasn't going to vanish into thin air each time Nick entered the house. And she'd never build Nick's male ego at the sacrifice of her self-confidence. They had to agree upon some guidelines. And help each other stick to them!

Pausing outside Clay's bedroom door, she smoothed her hands over her hair in case Clay had stayed up past his bedtime. Each night, this was part of her regular routine. Before she locked up the house and turned out the lights, she made certain he was safe in bed and sound asleep.

The light fixture in the hallway cast a beam across Clay's bed as she barely cracked the door open. Curled on his side at the edge of the bed with one arm under his pillow, he appeared younger than thirteen. Young and vulnerable. Sweet and defenseless.

Love and pride welled up in her throat. "Night, son," she whispered. "I love you."

He didn't respond. She hadn't expected him to. Each night these were the last words she spoke, often her last thought.

Silently, she turned and moved through the house to the pool enclosure. Her last thought tonight would still be of Clay, but she'd also be thinking of Nick.

As she slid back the door on its track, the night's humidity engulfed her. The cold snap had ended. An easterly wind scattered nimbus clouds across the pin-points of light above her. Somewhere in the distance a whippoorwill called to its mate.

Her eyes adjusted to the darkness. Nick was stand-ing beside the pool staring into the water as though it held the solution to their problems. She crossed to his side and laced her fingers through his.

While she was tucking Clay in, Nick had come to grips with his feelings. For him, whatever problems they faced weren't insurmountable. As long as they kept the lines of communication open, which had been impossible in his first marriage, he and Marianne could find acceptable solutions.

"He's asleep," she said.

"He could have woken. Now that I can be rational, I'm honestly glad that you stopped us. Clay is part of you, Marianne, an important part of who and what you are. I wouldn't want to offend him. It's important that we get along."

"You're good with him, Nick. I can tell that he admires you. But that doesn't mean he'll accept you as more than my casual friend or a business acquaintance."

"Kids are supposed to be resilient. It's also possible, if I don't rush my fences, that he'll adapt more easily than you imagine. Has his father remarried?"

"Ed remarried three years ago."

"And?"

"Clay went through a rough period. He loves his dad. In the back of his mind I think he'd hoped Ed and I would get back together. Once he realized Ed meant to go through with the marriage, he finally came around to being civil to Ed's wife." She had to be completely honest with Nick. "But he swore that even if I drop dead tomorrow he'll never call her Mother."

"Clay's loyalty to you and his father doesn't bother me."

Nick viewed that loyalty as a safety net that could keep him from falling into a bottomless abyss if some unforeseen tragedy happened to Clay. He wanted the bond between Ed and Clay to be strong and unyielding.

"Do you think I was wrong not to have men friends in our house?" When Nick didn't reply, she lifted her face and sighed up at the full moon. "I don't know why I didn't. When Clay was little, it seemed too much of a hassle. There weren't enough hours in the day. By the time I had taken care of both Clay and my job, I couldn't drum up the energy to be excited over dating." She smiled crookedly. "And frankly, men in their twenties must prefer women without encumbrances.

They wanted my undivided attention, which I couldn't give them.''

The moonlight's pale rays filtered through the arched screens overhead. Her eyes appeared dark. The golden highlights in her hair changed to shimmering silver and shadows. In sunshine, moonlight or shadows, Marianne radiated her own special loveliness, from the inside.

"I don't consider Clay a drawback, only a complication," he answered.

"He does complicate things," she agreed dryly. "For us to do more than hold hands we have to be...sneaky? Conniving? That's not setting a good example for Clay, is it?"

Her eyes dropped and she shook her head. Nick caught her chin in the crook of his forefinger.

"Try discreet. Circumspect. Like any adult should be around any teenager. Clay should know we're seeing each other. I'll do my best to make him a part of our relationship. What takes place between us when he isn't here is private—just between you and me.''

Marianne smiled. "You know, I used to dread the weekends Clay spent with his father. After I'd run my errands, I'd sit around here feeling sorry for myself for being left alone and lonely.''

"Sweetheart, you should know by now I don't want you to be alone or lonely. I want you with me.''

"I feel the same way, but that's a little scary, too.''

"Scary? Why?''

"I've adjusted to having my life revolve around Clay and Talent Plus. Come good times or bad, rain or shine, I know they'll be here.''

"I can hear what you're thinking...'will you?''' His hands molded to the rounded shape of her shoulders.

"I didn't walk out on my wife, Marianne, if that's what you're wondering. She left me."

She felt his fingers tighten. His lips parted, closed, then opened to speak. She put her fingertips against his lips.

"You don't have to make explanations, Nick. Just knowing you weren't the one who left is reassuring to me. Don't say any more. Not now."

His fingers slid to her wrist. "I should, but it's difficult to talk about the reasons for my divorce. When I left North Carolina I shut the door on all the thoughts that if only I'd done this or that I might have saved my marriage. Guilt and shame were driving me crazy."

"I felt the same way. Do you suppose the marriage partner who is left behind suffers the longest?"

"Perhaps. Within a year of our divorce Velma had remarried and gotten pregnant."

"Did you want children?"

Nick's lips turned down. "She didn't."

"Ouch?"

"Yeah. It hurt, but I'm over it. I don't love her, Marianne. I'm glad she found happiness with another man." He gazed steadily into her eyes. "I want you. I care for you."

"I want you," Marianne repeated later, looking at her reflection in the mirror while she brushed her hair its final one-hundredth stroke. "I care for you."

In the sanctity of the master bathroom, she admitted freely that had circumstances been different she would be curled up beside Nick now, not worrying about waking up to a tangled mass of hair.

Had she been younger, inexperienced, naive, as she had been with Ed, she could have skipped her heart-to-heart talk with Nick and let passion blind her.

"It would have been wonderful to wake up with Nick beside me," she said, hugging her arms about herself.

A mental image of them entwined in each other's arms replaced her image in the mirror.

No, she scolded silently. Your imagination has gotten you into enough trouble lately. She straightened her shoulders. I'm glad to be older and smarter. A mother. A businesswoman. I wouldn't trade any of that for sex.

She grinned. Nick hadn't asked her to make a trade. He wanted her just as she was. She didn't have to change to please him.

"And Nick doesn't have to change to please me, either."

Placing the brush on the counter, she languidly crossed to her bed. She flipped back the coverlet and top sheet. With a soft sigh, she slid between the sheets.

It took her as little time to fall asleep as it had to begin falling in love with Nick King.

Chapter Nine

By noon on Monday, Marianne prayed for temperatures to drop again. Beach flu had hit her clients full force. No one wanted to be cooped up in an office when they could be building sand castles and grabbing sun rays.

Fortunately for Talent Plus and Marianne's sanity, she'd been able to reach Jayne at home by telephone before Jayne left for King Enterprises, as planned on Friday. Her second call had been to Lou to inform her of Nick's letter of apology and his bonus check. Graciously, Lou had agreed to finish out the assignment after all.

And then the telephone lines had gone berserk!

To round out the morning, at noon the school nurse had called. Clay had contracted a mysterious ailment that sounded suspiciously like Incomplete Homework Infirmity. He was too ill to attend his fifth period

English class, but he knew he'd feel better by the time he had to go to baseball practice. Mentally kicking herself for not having checked to make certain Clay was prepared for his classes, she'd informed the nurse that she was on her way.

She had signed Clay out at the attendance office and had entered the clinic.

"Mrs. Clark," the nurse greeted cordially, "I'm glad you're here. Clay seemed to feel much worse after he spoke to you."

Minor guilt pangs stabbed Marianne. Because she was needed at Talent Plus she'd come close to telling the nurse to send Clay to class. Marianne followed the nurse to a small cubicle.

Clay groaned as he sat up on the cot.

"I'd better get him home and into bed," Marianne said, worried by how flushed his cheeks appeared. "Come on, son. I'll take your book bag. The car is out front."

Feet shuffling, Clay followed his mother out of the clinic to the car. "If I don't have a temperature, can I go to practice later?"

"We'll see how you feel. There must be a flu bug going around. We're swamped at work." She wanted to get him home before his stomach started churning.

Clay tossed his book bag in the car, wishing he'd written the dumb old limerick last night. This was all his mother's fault to begin with! She should have been helping him instead of yammering to Mr. King.

"How are you feeling, Clay?" Marianne touched his forehead. It felt cool to her. Other than the sour look on his face, Clay seemed normal.

"It's just a headache, Mom." He made a production out of snapping his seat belt while he thought of a way to convince his mother to let him go to ball practice.

"Okay, love," she soothed, patting his leg. "We're almost home."

As they entered the garage door, the phone began ringing. Clay dashed for the portable phone. "I'll get it."

"Let it ring, Clay. It's probably Jayne checking on you. She'll call back."

"It could be Brad." He grabbed the receiver. "Hello?"

Brad? The boys had separate lunch periods and different classes. She got the aspirin bottle and turned on the faucet. How would Brad know Clay had come home sick? Marianne gave her son a wary glance.

"It's for you." Clay rubbed his forehead. "Some man."

"Get a glass of water." She exchanged the tablets for the telephone. "Here's your pills. Go lie down. I'll be with you in a minute."

"Hello?"

"Marianne, is Clay okay?"

The familiar sound of Nick's voice sent a shiver of pleasure up her spine. "Nick? How'd you know I'd be here?"

"I called the office to see if you'd like to go out for lunch. The lady who answered the phone said you'd gone to pick up Clay at school."

She glanced at her son, who was piddling with the water running in the sink. Marianne made a shooing motion with her hand when he glanced over his shoulder at her.

"He says he's got a headache and achy joints. Could be the flu, I guess. He's on his way to bed, *right now*."

"Yeah, yeah, Mom. I'm going. Don't rush me."

Clay turned off the faucet and took the aspirin, making a face as one of the pills dissolved on the back of his tongue.

"He's too sick for school, but he wants to go to baseball practice," Marianne said with a grimace.

"Do you think he has an early case of spring fever?"

"Could be. He isn't the only one, if that's the case. The entire population of central Florida seems to be suffering from the same affliction."

Nick chuckled. "My father had what he called a miracle elixir for school-itis. Cod liver oil. Have you ever smelled cod liver oil?"

"No. I can't say that I have."

"Well, believe me, getting it past your nose is only secondary to what it does to your taste buds. All Dad had to do was open the refrigerator and pull out the bottle to get a miraculous, instantaneous recovery. My attendance record at school was nearly perfect!"

"But what if you weren't faking it?"

"Cod liver oil is an old-fashioned cure-all. I can still hear Dad say, 'What you've got it'll get rid of, and if you don't have anything it'll cure you anyway.' I'd offer to stop by the pharmacy and pick up a bottle for you, but Clay would have a fit if I brought you chocolates and brought him cod liver oil."

"I think I'll stick with modern medicine. If he is faking, I want to know why. He must be sick. His stereo isn't turned up full blast. Listen, Nick, I appreciate your calling and inviting me to lunch. I've got to take care of Clay, though. Can I have a rain check?"

"Anytime. Tell Clay I hope he gets to feeling better. Bye."

While his mother talked on the phone, Clay stretched out on the bed with his English book and spiral notebook. Impatiently he tapped his pencil on the blank page, then inspiration hit him and he began writing:

There was a young mother named Marianne Clark,
Who thought her kid being sick was a lark.
She giggled on the phone
While he bled from his bones.
She'll be sad when he runs off to the baseball park.

Not bad, Clay decided as he read it silently. The rhythm is a little off, but it does rhyme. Why couldn't I think of this last night?

Feeling considerably better, he looked at the clock on his dresser. He could make it back to school before the end of the fifth period if his mother drove like a maniac.

"How are you doing?" Marianne asked as she crossed to the side of his bed.

"Those pills worked really fast—just like in the commercials." He swung his legs off the bed and reached for his shoes. "You can take me back to school now."

"Whoa, fella." She pushed lightly against Clay's shoulder. "Those pills don't work that fast."

"Don't! You're going to mess up my homework paper."

"Homework paper?" Picking up the notebook, she pointed it at him. "How could you have homework from English when the class is still in progress? Is this the work you were supposed to finish last night?"

A dull thud inside Clay's head made quick thinking impossible. He felt cornered, trapped. No matter what he did lately his mother was on his case.

He grabbed the notebook from his mother's hand to prevent her from reading the contents. Closing it, he asked, "How do you expect me to turn my homework in when I'm not there?"

"I guess you can't." Her suspicions ebbed. Clay was a conscientious student who'd never given her problems at school or at home. Why was she questioning him as though he was a potential dropout, a juvenile delinquent? His attendance was excellent, without Nick's cod liver oil treatment. She felt guilty as hell for having misgivings. "You get some rest, Clay."

"Mom, I'm better! I don't want to miss ball practice!"

She fluffed his pillows. "It's only a practice session."

Frustrated, Clay threw his notebook in his book bag. "I might loose the catcher position and it'll be your fault!"

"The coach isn't going to punish you for being sick."

He won't, but you are, Clay railed silently, flopping his head on the pillows and giving his mother a hostile glare. What does she care if the coach puts me in the outfield? She's too busy with Mr. King to watch the game anyway!

"Can I get you anything?"

"No." It really burned him that he had to miss baseball practice because she hadn't helped him last night when he had needed her.

"I'm going to go make some business calls. You call me if you need anything." She had crossed the threshold when she remembered Nick's message. "Mr. King said to tell you he hopes you get to feeling better."

She'd left the bedroom when Clay mouthed, "I hate you! I hate him, too." This was both their faults! He'd have had his homework finished if Mr. King had gone home when he was supposed to go. But no, he'd stuck around to watch television. He could have watched the boob tube at his own house!

Clay folded a pillow over his head. Mom likes Mr. King more than she likes me. She's always on Dad for giving me expensive gifts. That weight-lifting equipment had to cost more than the skateboard! But she didn't say boo 'cause she wants Mr. King over here three nights a week. She'd never have time to help with schoolwork.

She'll be sorry, Clay vowed. He'd flunk seventh grade 'cause his homework sucked, and get kicked off the baseball team, for sure. He didn't need a crystal ball to predict the future. And when he grew up and turned out to be a bum, it'd be all their fault!

Hunkered down with two-thirds of her torso in the cabinet, Marianne said to Clay, "Okay. I surrender. Where'd you put the colander?"

"I don't know."

"You unloaded the dishwasher."

"I don't know what a colander is. How do I know where I put it?"

Marianne's patience grew thin. "It's the thing I use to drain noodles. It's white. Plastic. With holes."

"Oh that? It's in the backyard."

"You put it away in the backyard?" Marianne groaned.

"Brad buried one of my plastic soldiers. I used it to sift sand."

"Go get it."

"Mom!" He strung the words out until he hit three separate notes. "I'm doing my homework. I don't want to miss practice again tomorrow."

Annoyed, Marianne felt her temper flare. "You have to the count of twenty, young man. When I reach twenty the colander had better be in my hand. One...two..."

"I'm going." He pushed his chair back and lazily rolled to his feet.

"Five...six..." She needed the numbers exercise to keep her from chasing after her son with a skillet in her hand! Since yesterday, he had been testing her level of tolerance. Nothing suited him. Not the clothes she'd laid out for him to wear. Not the breakfast she'd cooked. Not the hug she'd tried to give him before he left for school. She'd been five minutes late arriving home from work and Clay had acted as though she'd committed a capital crime. Asking him to do his homework at the kitchen table so she'd be able to help him had caused moans, groans and a series of you're-picking-on-me looks.

Didn't Clay realize she was rushed because Nick would be here at any minute to work out with him? A little cooperation was all she needed. Was that too damned much to ask?

"Eighteen..." She raised her voice when she saw Clay slowly ambling across the pool deck. "Nineteen!"

Clay increased his pace infinitesimally.

"Nineteen and a half!" She crossed to the door and opened it in case Clay couldn't hear her. "Nineteen and three-quarters."

Tossing the colander toward his mother like a Frisbee, he shouted, "Twenty! Made it!"

Marianne managed to catch it. "You're asking for it, son," she warned solemnly.

"What's wrong? I got it to you before you reached twenty."

"I don't appreciate how you got it to me. You'd better change your attitude or you'll be missing practice tomorrow, too."

He could tell she wasn't bluffing. Tempted to push her a little further, but knowing she'd follow through, he mumbled, "Sorry."

Marianne doubted his sincerity. "You're going to be if you keep pushing me. Dinner will be ready in ten minutes. I want you to get busy and get your homework finished. Do you understand me?"

"Yes, ma'am." Fuming silently, he strode to the table and slouched down in his chair. He understood her. She'd make him miss baseball, but not weight lifting. Heaven forbid she should have to call Nick and tell him not to come over here! His mother didn't care a whoop or a holler about his muscles. She just cared about Mr. King!

Chapter Ten

"Who stepped on Clay's tail?" Nick wrapped his arms around Marianne's waist as she stood in front of the sink, her wrists deep in soapy water. "You?"

Marianne dropped her head back on his shoulder. For a moment, just for a second or two, she needed a strong shoulder to lean on. His lips nuzzling the side of her neck had to be the nicest thing that had happened to her since Sunday.

"Me. But it was purely unintentional."

"Want to tell me about it?"

"It's typical teenage rebellion, I suppose. Nothing serious."

She could handle this minor flare-up between her and her son. And yet she found herself needing to talk to someone about Clay's odd behavior. Maybe Nick, being a man, could give her input from the male's viewpoint.

He lifted her hair off her neck and liberally peppered light kisses there. "Clay's in the garage aggressively attacking the weight machine. It might be good for you, too."

"What? Lifting weights?"

"No, sweetheart, letting off steam. Bottling it up eventually leads to a major explosion."

Nick's endearment and his encouragement to unload her problems on him was irresistible. She raised the sink's stopper and let the water drain while she dried her hands.

She turned around in his arms. "I made him do his homework at the kitchen table, which he hates. I made him clear off the dinner table, which he also hates. And when he dropped his plate on the floor I made him clean up the mess. He didn't love that, either. On a popularity scale of one to ten, I score in the minus-five range."

Nick softly kissed her, showing Marianne she ranked much, much higher with him.

"Any suggestions?" she murmured.

"I'm hardly qualified in the child-rearing department."

"You're a man, though." Her hands found a temporary home on his chest. As usual, he was dressed in the latest casual sports outfit, a coordinating shirt and slacks in navy blue with white accents. "You were a teenage boy. What did your mother do?"

Grinning, Nick replied, "Turned me over to my dad."

"More cod liver oil?" Marianne asked, chuckling at Nick's automatic grimace at the mere mention of the home remedy.

It made Nick feel good to know he'd made her smile. "No. Actually, he was a great believer in letting me face the consequences of my actions. Homework was my responsibility. If I didn't do it and received bad grades, *then* I studied at the kitchen table."

"Clay is a good student, but . . ."

"Then why punish him before he commits a crime?"

"I don't think of him being close to me, where I can help him while I'm fixing dinner, as punishment."

"Does Clay?"

"He'd prefer to be in his room with the stereo blaring while he studies." Marianne lifted one eyebrow. "Do you think I should let him do that?"

"I did when I was his age. Boys his age are asserting their independence. Cutting the apron strings, so to speak. The noise may bother you, but he probably blocks out the music when he's concentrating on his work." Nick glanced at his wristwatch. "Sorry, but I'm going to have to get back out there. He wants to do a set of bench presses. I have to spot for him."

"Spot?"

"Make certain the barbell doesn't fall on him."

"He's been working out with those barbells alone. Is that dangerous?"

"He could have been hurt." Nick dropped a swift kiss on her lips. "I've got to get out there."

Marianne watched him leave the kitchen before she picked up the damp dishcloth. Did Clay think she was punishing him? Was she binding him too close to her? But how could Clay learn with drums pounding and guitars wailing in the background?

Reluctant to change her tried and true methods, Marianne circled the cloth on the center counter at the same pace the questions circled in her mind.

* * *

"Don't use a rubber pad!" Nick called, arriving ten seconds too late.

Clay had stretched out on the bench beneath the barbell. Looking at the number of weights on the bar, Nick's concern grew. He had just given Marianne advice on not being overly protective, but here he was about to lecture Clay.

"I always use a rubber pad. I bounce the bar off the pad to get lift at the bottom part of the movement."

With the amount of weight on the bar Clay was damned lucky it hadn't bounced off the pad onto his neck or face. In high school Nick had witnessed a serious injury with this same setup. At risk of hurting Clay's fledgling ego, he had to prevent an accident.

Moving into the spotting position with the bar within easy reach, Nick said, "Isn't the object of doing a bench press to place maximum resistance on the muscles?"

"That's the main idea," Clay answered, grunting as his muscles strained to lift the barbell off the rest. His hips came off the bench in a bridge position, which stressed the more powerful lower pectoral muscles. "Got it. No sweat."

The bar shifted to the right precariously. Nick steadied it, then assisted Clay in lifting the bar back to the rest.

"The pad and lifting your hips is a double cheat," Nick said bluntly. He began removing the cast-metal plates. "Any trainer worth is salt will tell you that. The trainers that don't are snickering behind your back because the only thing you're boosting with that amount of weight is your ego. And they know it and they aren't impressed."

Peeved, Clay tossed the rubber pad on the floor. "I wasn't cheating. I didn't know better."

"Now you do. Put your hands on the grooved knurls. If your hands get sweaty, they won't slip. Let's give this a try."

"I can do this by myself," Clay said. "You don't have to hover over me like a mother hen."

"Even the pros use spotters. What's your problem? Do you want your nose flattened to the back side of your skull?"

"No. I'm not that hardheaded."

Clay lifted the bar in one smooth, steady motion and silently counted the number of repetitions.

"You're doing fine, Clay," Nick praised. "Keep up the good work and I'll let you beat me at a game of Ping-Pong."

Clay grinned. Mr. King wasn't a bad guy. He just wanted things done his way. Flat on his back looking up at the set of muscles bulging beneath the man's shirt, Clay wasn't inclined to argue with success.

"Someday I'm going to be built like you," Clay complimented. Bigger, he silently added.

He jumped up. "Here comes Brad."

"I want you two to spot for each other on the weight bench," Nick said. "Okay? You help each other while I visit with your mother for a few minutes."

"Aren't you going to watch Brad work out?"

"I'll be here before he gets finished with the warm-up routine."

"Brad isn't going to do what I tell him to do. He'll argue with me."

Nick glanced wistfully toward the door leading into the kitchen. What was it he'd said to Marianne about taking the consequences for one's actions? He'd offered to teach the boys how to lift while they tested the equipment. The consequence was sacrificing time with Marianne.

"I'll watch," Nick conceded. His acquiescence earned him a heart-winning smile from Clay. It was easy to understand why Clay's recent behavior distressed Marianne. When the boy got what he wanted his face lit up with pleasure in a way that would make the coldest of hearts melt.

"Hiya, Mr. King," Brad greeted, continuing to run in place as he spoke. "I did my warm-up exercises at home—toe touches, push-ups and jumping jacks. Can I get started?"

"Curls first, Mr. King?" Clay asked.

"First, let's drop the mister. Trainers and athletes call one another by their first names. Mine is Nick."

"All right!" Clay responded, holding up both hands toward Brad. "Gimme five!"

Brad slapped Clay's hands. "Thanks, Mr.—I mean, Nick."

Nick watched the two teenagers, both pleased at being treated like men. Without quarreling, Brad listened to Clay give instructions. While Nick observed them, he realized how much he enjoyed working with beginners. Their willingness and enthusiasm made him reconsider his written policy restricting membership at King's Gyms to people over sixteen. The manufacturer of this new equipment might have a brilliant idea.

An hour later Brad departed, and Clay was "pumped"—filled with a euphoric feeling brought on by exercise. He rushed into the house, grabbed his mother around the waist and gave her a bear hug.

"Mom, it's great. I feel twice as strong as I did yesterday! I invited Nick to stay for a glass of lemonade. Is that okay?"

Marianne didn't know how Nick had performed the magical change in her son's attitude, but she felt profoundly grateful for his assistance. "It's mixed and in the refrigerator."

"I'll get it, Mom," Clay offered, pushing her out of the kitchen. "You and Nick go on in to the living room and relax."

Not wanting to put a damper on Clay's ebullience, Marianne didn't blink an eye at the use Nick's given name. "Thanks, son. That's very considerate of you."

Considerate is an understatement, she thought, as she sat a respectable distance away from Nick on the sofa. She was the fetch-and-carry person around their home. Clay's offering to serve beverages was nothing short of a radical change.

"What did you do to him?" she asked Nick quietly.

"Exercise is a stress buster, remember?"

Marianne nodded. He'd told her that the night they'd met.

"Fresh frozen lemonade," Clay announced, laughing at his own joke. He gave Nick a glass, then served his mother. The distance between the grown-ups widened when he wedged in between them. "Thursday, Nick is going to take me and Brad on a tour of King's Gym, if it's okay with you. He says there's a company policy against kids our age being members, but he's thinking about changing it 'cause of this equipment and 'cause me and Brad are doing so well."

"Would you care to join us?" Nick invited.

Marianne opened her mouth to tell Nick she had a late appointment Thursday, but Clay answered for her.

"She can't. We're going right after school. Mom has to work. She's got a big deal cooking with a new company that's moving their international headquarters to Orlando."

"Uh, son..."

"Right, Mom?" Clay didn't wait for an answer. "Besides, she's not into sports activities. She likes to watch me play, but that's about it. Huh, Mom?"

"Well, I might consider an aerobic fitness class."

Clay winked at Nick. "She wouldn't last a week. It would be like the bike she bought. She never rides it. She only plays Ping-Pong 'cause I nag at her. Two thousand years from now she'll be one of the reasons human beings have huge brains and no arms and legs."

Marianne rubbed her arms as though they had begun to atrophy. "Thanks a lot."

"Chill out, Mom. So you aren't an athlete. You have other good qualities." Clay nudged Nick's arm, then rose to get out of harm's way as he said, "Give Nick and me a day or two and we'll come up with a list to prove it."

"Notice Clay moved before he started his mouth rolling," Marianne said to Nick. She wiggled her fingers at her son. "I may be nonathletic, but I can tickle Clay until he squeals for mercy."

"I just don't want to hurt her," Clay quipped. Imitating Nick's masculine gait he sauntered toward his room. "I have a couple of math problems to do. See ya, Nick. G'night, Mom."

Marianne heard Clay's door close before she said, "You're good with him. It's a shame you don't have children."

"You aren't so bad yourself," Nick responded lightly while thinking frantically. She had begun to in-

clude him in her family, and as a result he felt he had
to correct the mistaken assumption she'd made. Difficult as it was for him to deal with his grief, Nick wanted
to tell Marianne at least the bare facts. "I was a father."

Divorce ends a marriage, not parenthood, Marianne thought, puzzled by his use of the past tense.
"Was?"

She drew a quick breath as she saw Nick's expression change to one of deep pain. "My daughter died,"
he said shortly.

She could only imagine his anguish, but as a mother
she understood it had to be unbearable. A parent's
worst fear had to be the loss of a child.

"I'm sorry, Nick." She entwined her fingers around
his to convey her sympathy. What else could she say?
Words of comfort often hurt more than they helped.

Nick didn't want Marianne's sympathy. Not even she
could relieve his burden of guilt. He'd seldom allowed
himself the privilege of speaking Crissy's name, and he
hadn't spoken about her death to anyone... not even
his wife.

His fingers tightened on Marianne's hand. For days,
even weeks now, he could avoid thinking of Crissy. But
the mention of her name brought back the agony in an
instant. It took him the strength of Samson, who had
blindly destroyed pillars in biblical days, to part his lips
and say, "Crissy drowned."

Silently, Marianne reached for him. His shoulder
muscles were rigid and his back erect, as though tensed
for a blow. She felt a shudder course through him as
she groped to find the right words.

"It was my fault," Nick said. "I'm the one who
bought the house with the backyard pool. I'm the one

who took her to water safety classes, fat lot of good they did.'' He let go of Marianne's fingers to rake his hands through his hair. ''Crissy asked me to go swimming with her, but I was planting a flat of summer flowers in the front yard.'' For a moment he stared at his hands as though he could feel the soil on his hands. He wiped them on the sides of his slacks, balled them into fists and shoved them into his pockets.

''I told her to change into her swimsuit while I finished the yard work. Crissy gave me a bear hug, ran up the front steps into the house. It only seemed a few minutes later that I heard a high-pitched scream coming from the backyard. I ran around to the pool. Velma was standing there with Crissy limp in her arms. Everything blurred into a swirl of color for a moment. Blue water streaked with a tinge of red. And the keening whimper Velma made. I waded in and pulled both of them from the water. Velma ran in to call 911 while I tried to resuscitate Crissy. But I couldn't get her to come back to life, and neither could the paramedics when they came.''

Nick rubbed his eyes with his knuckles to erase the mental picture of Crissy sprawled lifelessly beside the pool.

''She must have hit her head, fallen into the pool. It wouldn't have happened if I hadn't planted those damned flowers. Oh God, what a waste. She was so young, so full of life. She never even knew what going to first grade was like. Never went to the dances . . . the prom. Never fell in love. She never had a chance to do any of those things. Such a damned waste! Why couldn't it have been me?''

Marianne bowed her head, unable to give him an intelligible answer or even to look at him. Accidents happened. There had been many a time she'd held her breath while she watched Clay doing his skateboard stunts. There was no stopping him on his bike, either. But she also knew that if anything ever happened to Clay, she would never stop blaming herself, either.

"They think they're invincible" was the best she could come up with.

"And they're so fragile. It happened so fast."

Marianne reached up to brush away the lone tear caught in the laugh creases at the corner of his eye. "Tell me about the two of you."

"The two of us?" Nick repeated.

"Only about the good times."

Nick shook his head. Crissy's drowning had overshadowed his pleasant memories. He couldn't remember anything specific.

"The little things," she prompted softly. "Like how she crawled or held your finger. Or how she giggled when you pushed her in a swing."

Images, like priceless snapshots, flashed in Nick's mind. And yet, he couldn't speak. His lips had fastened his suffering inside his mind as securely as her small body had been sealed in her coffin. He dared not speak of her for fear of going completely mad.

"I remember Clay's second Halloween," Marianne said to prod his memory. "I'd never given him candy. A friend of mine, who had a daughter Clay's age, invited us to her house. Nell gave both the kids a paper cup with candy shaped like kernels of corn. He dumped the kernels on the floor and carefully put them one by one back in the cup, like dropping clothespins in a bottle. Then he emptied the cup again. Only this time, Nell's little girl quickly confiscated his candy. Horrified that she'd eaten his toys, he came running to me, begging me to pry them out of her mouth. Funny, but he seldom eats candy, even now."

"Crissy had a ballerina costume." Nick's jaw locked as he prepared to feel an explosion of pain ripping through his head. For a second or two he held his breath, waiting for icy numbness to encase him. They didn't happen. He felt Marianne's warmth wrapped around him, but no pain, no bone-freezing cold. The clearest image yet formed in his mind. He could see Crissy laughing up at him with her dark curls bobbing and her eyes bright with love as she pirouetted in circles until she was dizzy. "She held up two fingers and said, 'I'm two in a tutu.' Two in a tutu," he repeated, cherishing that memory. His taut facial muscles relaxed slightly. He gave Marianne a small smile.

"Clay loved to peek at his Christmas presents. Still does," Marianne said, encouraging Nick to find other treasured recollections.

"Crissy spent hours shaking and rattling her gifts. She'd guess at what the boxes contained. I bought her a ring and wrapped it inside a big box." He stared at Marianne through unseeing eyes. "I wonder what happened to it? And the little heart-shaped necklace I gave her." Where were her dresses and toys? Her child-size furniture? He couldn't remember. One day Crissy's belongings had been in her bedroom and then they'd disappeared. "They vanished without a trace...like Crissy."

Marianne could only assume Nick's wife had packed Crissy's belongings. Each of them must have carried the burden of their daughter's death alone. At a time when it should have been natural for them to lean on each other for support, they must have grown apart.

She held him fiercely against her, but she knew it wasn't enough. Just as Nick had searched the nooks and crannies of his mind trying to find the child's trinkets, Marianne searched her heart for the right thing to say. If it had been humanly possible to absorb even a small portion of his bereavement, she would have.

She spoke haltingly, stumbling to find what would help her if something happened to Clay. "Crissy's memories are alive, Nick. But only if you let them live. It's wrong to bury them. They are the last precious gifts Crissy gave you."

Nick stared at Marianne as though she'd spoken in an alien tongue he couldn't comprehend. The idea of rejecting anything Crissy had given him was beyond his powers of comprehension. He'd been proud to paper his office walls with her crayon drawings. Seashells she'd given him had lined the front of his bookcase. Things that were of no material value to anyone had been his prized possessions. And yet after her death he had packed them all away, unable to bear the sight of them.

The thought of repudiating Crissy's last gift of love brought a rush of tears to his eyes. "I loved her."

"No," Marianne whispered. "You love her. Love that strong is eternal. It doesn't die." She lightly kissed away the droplets of tears on his cheeks. They tasted of salt... and of age, from the years he'd contained them in his heart. "You can't deny Crissy's love or memories of her. They're a blessed part of you."

His vision blurred. The memories he'd long denied rushed from the recesses of his mind as though Marianne had unlocked them from where they'd been imprisoned. For now, they were too precious to share. He felt a compelling urge to be alone, to examine in solitude these emotional treasures Marianne had unearthed.

Explanations were impossible. He could only show how deeply she'd touched him, how deeply he was indebted to her, by burying his face against the crook of her neck. Great sobs racked his broad shoulders with shudders. With the tears came a release from a pain worse than death.

Marianne held him, gently stroking his nape and shoulders, letting his tears and the grief he'd bottled dampen her skin. Silently, she wept, too. She wept for Crissy, for Nick and for a woman she'd never met.

But all that mattered to her was Nick.

Crissy was in heaven. Velma had made a new life for herself with another man and his child. Only Nick had continued to suffer in silence.

He needed her.

Chapter Eleven

"You've got oscars, Daddy." Crissy had giggled with delight as Nick tickled her tummy with his night's growth of whiskers on his chin. Nick smiled as he shaved. Oscars, he thought, remembering other words she'd changed to make them easier to pronounce.

He'd been awake much of the night, but he felt revitalized, at peace with his memories. He didn't need his morning run to get his heart pumping. Was it possible, he wondered, that symbolically he'd been running away from himself? That he'd physically forced his body to the limits to keep his mind under lock and key?

Nick splashed cold water on his freshly shaved face, then rinsed his razor. As he dried his face he peered at the reflection in the mirror. Grief had left distinct marks. Fine lines etched his brow. Creases, like the imprints of crow's feet, were clearly visible. But such marks were unimportant.

As he folded the towel his thoughts turned to Marianne. He needed to call her. She'd been such a comfort to him. What he and Marianne had shared was what he should have been able to share with Velma. They hadn't. They'd barely been able to look at each other. Guilt is a great silencer, Nick thought.

He hung the towel on the rack, crossed to the phone beside his bed and dialed her number.

"Clark residence."

Recognizing Clay's voice, Nick said, "Good morning, Clay. Can I speak to your mother?"

He wasn't prepared for the sound of Clay bellowing for his mother to pick up the extension in her room. He had to hold his phone at arm's length to keep from having his hearing impaired. "She'll be right with you, Nick."

Crissy hadn't yelled. She'd preferred to chatter with the caller. Nick smiled as he remembered coaxing Crissy, often resorting to bribery, to get her to put down the phone and go get her mother.

"Good morning, Nick." Marianne had barely slept for worrying about him. "How are you?"

"Better than I've felt in years," he replied candidly. "I hope you weren't worried."

She matched his candor. "I still am."

"Don't be, Marianne. It's almost like I was a willing amnesia victim, only I'd suffered a blow to the heart not the head. When the good memories started coming back they sort of overwhelmed me. I dreamed of Crissy last night. Pleasant dreams, not nightmares. Does that make any sense to you?"

"Yes. Just don't shut me out," she said, revealing her fear of being excluded from an important part of his life.

"I would have liked to tell you about Crissy the first evening I had pizza at your house." His voice lowered as he admitted, "But I blamed myself for what happened to Crissy. I was afraid you'd think less of me."

Marianne knew what he meant. She could be ten miles away from Clay when he skinned his knee but she'd be the first to put the blame on her own shoulders. An inherent part of being a parent was accepting blame and feeling guilty.

To erase any doubts from his mind that she in any way held him remotely responsible, she said, "Accidents happen, Nick. I don't think less of you."

"I won't shut you out from now on. We'll talk about Crissy, Marianne. I want to talk to you about her. About us."

Clay had entered Marianne's bedroom. Impatiently, he shifted from foot to foot until he couldn't wait any longer. "Mom! You're going to make me late for school!"

"I heard him, Marianne," Nick said. "Is Friday night okay with you? Say a quiet dinner out...with no interruptions?"

She held up her hand and raised her forefinger, signalling Clay to be patient for just a second longer. "I'd like that, Nick."

"Remind him about Thursday," Clay prompted, edging closer to the bed where his mother sat.

"I heard him. Tell Clay I'll pick up him and Brad and anybody else he wants to invite at school. We'll stop for hamburgers on the way home from the gym."

Marianne had to get her hat, purse and shoes before she could depart. "You tell him. I'll work around whatever arrangements the two of you make for Thursday."

She dashed into the walk-in closet when Clay took the phone. Red hat, shoes and purse in hand she motioned for Clay to get a move on. She dropped the high-heeled shoes on the floor and shoved her nylon-clad feet in them while she unloaded the contents of her black purse into the one she'd be carrying.

Eavesdropping, she noticed Clay and Nick had gone beyond discussing the plans for Thursday. Sunday afternoon seemed to be the topic of conversation when she said, "I'm out in the car. Let's go."

She'd backed the car from the garage when Clay finally made an appearance.

"Nick invited us to go hydrosliding Sunday. Did you know he lives right on the lake? He's got a speedboat and everything! You don't mind fixing a picnic basket, do you?"

Marianne chuckled over Clay's enthusiasm. She backed the car down the drive and headed toward the school before she answered, "No, I wasn't aware his house was on the lake, and no, I don't mind fixing a picnic basket."

"Fix food for four." Clay had difficulty wrapping his tongue around the twister. "Bet you can't say that three times real fast."

She tried, but failed. Laughing, Clay made the same attempt. He sounded as though he'd just inhaled a mouthful of crackers. Unwilling to admit defeat, they both tried again until they were laughing too hard to be making intelligible words.

In high spirits, Clay did something that completely flabbergasted Marianne before he got out of the car.

In broad daylight, in the front drive of middle school, with his friends sitting on the steps waiting for him . . . he hugged her.

Clay's hug had to last Marianne until Friday after school when his father picked him up for the weekend. The wait was worthwhile because his hug came accompanied by a kiss on her cheek.

Since Nick had given her a glimmer of insight into why Clay reacted negatively to her suggestions and direct orders, she'd radically modified her approach to getting routine jobs accomplished.

After dinner, instead of hassling Clay to clear off the table, she went to the dishwasher and loaded the cooking utensils. With or without the plates, knives and forks, she started the machine and left the kitchen. Clay quickly realized he had to unload the dishwasher twice as often if he didn't get the table cleared off promptly.

She'd eased up on checking over his homework. Clay did his homework with the stereo speakers thumping out a heavy beat. He made a point of showing her his papers.

To her surprise, Clay had been the one to notice the grass in the yard needed mowing and did the chore without complaint. And, to her complete amazement, after two nights of sleeping in an unmade bed he'd changed the sheets and done an admirable job of remaking it.

Along with asserting his independence Clay was gradually learning that he had to accept responsibilities.

Normally, watching Clay drive away with his father disturbed her. She'd built her schedule to revolve around her son. When he was gone, it was as though her axis was gone. She missed him, dreadfully.

This evening she almost felt a twinge of guilt as she anticipated pampering herself in a leisurely bubble bath, taking her own sweet time getting ready for her date with Nick. Almost, but not quite. Along with the realization that Clay could assert his independence came an awareness of the segment of her own life that was independent of her son.

With her hair piled on the crown of her head and held with a lacy ribbon, she submerged neck deep into the churning water of the whirlpool bathtub. Fragrant bubbles lightly caressed her. Blissfully her thoughts settled on Nick.

She'd underestimated him. At After Hours she'd perceived him as little more than an attractive man whose glossy picture she'd seen on a billboard. Admittedly, she'd been intrigued by him, fascinated by his charisma and his sense of humor. He was a man any red-blooded woman would weave lustful daydreams about.

Like a circus clown, Nick had painted a happy smile on his face that had made his personality one-dimensional—the type of man a woman could have a brief affair with. His kisses had made her toes curl, awakening the passionate side of her soul, but her physically wanting Nick had scarcely qualified him for a lasting relationship. He had been a fine playmate for her and Clay, but not to be taken too seriously.

Marianne held up a washcloth. Slowly, she twisted it, letting the droplets fall on her face.

She'd had clues there was more to Nick than a handsome face attached to a well-developed body. And then she'd gotten to know him, gotten beneath the surface. To her amazement, she'd discovered he cared about his work and the people who worked for him, and he'd shown a keen interest in Clay. But it was only when Nick had stripped off the clown's greasepaint by revealing his personal sorrow that she'd begun to care deeply for him.

Care deeply? As in love? She dipped the cloth in the bathwater, held it over her breasts and let the droplets trickle between them. Her nipples hardened in response. How deeply could one care before one was irretrievably in love?

The sound of the doorbell ringing snapped her out of her reverie. She leaned forward until she could see the clock on her nightstand. It was only six o'clock. Nick had relayed the message through Clay that he'd pick her up around seven. She levered her body upward until her shoulders and arms surfaced from beneath the water.

"Brad?" she shouted, wondering why Brad was at the front entrance. When the garage wasn't open he came around through the pool area. "Clay isn't home. He's with his father this weekend."

The doorbell pealed again. Marianne groaned. It had to be a door-to-door salesman. Pests! They'd been so bothersome lately she'd posted a small sign under the doorbell.

"There's nobody home," she bellowed, slapping the washcloth against the surface of the water. "Can't you read the No Solicitors sign! Go away! I don't want any!"

"Marianne," Nick called from outside the front door. "It's me."

Silver-tongued salesman, Marianne thought, grinning. She thought she knew the meaning behind Nick's early arrival. Was he as anxious to see her as she was to see him?

"It's unlocked, Nick. Come on in and make yourself at home." She heard the door open and shut. She pushed her toes against the button to open the drain. "I'm in the tub. You're early, aren't you?"

Nick checked his watch. Only an hour or so, he mused. Considering the fact that he'd gone home at noon, showered, shaved and changed clothes by one o'clock, it seemed as though it had to have been after seven when he left his house. There were some definite advantages to owning his own business!

"A little," he called.

Unlatching the shower nozzle from its holder, she turned on the faucet to spray the residue of soap from her skin. "Clay said you would be here at seven."

"Reservations are at La Maison, at seven."

He followed the sound of her voice to the master bedroom. He could hear water gurgling down the drain. The old-fashioned scent of lavender drifted from the bathroom into her bedroom. A mint-green bedspread covered her bed. Drapes held the same green muted by peach-colored tulips in disarray, climbing from the floor to the ceiling. Pillows of the same fabric had been tossed on the king-size bed.

The room suited Marianne. Feminine, yet not frilly. Neatness tempered by a touch of informality. Serenity with a wild dash of spontaneity.

Nick swallowed thickly as a mental picture of her flirted with reality. Would her lingerie reflect the same facets of her personality? Nothing black or red, he thought, too blatantly sexy. No granny gowns with white lace, either. Pajamas? Uh-uh, too masculine. Each thought came with a visual image of her. No, Marianne would wear a long, flowing gown.

The image of her reposing on the pastel coverlet made his palms damp. Secure in the knowledge that they were alone and weren't likely to be interrupted, his imagination took a sharp turn away from the room's decor and her clothing. His thoughts grew increasingly primitive as his heart began to thud heavily in his chest.

Marianne poked her head into the bedroom. She wore only a white satin robe. It might have been made of synthetic fibers, but it moved with the flow of sheer silk. The humidity in the bathroom had wildly arranged her hair in loose curls around her face. Her sixth sense, woman's intuition, told her he was closer to her than he was to the brocade-covered chairs in the formal living room.

What to say, what to do, she thought, her skin suddenly warmer than it had been in the hot tub. Why couldn't she be one of those sophisticated women on television who pranced half-dressed in front of men they'd just met? Nick wasn't a complete stranger, for heaven's sake. And she wasn't a reluctant virgin!

But that didn't mean she was going to make a flying leap to the bed with her arms open wide. Everything in moderation, she decided, searching for a happy medium between being boldly crass and being a cold fish.

She decided to invite him into her bedroom—but not into her bed. Not yet, anyway.

"Uh, Nick," she stammered, having difficulty putting her happy medium into action, "uh, why don't you take a seat on the chaise longue and talk to me while I get dressed?''

One look at her had Nick clearing his throat to make speech possible. She wore a robe. No gown. Simple, and yet sexy as hell! His legs felt like logs of hickory, inflexible, as he moved to the chair she'd offered.

He opened his mouth to speak, but shut it when he realized how inane it would be to ask how she was. A blind nitwit could see she was great!

You're making her nervous, too. Say something, anything, he thought.

''How dressy should I be tonight?'' Marianne asked, sedately crossing the bedroom to her closet. The ten-mile marathon Nick had run last Saturday had to have been shorter, she mused.

Nick tried to think of something clever and suave to reply. Nothing came to mind other than how absolutely beautiful she looked at this moment. He knew he was staring, but he couldn't take his eyes off her.

A surge of desire pounded through his veins. He wanted Marianne so badly he could remember the taste of her mouth—sweet, indescribably sweet.

Get up and go in another room, he commanded silently. You're going to scare the hell out of her by staring as though she's the first woman you've seen in centuries. And if he stood Marianne would need only one glance to be convinced he had only her on his mind...undressed.

Marianne's fingers shook as she moved hangers without being able to make the simple decision of what she should wear. She could feel Nick's eyes on her. Should she have asked him to go into the other room? It had seemed coy and silly when she first thought of it. After all, they weren't Clay's age. Nor were they strangers. Nick had told her things he'd been unable to share with his ex-wife!

Then why, oh why was she blushing? How could she blush when she felt as though the entire heat from her body centered between the juncture of her thighs?

She felt like a complete nincompoop hiding in her closet to avoid facing Nick. But the moment she turned around, he'd know what was racing through her mind.

Deciding that wasn't bad, she slowly turned toward Nick. As their eyes met, the dark fires in his eyes were fueled by the passionate green depths of hers. Her yearning collided with his longing. In response, she lifted her arms, her hands palms upward in the age-old gesture of welcome.

"I'm afraid to move," Nick said. "In case I'm dreaming this."

"You aren't dreaming." Her fingers beckoned him to come to her. "Touch me?"

"Are you doing this out of pity?" he asked, unable to convince himself what he felt for her was mutual.

"Pity is the last reason I'd share my bed with you." She shook her head. The ribbon conceded its battle with the pull of gravity, falling from her hair. Absorbed in her feelings, Marianne didn't notice the curly mass cascading down her shoulders. Nick did. Seeing the silky flame-colored hair spilling freely against the white sleekness of her robe brought him to his feet. "We've both had difficult periods in our lives. But we've both survived. Survivors don't need pity. Pity would destroy your courage."

"I'm not courageous, Marianne."

"You are, Nick. You've been to hell and back. Isn't the worst behind you? What could you possibly fear?"

He replaced the lace ribbon, catching her hair, lifting its weight with his fingers as he looked deeply into the dark centers of her eyes. He saw only loveliness, inside and out. With her strength, he could learn to control the one remaining fear that could cost him his sanity.

"Nick," she whispered, placing her hands on his smooth face, aware of his need for complete honesty between them. "What takes place between us has nothing whatsoever to do with pity. It only has to do with my caring for you, wanting you, in the most intimate sense."

What occurred for the next few minutes made Marianne wonder if she'd ever experienced love. Nick held her, just held her. Their bodies swayed ever so slightly as though their hearts provided the softest strains of music.

He stroked his fingers across her lustrous robe, giving her pleasure and taking pleasure in the giving. He had the physical power to crush her against him, and yet his hand could not have been more gentle.

Marianne summoned her own courage. With a twist and a flick, the belt knotted at her waist slithered free. The front of her robe parted of its own accord.

"You're so lovely, Marianne," he said softly. His fingers followed the path of her lapel. "That's the first thought I had when I first saw you. I just didn't know how lovely."

His lips tenderly traced the path his fingers had taken. The slightest of shrugs and her robe made a pool of snowy whiteness around them. He inhaled the lavender fragrance of her skin and tasted her sweetness with his lips and tongue as he began to dispense with his clothing.

She helped him.

Her craving to feel the texture of his skin against hers quickly became an obsession. Her fingers loosened his tie and stripped it from his neck. She didn't notice where she tossed it or where it landed. He must have risen to his feet, for her fingers made quick work of the row of pearlized buttons down the front of his shirt. She removed his jacket and shirt in one deft motion. With the same reckless abandon she dispensed with his belt buckle, zipper, slacks, underwear, loafers and socks. What could have been awkward or difficult, between the two of them, was effortless.

With clothing no longer a barrier Nick lifted Marianne, pushed the coverlet back and placed her on the palest of pink satin sheets. He gathered her close, his lips touching hers with a euphoric sigh.

She melted against him, flowing, clinging to his larger, stronger body. Her heart slammed in her chest as his hand covered her breast and his tongue whispered a silent primitive language that only lovers understood.

His hands moved over her slowly, then increasingly fast, confident that each subtle shift of her body, each small sound he heard, was a clue to what gave her the most pleasure.

She explored him, tentatively at first, pausing to marvel at their differences. Her fingers followed the contours of the muscles sheathing his back and shoulders. Compared to him, she was only ounces more than skin and bones. Her fingers, pale as moonbeams, were swallowed in the shadowy darkness of his thick hair. Only the lively color of her hair equaled his bold physique.

As his lips left hers and moved to the peaks of her breasts, he rolled one taut point between his tongue and the roof of his mouth. He buried his face in the deep cleavage he made by cupping the underside of her breasts. Her fingers pressed against the short hairs at his nape as his lips and teeth teased her. Eager and wet, his lips moved from one nipple to the other, neglecting neither.

Seeking relief from the tight coil of pressure building inside of her, which had lain dormant since Ed left her, Marianne arched against the wide cradle of his hips. The virile length of him speared against her stomach.

She felt herself drawn to that frenzied height a woman never forgot, regardless of how many years had passed.

Nick's possession of her was hard, powerful. He plunged deeply and withdrew, then stroked her again and again. Her fingers dug into the unyielding flesh of his back as her legs snugly wrapped around his narrow hips.

She made small, imploring noises that could only have been Nick's name. He captured her lips. Frantically their tongues dueled as Marianne's lower body twisted, arched, plunged, then exploded as they reached the final height of passion. A tingling sensation started along the backs of her legs, spreading quickly to her thighs and stomach until some goose bumps of delight splashed across her chest. Her fingers clutched his buttocks, staying at the peak, savoring its height.

Then, slowly, they drifted down from the heights. Nick moved to his side, but he continued to hold her. They lay for a long while that way, softly murmuring, kissing, lightly touching the places that gave the other pleasure. Intent on each other, neither of them noticed when the first number on the digital clock changed from six to seven and finally to eight.

"You said you'd tell me about Crissy," Marianne said, feathering her fingers through his straight hair.

"I guess I felt the same way about her that you feel toward Clay. She wasn't perfect, but very, very close. She must have had a few faults, but I didn't see them." His smallest finger skated across Marianne's collarbone, then he held it up. "She had me wrapped around her pinkie finger."

"Did she look like you? Dark hair, black eyes?"

"Dark hair, hazel eyes and a saucy mouth."

Marianne brushed a kiss across his mouth. "Can't imagine where she got that from, can you?"

"Couldn't have been hereditary."

"Of course not," she agreed. She rolled her tongue in the side of her cheek. "Clay gets his smart mouth from his father's side of the family. Everybody on my branch of the family tree is sweet, kind and considerate."

"Of course he does," Nick concurred with the same false note he'd heard in her voice. "And his red hair, too?"

"I admit responsibility for the hair color. He wants to dye it."

Nick chuckled. "Crissy cut hers."

"Do all kids do that? Clay got hold of a pair of scissors and whacked his off." She rolled her eyes toward the ceiling. "I thought it would never grow back. It was almost as bad as the time he fell asleep with a wad of bubble gum in his mouth and I had to cut out hunks of his hair. I seriously considered snipping off the ends of my hair and pasting them on his bald spots.''

Nick rolled over and pinned her beneath him. Picking up several locks he fanned them across her pillow. ''You have magnificent hair.''

''Umm. I know how Clay feels. I started wearing hats long before they were fashionable. Strange how they became my fashion signature. I had forgotten the reason I started wearing them.''

''Lou wore one to work yesterday.''

''Black, with a silk magnolia pinning up one side of the floppy brim?'' Marianne's voice lilted with laughter. She could tell Nick hadn't been wild about the hat.

''That's the one.'' With his hand covering one of her breasts he could feel her restrained giggles. ''What's so funny?''

''Lou calls that her victory hat. She wears it on the last day of a tough job.''

''I swear to you, Lou has never had a more cooperative, kind, softly spoken boss. I even made morning coffee for her!''

''So you say,'' she replied saucily, wiggling against him. ''We'll see what Lou writes on the evaluation form she files on you. She'll probably recommend Talent Plus drops you as a client.''

Nick groaned, but it had nothing to do with his employee relationships. Fully recovered, he wanted Marianne with a stronger intensity than when he'd first entered her bedroom.

''I take my employees' recommendations seriously,'' she teased. Her needling him ended abruptly as Nick began taking small love bites along her neck and shoulder. ''Lou gave you a glowing report.''

His lips circled her breast, suckling it hotly until her knees bent and pressed together to still the budding desire that began to tie love knots low in her stomach. Stunned by how quickly her body responded to him, she murmured, "Nick, you'd better stop tormenting me or..."

She gasped, unable to complete her thought as the heel of his hand firmly rotated against the feminine triangle of dark auburn curls.

"Or what, love?"

Any threat she could have made would have been an empty one. There was only one lucid thought in her mind. "I want you, Nick."

Chapter Twelve

On Sunday morning a winter storm depression off the Atlantic coast gusted sheets of pounding rain into central Florida. Nick awoke to the sound of heavy raindrops scouring the skylights over the bed. Drowsily, he nestled Marianne closer to him as though to protect her against nature's downpour.

Marianne awakened slowly. "It can't be raining," she whispered, unwilling to disbelieve the weatherman's prediction of fair and sunny.

"It can and is."

"Make it stop," she groaned, shifting her position until she faced him. Since Friday evening, he'd thoroughly convinced her that he could accomplish the impossible. She'd lost track of how often he'd aroused her to a feverish pitch and masterfully claimed her. "You can do it."

Storms seldom last more than twelve hours, unless driven by a hurricane, Nick thought. "Could you give me twenty-four hours?"

"Uh-uh. Clay is supposed to be home at noon. We're going out on the boat, remember?"

"With you in my arms I'm lucky to remember my name." His lips moved against her brow as he inhaled the fragrance of her hair. "You're insatiable."

She lightly tugged the hair on his chest. "Me? What about you?"

"I'm merely a willing slave to your sexual whims," he teased, smiling as he closed his hand over her fingers. "Don't."

"Don't what?"

His eyelashes parted, letting her see how easily she could rekindle the smoldering embers of his passion for her. "Don't start anything you're too sore to finish."

Marianne hated to admit it, but he was right. Her mind was willing, but her body felt fragile. "We'd better get up."

"Why?" Knowing discretion was a major factor in their being together, he wasn't looking forward to wasting the precious moments they could share. "Don't you like to cuddle?"

"Unless a troop of good fairies straightened the family room after you carried me in here, the pillows and wineglasses, et cetera, et cetera, won't leave much to Clay's fertile imagination."

Bolts of lightning shot from the gray clouds as Clay slammed the front door and strode toward his room without saying a single word to Nick or his mother.

Intolerant of her son's rudeness, Marianne ignored Nick as he shook his head at her, and followed Clay.

He'd turned his stereo up to full volume and flung himself spread-eagle across his bed before she reached his door. Given the choice between screaming at the top of her lungs to be heard or turning off his equipment, she compromised by lowering the volume.

Prepared to read Clay the riot act, starting with page one, she backed off when he lifted his head. Although he'd rubbed his knuckles in his eyes to conceal his tears, they were red-rimmed.

Instantly she knew something awful must have happened at Ed's house. "What happened, son?"

"I'm never going back to Dad's house. Never."

Marianne moved to the side of his bed. "Why?"

"Because he breaks his promises." He twisted his knuckles in his eye sockets to dam the flow of tears. "Dad promised he'd get me a moped bike for my fourteenth birthday and he's backing out of it."

This was the first Marianne had heard about Clay getting a motorized vehicle. Had Ed discussed it with her, she'd have put her foot firmly down.

"And that's not all," Clay said with a sniff, wiping his eyes on the sleeve of his shirt. "Do you know why he won't buy one for me?"

"No." It was too much to hope that Ed had reconsidered and decided a moped was unsafe. Out of the corner of her eye, she saw that Nick stood in the doorway. "Why?"

"Because he has to save his money." He paused as a rush of tears clogged his throat. "Eileen is going to have a baby! Soon!"

Marianne dropped beside Clay. Her son fell into her arms. She held him tightly against her chest. Sympathy was all Clay needed to change his silent flow of tears into bone-jarring sobs.

She wasn't surprised by Ed's announcement. Eileen was young and healthy. Naturally she'd want children of her own. Marianne was just surprised this crisis hadn't occurred before now.

The mistake she'd made was not preparing Clay to accept that eventuality. She'd considered it Ed's responsibility and had kept silent. Obviously, until today Ed had also kept his mouth shut.

As she rocked Clay in her arms, a hard kernel of old bitterness left a rancid taste in Marianne's mouth. How like Ed to turn their world topsy-turvy and then ride out of sight, leaving her sitting directly in the wake of the difficult aftermath.

Between racking sobs, Clay cried, "He doesn't love me anymore. I know he doesn't. That's why he's so happy about getting another child."

"Shh, sweetheart. Your father does love you. Their having a baby doesn't mean he'll love you less." She rubbed his back to soothe him the same way she'd done when he was smaller. "Love isn't measured by cups or tablespoons. Shh, love. You wait and see. It's going to be okay."

Clay lifted his head and hiccuped. "Promise?"

"It'll take time for you to adjust to the idea, but yes, I promise the hurt will go away," she pacified. "We both love you. That will never change."

"You'd have been proud of me, Mom. I was mad as blazes, but I didn't blow my top. I just told Dad that I wanted to come home early 'cause I had important things to do."

As Nick silently watched, his heart ached for the boy's uncertainties. He wanted to do something, but didn't want to intrude.

"You know I'm proud of you, Clay." She reached to the bedside table for a tissue and gave it to him. "I have a good idea. Why don't you and Nick go work out on the equipment and then we'll go to the movies?"

Nick stepped forward where Clay could see him. "It will make you feel better."

"I doubt it, but I'll give it a try." He wadded the tissue into a small ball and lobbed it into his waste can. Looking up at Nick, he asked, "Do you know any manufacturer that has some mopeds that need to be tested?" He glanced down at his running shoes. "I'm getting mighty sick and tired of using the shoe sole express."

Chuckling at Clay's weak attempt at humor, Nick said, "Mopeds aren't standard gym equipment. Sorry."

Nick decided this wasn't the right time to add that even if his warehouse had been overstocked with mopeds he wouldn't offer to bring one to Clay, after having watched him on the skateboard ramp. With Clay holding the handlebars a moped could be a lethal weapon pointed at the boy's head.

Before Nick and Clay made it into the garage the phone rang.

"It's probably Brad," Clay said as Marianne picked up the phone. "Tell him to come on over."

Marianne narrowed her eyes as she recognized the voice on the other end of the line. Not pleased with Ed's lack of sensitivity, she momentarily considered hanging up on him. But what purpose would that serve? The rift between father and son needed to be narrowed, not widened. Clay brooding for two weeks, until he visited his father again, would only magnify Clay's hostility.

"It's your father, Clay." She put her hand over the mouthpiece. "He says he has some good news that he wants to share with you."

Clay's chin wobbled as he said, "Tell him I'm busy."

"Is that what you really want me to tell him? Remember, you held your temper. He doesn't realize how upset you are with him."

Stalking to the phone Clay took it from his mother's hand. "Yeah, Dad?" As Clay listened, his lips tightened and his face turned brilliant. "Yeah, Dad. Great news. Hey, I gotta go. Bye."

He slammed the phone down. "Eileen got on his case after he got home 'cause he didn't share all the *wonderful* news. She may have twins!"

Congratulations, Ed, Marianne thought. You've just been given the Obtuse Man of the Year award by your son.

If Marianne was proud of Clay for controlling his temper, he earned Nick's approval by straightening his shoulders and marching toward the garage.

Nick pressed the garage door opener to get some fresh air. Without being reminded, Clay immediately started the series of warm-up exercises. Nick dropped to the floor beside him. For several minutes neither of them spoke.

Two babies! Clay thought, gritting his teeth. No wonder Dad couldn't afford a moped. He'd be spending all his money on diapers and bottles. They'd probably have to buy a bigger home, too. Not that he wanted a stinking old moped anyway. If his dad spent one red cent on him for his birthday, he'd give the gift back to him.

At least Mom loves me. She isn't going to start a new family and forget about me. She has me and Talent Plus. That's enough for her.

He glanced over at Nick. Or was it? How come Nick was here when he got home? He and his mother were supposed to take a picnic basket and go to Nick's house.

"So, Nick, what did you do this weekend?" he asked, trying to sound casual.

"Not much. Watched television." They had watched for all of ten, maybe fifteen minutes, Nick justified silently.

"Did you visit with Mom?"

"Yeah. I came over." Nick grew increasingly wary of the direction Clay's questions were leading to. He wouldn't lie and he damned sure wasn't going to start feeling guilty.

"You kind of like her, don't you?"

"I like both of you. Otherwise, I wouldn't be here."

"Yeah, but you like her a lot, don't you?"

"Yes. I do."

Clay shoved himself to his feet. The next thing you know, Clay thought bitterly, Mom will marry Nick and they'll be spending all their time making twins! He'd had about all the "wonderful" news he could take for one day. He wasn't going to ask another leading question because he didn't want to hear the answer.

He liked Nick, but he wasn't going to lose his father's *and* his mother's love.

If he'd caused major problems before his dad had remarried, there wouldn't be little crumb-crunchers growing inside Eileen's stomach.

"I don't need your help on the equipment," Clay said, asserting himself when Nick started to adjust the pressure on the bar.

"Clay, I can see you're upset. Would you prefer to work out alone?"

No way was Clay going to let Nick go in the house with his mother. He moved from the new equipment to his barbell bench. Since Nick insisted that he have a spotter, he could do it himself.

"Nope." His hands felt clammy as he touched the metal bar. His arms felt as though they were made of rubber. "You can spot for me."

"I'm ready when you are," Nick said, prepared to catch the weights if Clay dropped the bar. "Breathe naturally."

How can I? Clay wondered. He felt as though his whole world was crumbling down on him and he was too weak to hold it in place.

"Eight repetitions. One...two..." Nick could see that Clay was having trouble balancing the bar. What had been easy for him the past week was causing difficulty today. Nick couldn't give the solace to Clay his mother had given him, but he could give praise and encouragement. "Take it easy. You're doing just fine, son, just—"

Clay heaved the bar back up on the rack, then rolled off the bench. "I am not your son and never will be," he shouted. "I have a father. I don't need you or him, and I don't need your dumb old equipment." Feet spread, hands on his hips, chin jutting forward, Clay looked ready to physically defend his home against this man twice his size. "This is my home. Why don't you take your stuff and leave? I don't want you here!"

Stunned and appalled, Nick stepped backward. The last thing he wanted to do was get into a brawl with Marianne's son!

"Calm down, Clay. I wasn't claiming a blood relationship with you." Trying to bring levity to this explosive situation, he said, "Rowland Martin, the bass fisherman, calls whoever is in his boat 'son.' Taking your frustration out on me isn't going to solve your problem."

"You aren't fishing for bass. You're trying to get your hooks into my mom." Clay pointed his finger at Nick. His voice cracked as he yelled, "You are part of the problem. Get out of my garage. Now!"

"Okay, Clay. I'll leave. You need time to cool off and get things into perspective." Nick moved toward his car. "Tell your mother I'll be talking to her. Soon."

"You don't have to call her and snitch," Clay shouted, wishing he'd had the guts to yell at his father. "I'll tell her I don't want you in our home!"

From inside the house, Marianne heard Clay screaming at Nick. What the hell is going on out there? she wondered, dashing across the living room and heading straight for the garage. She burst through the door just in time to see the headlights of Nick's car backing down the drive.

"What have you done, Clay?" She grabbed her son's arm and wheeled him around to face her. "Why were you shouting at Nick?"

"I don't want him here," Clay answered with defiance in his voice and a hardness in his eyes. "It's my home, too. I should have some say as to who comes and goes around here. I told Nick to get out and never come back."

Marianne came close to bending her son over her knee and wearing out the bottom of his blue jeans. She'd never spanked Clay, and she was beginning to think she'd spared the rod and spoiled the child.

It took every ounce of restraint she could drum up to keep her voice calm as she said, "Young man, you listen to me very, very carefully. You may think you're a thirteen-year-old dictator in this household, but I have a news flash for you. I think you're getting too damned big for your britches. You don't yell at *any* adult and you don't order my guests out of our home. Is that clear?"

Clamping his lips into a straight line, Clay refused to respond. He should have known his mother would take Nick's side without asking him why he'd ordered Nick off his property. His mom and dad were alike. Neither of them cared how he felt about anything!

Marianne's chest heaved with suppressed anger. She dropped Clay's arm, afraid she'd give in to the impulse to shake him until his teeth rattled.

"Furthermore, young man, you will march straight to your room, unplug the stereo, sit down on the bed and think about what you've done." She moved to one side of Clay and started backing him toward the door. "I'm going to think about it, too. Later, when we're both feeling civilized, we'll talk about this. Until that time? No stereo. No television. No telephone. No nothing. Now, turn around and get moving."

Without a word, Clay followed her orders. He wouldn't give her the satisfaction of seeing him cry. He'd never apologize. Nick was trying to take his father's place. Clay vowed never to let that happen.

Standing alone in the garage, Marianne had the urge to pick up something and throw it as hard and as far as she possibly could. She could not believe her son had behaved in such a despicable manner. She refused to make excuses for him or to feel guilty for isolating him.

She heard a horn toot in front of her house. She prayed Nick had waited to speak to her as she hurried out to the driveway. Seeing his car at the end of the drive she gave silent thanks. Briskly, she jogged through the rain toward it.

Nick waited for her inside his car. After Clay had spouted off, Nick had driven around the block. He realized Clay was so emotionally distraught that he might blow up at his mother. He wanted to be there in case Marianne needed him.

Sliding in beside Nick, Marianne wiped the rain from her face and said, "I'm so sorry . . . embarrassed . . . humiliated . . . disappointed."

She would have gone on, but Nick put his arm around her shoulders, shook his head and put one finger over her lips.

"You aren't to blame, sweetheart." He heaved a thoughtful sigh. "Frankly, I'm not certain Clay is, either."

"That's generous of you, Nick. I wouldn't blame you if you squealed your tires getting out of here as fast as you could."

"Why? Because your teenager is feeling unloved by his father and he threw a childish tantrum?"

"Don't make excuses for Clay's misbehavior. I truly thought I'd brought him up to control that redheaded temper of his. He will apologize to you."

Nick doubted that making Clay grovel was a good idea. "What do you think is going on in his mind right now?"

"He's probably wondering if I'm going to let him go to baseball practice after school tomorrow," she replied with brutal candor. "He's gotten into the habit lately of thinking of his own best interests first. That's what this whole thing is about, isn't it?"

"In a way, you're right," Nick agreed. "But maybe you ought to put yourself in his shoes. Clay must feel as though he's being displaced by a baby in his father's home. And, when he arrives home and finds me there, he feels as though he's being displaced by me in your home. Where does that leave him?"

"In his room with no stereo, no telephone and no TV!"

Nick squeezed her arm. "C'mon, Marianne. You're as angry as he is."

"That is precisely why he is in his room and I'm out here. I don't get angry often and I don't hold a grudge longer than a decade, but when I am angry there is no reasoning with me. I'm as mean as an alligator with his mouth taped."

"You don't feel the least bit sorry for him?"

"I'm only sorry that he took his frustration out on you. Couldn't he have waited until you left and blown his cork at me?"

"You aren't the one he's mad at. He's drawn a territorial circle around your home, with you on the inside and anyone who threatens to take your love on the outside. You see him as a kid blowing off steam. Clay sees himself as a man protecting his territory."

Marianne couldn't comprehend that sort of male logic. "That would be fine if I was a valuable figurine covered with precious gems and you were a burglar, but that isn't the case." She brushed a damp curl back from her face. "I am not a piece of property... or a meaty bone that should be fought over. Doesn't that strike you as a tad uncivilized?''

"Mothers are civilized. Thirteen-year-old boys can be little barbarians.''

Marianne bit her lip thoughtfully. Men were so damned different from women. A simplistic viewpoint, but true.

How could she guide Clay toward being a well-rounded, rational adult when she did not understand what motivated his behavior? Did being a single mother get tougher as one's son grew older?

She'd raised Clay, but Nick had insights into her son that only a man could have.

"What do you think I should do?''

"Exactly what you have been doing. Love him and show it. Guide him, but not with an electric cattle prod. When Clay feels secure he'll get back on the straight and narrow.''

"You don't think I should punish him?'' she asked skeptically.

"Don't misunderstand, Marianne. I'm not saying Clay doesn't need boundaries. He expects them. Remove them and he'll be dead certain that you don't care about him. But don't make him grovel, especially to me. You'll only make him hate me.''

"You think he'll come around? About us, I mean?''

Nick gave her question consideration for several seconds. Clay resented him, with what the boy thought were good reasons. It would take time and patience, but with maturity Clay would reconsider his position and make an about-face.

"We both know Clay is basically a good kid, Marianne. You've taught him the difference between right and wrong, fair and unfair. You can't lose faith in Clay.

He's your son. Let's take it a day at a time and see what happens."

Marianne covered her face with her hands. Deep in her heart, she knew what Nick had just said was true. She had to believe in Clay's innate goodness.

He placed a gentle kiss on her lips. "Can I call you at Talent Plus for the latest news bulletin?"

"Please do." She glanced through the windshield at the dark window in Clay's room. "He's going to miss you, and I am, too."

"Good. I'll miss both of you."

She reached for the door handle. "I'd better go inside."

Nick detained her by hooking his hand at her nape and giving her a swift hard kiss. "I had a lovely weekend, Marianne. I'll be thinking of you."

Chapter Thirteen

"This has gone on long enough," Marianne said to Nick on the telephone at her office. "Clay is cutting off his nose to spite his face." My nose, too, she silently added. "Tuesday he pushed the weight-lifting equipment up against the wall, and Thursday he covered it with a sheet. He must make forty trips a day through the garage to stand and gaze at it with a wistful expression on his face."

"You didn't forbid him to use it, did you?"

"No. Brad pesters him to use it on a daily basis, though. For once, peer pressure is a positive influence. I overheard Brad tell Clay he was being a jerk. My son didn't wrestle him to the ground and make him take it back."

Nick swiveled his desk chair toward the window overlooking the park. This was the fifth day of the standoff. Clay neither attacked nor retreated, and Nick didn't either.

When their work schedules allowed it, he and Marianne met for lunch. Nick was jogging a lot, pumping iron and standing in the shower stall with cold water dripping down his tense body. Mentally he was long on patience, but physically he was short on I-won't-intrude power.

"Anything else?" he asked.

"I went to the doughnut shop that has the King Enterprises billboard near it. Usually Clay goes in with me because he likes the yeasty aroma and to pick out the kind of doughnuts he wants. He sat in the car and stared at your picture. Dammit! He misses you. I miss you! Why are we letting Clay's stubbornness make all of us miserable?"

"Maybe it's time to give him a gracious out. Can you think of something that would allow him to back down without losing face?"

"Well, I could point him in your direction and give him a good swift kick where it would do him the most good," Marianne joked. "I still think he owes you an apology."

Silently Nick agreed with her. It had to come from Clay, though. And it had to be sincere. Otherwise, this problem would constantly crop up.

"What do you think of my inviting both of you out on the boat Sunday? We'd be on neutral territory—the lake—away from both of our homes. He could bring Brad along if he needs reinforcements."

"I don't know, Nick," Marianne said, thinking out loud. "Is there some way we could arrange to accidentally bump into one another?"

"There's a park on Lake Monroe, up in Sanford. If you rented one of those two-seater sailboats and I just happened to be out in my boat..."

Instantly Marianne warmed up to his idea. "Clay would have his options open. He'd have an opportunity to get back in your good graces or continue to be a stinker."

At least she'd have a chance to see Nick, Marianne thought. Only hearing his voice wasn't enough. There were times when she'd awaken in the middle of the night and reach for him. Cuddling up to a telephone wasn't nearly as satisfying as touching Nick.

"Either way, we'd have a better idea of what he was thinking. This trying to outguess him is slightly maddening."

"Slightly? It's thoroughly maddening. It's like fighting a battle of wits knowing I'm unarmed!"

Nick chuckled. "How are the two of you getting along?"

"I hug him even when he pretends to resist, and he still asks for his nightly glass of water." Marianne picked up a pen and doodled a kingly crown on a sheet of paper. "His school grades will be out next week. I'll have the final results on studying with or without the stereo playing pop music." She paused, then said, "I talked to Ed. I thought he needed to know his son is going off the deep end."

"What did he say?"

"Nothing helpful. He's sure I can handle the problem." She appreciated Ed's vote of confidence, considering he still liked to inflate his ego by thinking of her as the woman he had outgrown. Five minutes into the conversation she'd quickly realized Ed wouldn't help straighten Clay out. He wanted to be the good guy, as usual. She'd chewed him out royally and hung up. Nick had shown far more fatherly concern than Ed had, much to Nick's credit. "Clay isn't the only one disappointed by Ed's insensitivity. I thank my lucky stars I have you to talk to."

"The feeling is mutual, sweetheart." Nick noticed Irene watching him with a gigantic smile on her face. "Just a second. I need to close my office door. Irene has big ears and doesn't mind using them. She's also become extremely opinionated."

While she waited for Nick to come back to the phone, Marianne wondered what Irene thought of her. "What is Irene's opinion of me?" she asked when Nick returned to the phone.

"Since you arranged for her mother to go to the Youngsters' Place, she's become extremely biased about anything concerning you." In a hushed voice he added, "On her lunch hour yesterday she went hat shopping. Does that tell you anything?"

"The millinery shop is doing a great business and we both should invest in it?" Marianne teased, definitely flattered.

"Or you could open your own hat shop. There are enough hats in your closet that you wouldn't have to purchase much of an inventory." He closed his eyes and asked, "Which one are you wearing today?"

"It's black with pink rosebuds on it that match my dress." Daring to add a smidgen of spice to the conversation, she whispered, "The rosebuds also match the tiny flowers embroidered on the lace of my underclothes."

Nick groaned. The telephone wire sizzled. Marianne grinned.

"You're a wicked lady, Ms. Clark."

"Well Mr. King, you did ask."

"That will cost me another couple of hours at the gym working off my frustrations. By Sunday I'll be so muscle-bound I won't be able to get into my shirts."

"I don't mind," Marianne quipped. "Wait until you see the swimsuit that matches my sunbonnet!"

"Delete wicked and replace it with cruel," Nick groaned comically. "And add another hour to my workout while you're at it."

Jayne stuck her head in Marianne's office and whispered, "Line three."

Nodding, Marianne said, "I have a business call on another line, Nick. I'll look forward to seeing you Sunday. What time?"

"One o'clock?"

"Fine. See you then. While I'm at church with Clay I'll send up a few prayers to the powers that be to intercede on our behalf. Bye."

Marianne switched to the other line and quickly dispensed with the minor problem of a new employee. She'd hung up the phone when Jayne came in and sat down.

"Did I hear you talking to Mr. King?" she asked, grinning broadly. "He calls here once or twice a day, doesn't he? Must be a difficult customer, huh?"

Marianne pointed her pen in Jayne's direction. "Since when have you developed this keen interest in my personal life?"

"Since you acquired a personal life. Clay is a sweetheart, but I'd have to rate your life as strictly PG-13," Jayne replied as she crossed her long legs and settled into the chair. "Are you blushing? Darn, I knew I should have kept the King account in my files."

"When Lou marched in here mad as a wet hen, you couldn't hand over the file to me quickly enough. Remember?"

Jayne held up two fingers an inch apart. "I came this close to replacing her, too. The fates must be working against me."

"I can certainly empathize." Fate, thy name is Clay, she thought silently.

The telephone rang. Marianne reached for it; Jayne was quicker.

"Talent Plus," Jayne answered, picking up Marianne's extension. "How may I help you?"

The way Jayne's face lit up, Marianne thought it had to be Nick.

"That's three receptionists, two filing clerks, then data entry and seven secretaries?" Jayne said, giving her boss the thumbs-up signal. "For two weeks. Could you hold for one moment, please, while I move to a computer terminal?" After she punched the hold button, she hurried to the outer office saying, "It's Pascal's Manufacturing."

Rubbing her hands together in delight, Marianne grinned. Her personal life was a muddle, but Talent Plus was doing great. Pascal's would be the third new company to go to contract this week. Talent Plus was growing by leaps and bounds.

At this rate she was going to have to put a larger ad in the daily paper to attract more temporary help. Better yet, she thought, there were several women who had been working on upgrading their skills, why not contact them?

At five-thirty, Marianne picked up Clay from baseball practice feeling as though she'd been pulled backward through a knothole in a board fence. Aside from her usual busy Friday, she'd tested nine women and added them to her roster.

Tossing his catcher's mitt and cleats in the back of the car, Clay climbed in. "Mom, you look pooped."

"I look better than I feel." She gave Clay a tired smile and patted him on his knee. A week ago he wouldn't have noticed how she looked. "Pizza tonight?"

Clay grinned. They were back in their usual routine, and he loved it. "It's Friday, isn't it? Sausage for me and a deluxe for you."

"I thought we might go up to Lake Monroe this weekend. We could rent one of those small sailboats."

"Could we take the fishing rods? One of the guys in math class said the crappie are practically jumping into the boat. Please, Mom, I'll even bait your hook and clean the fish we catch."

"I can't turn down a deal like that," she said, chuckling, fully aware that Clay was as squeamish about baiting hooks and cleaning fish as she was. "What brought on this change?"

Change? Clay repeated silently. He'd made the offer because he thought it was the manly thing to do. He didn't want any changes, though, not even little ones.

"On second thought, we'll stick to the equal-opportunity rule. I'll do mine and you do yours."

"What about the fish that jump into the boat?" she teased. "Who's going to clean them?"

"We'll flip a coin like we always do."

Marianne pulled into the garage. "Home again, home again..."

"Jiggity-jog," Clay said, completing the last line of the nursery rhyme.

Automatically his eyes focused on the white sheet draped over Nick's weight-lifting equipment. It resembled a huge ghost and it haunted his conscience. His keen sense of fairness recoiled with shame when he thought about what he'd screamed at Nick. Just because he'd been mad at the world, and his father in particular, didn't make what he'd done right.

Nick was mad at him. And he deserved it. He'd have felt a whole lot better if Nick had at least called him on the phone to chew him out for being an inconsiderate, ungrateful brat.

"Shall we have your pizza delivered to the car?" Marianne asked as she unlocked the house door. Through the windshield she could see Clay staring at the dashboard.

"I'll be right in."

Clay pinched his biceps. His muscles hadn't turned to mush yet, but any day he expected them to feel like cooked oatmeal. He'd already lost the power to throw the baseball superhard to the second baseman.

He opened the passenger's door and got out of the car. No one had told him Nick's equipment was off-limits. He was the one who had pushed it against the wall and thrown a dustcover over it.

Such a waste, he thought, reaching for the metal bar. Wasn't it supposed to be a shame for expensive equipment to go unused? Hadn't his own mother yammered at him for buying stuff and not using it? Or for putting food on his plate and not eating it? There was probably some kid in Africa who'd give his eyeteeth for this machine.

Clay groaned inwardly. He didn't have to go halfway around the world to find a taker. Brad, right next door, would go bonkers if he hauled it over there. Heck, Brad would carry it piggyback!

He thought about calling Nick. Cringing at the idea, he dropped his hand limply to his side. What would he say? "Sorry" sounded awfully puny. Also, apologizing implied he wouldn't come unglued at the seams again. "I miss having you around here"? That would be like giving Nick a key to the house.

If Nick started coming over to lift weights three times a week and his mother also saw him once on the weekend, she'd probably start liking Nick more than she liked him.

Turning his back on the equipment, he decided taking the risk of losing his mother's love, just to get big muscles, was stupid. She meant more to him than the equipment and the baseball team combined.

The best thing to do, he decided, would be to sacrifice the equipment by having Nick send one of his deliverymen over to get it. Maybe Nick wouldn't be so mad at him then. Nick was a man. He would know how much it hurt a guy to give up something he really wanted.

Clay entered the house feeling not quite so guilty. "Mom?"

"I'm in the laundry room. Bring me your dirty jeans, would you?"

Hustling into his bedroom, he pulled his dark clothes from the clothes hamper and carried them to the laundry room. His mother was folding clothes from the drier. He sidestepped around her.

"I'll load these in the washer," he offered. "I'll even spread them around so the washer won't get off balance and go wha-wham, wha-wham, wha-wham."

"Thanks, son."

Uncertain of how to broach the subject of giving the weight set back, he asked, "Are you going to be seeing Nick this weekend?"

"Why?" She folded the towel in her hands as she watched Clay shove his jeans in the washer. Nick's name hadn't crossed Clay's lips since the big blowup. Optimistically, she dared to hope Clay had had a change of heart. "Do you have something planned I don't know about?"

"Nope." He stuck his head inside the washer to avoid looking at her. "I thought you might tell Nick to have somebody come over and get his equipment."

Marianne's hopes shriveled. Clay wanted Nick and his gym equipment out of the house. This wasn't a good omen for Sunday's get-together.

"I don't know exactly when I'll be talking to Nick, but I'll mention the equipment to him." She placed the folded towel on the stack. "Are you certain you won't want to use the equipment?"

"Yeah, I'm certain." Proud of himself for doing something that felt right for a change, he lifted his head from the washer. "A cup of detergent?"

The satisfied smile she saw on Clay's face made her temper flare. A dozen unkind thoughts scurried through her mind, but she only said, "Yes."

Unloading the picnic cooler from the car, Clay called, "You packed enough fried chicken for an army. Are we going to eat or fish?"

"You have the appetite of a grizzly bear getting ready for a long winter." She heard Clay grunt as he lugged the food and drinks to the table nearest the lake. They'd agreed to fish first, eat, then rent a sailboat.

"You only had pancakes, eggs and sausage for breakfast. Are you weak from hunger already?"

"It weighs at least a ton, Mom."

They exchanged a brief look, then quickly glanced away as each of them pictured Nick and the weights he had given Clay.

To escape from his feelings of guilt, Clay ran back to the car, calling over his shoulder, "Where did you put the container of worms?"

"In your potato salad," she muttered, on edge about how Clay would behave when Nick appeared.

She'd spoken to Nick on the telephone after midnight, in bed, huddled under the covers. Sleepily, he'd agreed that Clay's wanting the equipment removed from the garage wasn't a good sign. The sexy tone of his voice had had her switching topics within seconds. An hour after she placed the call, she'd hung up the phone feeling intensely frustrated.

To say she was eager to be alone with him was the understatement of the century.

Louder, she called, "Behind the front seats. They can't take the heat."

"You can't, either. Do you want me to get your sun visor?"

"Yes, please." She scanned the width of the lake looking for Nick. Clay wasn't helping her nerves by being ultra considerate of her. He'd been good, too good. Except for cooking, he'd helped with all the housework. There was absolutely no way he could have found out about the planned "accidental" meeting, but Marianne felt as if she were in the calm eye of a hurricane.

"I brought the white stuff you put on your nose, too. Want me to smear it on you?"

"I'll wait awhile." She didn't want Nick to see her with her nose snow-white. "You'd better get your hook in the water or I'll catch the first fish."

Clay grinned. "I'll have a string full before you get the worm on your hook."

"You and what fishing pro?" Marianne quipped.

Handing her a fishing rod and the box of worms, he challenged, "I'll bet you a double-dip ice cream cone at the concession stand that I catch more than you do."

"You're on." Marianne grabbed what she needed and ran to the edge of the lake. Grimacing, she opened the container of worms. As she picked up a fat night crawler and dropped it, she made a face and said, "Yuck! What did you do, pick the squashy ones?"

Laughing at her, Clay dangled a worm in front of her face. "Give me your hook. I'll do it."

"I'll let you," she said, happy to concede. "I'll put the bobbers on the lines."

Within minutes both lines were in the water. Small ripples caused by the breeze made the red-and-white bobbers dip and sway lazily. Clay concentrated on watching his line; Marianne daydreamed about Nick while she watched for his boat.

"Look, Mom." Clay pointed toward his bobber. "The water is so clear you can see the fish."

Peering down, she replied, "Not around my worm I can't."

"Yeah. They're suspended." He jerked on the butt of his rod. His line reeled out. "Got one. Whoa, son." The fish stripped the line off the reel. "A whopper! Want to reel it in?"

"Are you sick or something? I used to let you reel my fish in to the bank."

"Whoa! There he goes again. Specks don't fight this hard. I must have caught a lunker bass."

Marianne felt a tug on her line. The bobber took a drive straight to the bottom. Her rod bent in half.

"Hey! I've got one, too!" she chortled. "Don't let yours cross my line."

The fish must have heard her and comprehended English. Both lines instantly zinged toward each other.

"Duck under my rod tip, Mom."

She raised her rod for him to duck under. He lowered his as she followed his directions.

"We're gonna lose them!" Clay squatted, then duck-walked under her line into the water. "We should have brought the net!"

The fish on Marianne's line broke the water's surface. A boat horn tooted. She glanced up and saw Nick waving as he idled directly toward her line. Clay had his thumb in the mouth of his bass and was holding it up for Nick to see.

The boat's propeller cut her line.

Under other circumstances Marianne would have been displeased, but when she saw the sappy grins on Clay's and Nick's faces, she couldn't have cared less about the fish that got away.

"How much do you think it weighs?" Clay asked Nick. "Looks like a ten-pounder to me."

"Shamu's cousin?" Nick teased, mentioning the trained killer whale at Sea World by name.

Marianne reeled up her empty line and said dryly, "Distant cousin. Way distant."

Clay waded to Nick's boat and dropped the fish inside it for safekeeping. Nick didn't look mad at him, but sometimes he couldn't tell with grown-ups. "What are you doing on Lake Monroe?"

"Checking out the boat. The engine was acting up. I thought it might be a fuel clog in the carburetor."

"It's cool looking." His hand trailed along the smooth aquamarine-colored hull. "Goes fast, huh?"

"Fast enough to pull a hydroslide or somebody on water skis. Want to try it out?"

Clay glanced at his mother, who shrugged, and then back up at Nick. "I didn't bring my hydroslide 'cause we were going to rent a skiff and go sailing."

"I have one."

"Mom?" Clay asked, wading back to the bank. "Wanna go for a speedboat ride with Nick? I'll let you hydroslide first." With his back to Nick he whispered, "That way I can talk to Nick, sort of man to man."

Inwardly crowing that Nick's plan appeared to be working beautifully, Marianne outwardly pretended to contemplate the idea of Clay's wanting to talk to Nick alone. She couldn't appear too eager or Clay would guess this "accidental" meeting had been arranged.

"We'll have to lug the cooler and the fishing equipment to the boat. Otherwise it might not be here when we get back." Quietly she reminded Clay, "You'll be Nick's guest."

"Yeah, I know. I won't be a jerk."

Marianne smiled. "Do I get to start the hydroslide ride from the bank?" she bargained.

"That's the sissy way to get started. You could really make Nick believe you're a star athlete if you skimmed across the water and hopped on it the way I taught you to do."

"I'll leave the role of star athlete in your department. In case you haven't noticed, I am a sissy." She gave him a mock blow to the chin. "And proud of it."

"So we can go?"

Before she could give permission, Clay was charging toward the picnic table shouting, "She says we can go with you, Nick."

"Do you need a hand carrying anything?" Nick shouted.

"No, thanks," Clay refused politely. "I'll get it. Just keep the engine warmed up."

The boat was close enough to shore for Marianne to see Nick wink at her. "I'll get the rope and hydroslide ready."

She smiled in return. As always, just the sight of Nick was accelerating her heart until she could feel it pounding in her chest.

Thoroughly pleased with how their little ploy was working out, Marianne removed the cover-up over her bathing suit, her sandals and her sun visor. The things I do for my son, she thought, as she braced herself for a shock. Her skin was hot and sticky from being baked in the sun. Timidly she stuck her toes in the water. "It's freezing!" she gasped.

"You'll get used to it in a minute or two!" Carrying the cooler on one shoulder as though it were weightless, Clay splashed into the lake. "Oops, sorry, Mom. Want me to bring the slide to you?"

"Can you do it without causing a tidal wave?"

She wiped the droplets of water off her bare shoulders and arms. Was it wisest to slowly ease into the water, letting it creep up her legs and torso an inch at a time, or to take the big plunge? Deciding to jump in and get it over with, she made a shallow dive into the water.

"Way to go, Mom!" Clay praised. He pushed the buoyant slide in her direction. "Heads up."

She stopped the board with her hands. "Take the keys out of my purse and lock it in the car, would you?"

While Clay made another trip to the table and the car, Marianne waded to Nick's boat. "Hi!"

"Hi, lady." Checking to make certain Clay wasn't watching he stooped and gave her a fleeting kiss. "Remind me to try that again later."

She folded her arms on the side of the boat and propped her chin on her forearms. Either the water had warmed or Nick's kiss had raised her body heat ten degrees. She certainly wasn't cold any longer.

"I'd say our strategy is working fine," she said, grinning up at Nick. "What do you think?"

"He acts like we're long-lost buddies, doesn't he?"

She nodded. "Clay and Brad have horrendous yelling matches and are best buddies within a few hours. Maybe he wasn't as angry as we thought he was."

"Shh. Here he comes," Nick said in a whisper. He raised his voice, improvising the tail of a casual conversation they could have been having. "I do a little water skiing, but I'm not an avid hydroslide fan."

"Wait until you see what Clay can do," Marianne bragged. "Brad's parents take them to Mount Dora Lake for a week in the summer. The boys do all sort of fancy tricks."

"Nothing dangerous, I hope," Nick said as he frowned.

Marianne saw his eyes darkened by a swift jab from his old fear. Would he ever completely get over Crissy's drowning? she wondered. "Stop worrying, Nick. We'll be with him. Clay won't do anything he hasn't done hundreds of times before."

Clay waded back to the boat with his hands full of their belongings. He dropped everything into the back seat. "Nothing I haven't done a hundred times on water rougher than this."

"Climb in," Nick said, offering his hand. "We'd better get going before your mother's lips turn blue."

"Take a good look at that slide, Mom. It's got fins that pop down to stabilize the tail end. There's no way you could fall off. Cool, huh?"

"Yeah, real cool," she agreed with a small shiver. "Toss me a life jacket and the rope. Let's get this show on the road."

"I've never pulled someone on a hydroslide, Clay. You'll have to give me a few tips."

Clay dropped the bright orange jacket and the rope handle. It plunked in the water near Marianne's hand. She grabbed both of them. As she put on the jacket and pushed the slide to the water's edge, she could hear Clay giving explicit instructions on what to do and what not to do.

"It's not like pulling a skier." Clay put on a life jacket as he spoke. "You don't accelerate to pop her out of the water real fast. You have to start Mom out slow and easy, then watch for her signals. Thumbs-up means faster and thumbs-down means slower."

Amused at the correlation between pulling her on the hydroslide and dating her, Marianne grinned. With her knees in position, she settled back on her heels and tightened the strap across her thighs. One final check to make certain the straps of her one-piece suit were secure and she gave Clay a sharp nod.

"Ready?" Nick shouted. He'd turned the bow of the boat toward the channel. "Take up the slack?"

The rope handle tugged her arm's sockets. Getting a firm grip, Marianne shouted, "Go for it!"

The boat steadily surged forward, towing Marianne. Exhilarated, she started laughing as the boat picked up speed. She shifted her weight and the board responded by zigzagging on the surface.

"Keep an eye on her," Nick said. "I'll watch for other boats."

"Whooeee!" Clay yelled. "You should have seen her jump the wake."

Nick pointed to the camera on the dashboard. "Why don't you take some pictures?"

"Will do." After he'd taken several shots, Clay returned the camera to the dashboard. Standing close to Nick, he said, "I'm sorry about last Sunday. I was a stupid jerk. Do you think maybe you could forget it happened?"

Nick grinned and put his arm across Clay's shoulders to give him a manly hug. "Consider it forgotten, Clay. I'm sorry my slip of the tongue upset you."

"Friends?"

Nick felt a lump in his throat. Clay would never be his own child, but Nick realized he truly cared for Marianne's son. "Yeah. Friends."

"Uh-oh! She didn't make that last crossover. Swing around and pick her up."

Laughing at the joyride she'd taken, Marianne dipped her head back to wash the stray hairs from her face. "Your turn," she shouted at Clay over the loud purr of the engine.

While Nick gave her a helping hand up the chrome ladder on the back of the boat, Clay gave an earsplitting yell and jumped overboard.

Nick handed her a towel. Aware that she had to be dying of curiosity, he said, "Clay apologized and he meant it."

"Thank heavens." She sighed. She patted her face dry. What she wanted to do was throw her arms around Nick's neck and smother him with kisses. "What about you and me? Did he say anything about us dating?"

"No, but I don't think he objects." He watched her dry her arms and legs, wishing he could do it for her. "We'll just have to be careful to make certain he knows he's loved by both of us."

"Do you? Love him, I mean?"

"What I feel for Clay is close to how I felt about Crissy." He turned toward the back of the boat and watched Clay preparing to mount the board. How could he not love Clay? In many ways the boy was a carbon copy of himself at the same age. "I guess if I'd had another child, a boy, I would have loved him, too, but differently than I loved my daughter. It scares me a little to know Clay could wrap me around his finger the way Crissy did. What if something happened to him?"

It was on the tip of Marianne's tongue to repeat her first question: "What about you and me?" Clay's shout of "Ready when you are" stopped her. She wrapped the towel around her shoulders and hugged herself.

She lacked Nick's patience, but she had no choice but to wait. If he loved Clay there was a strong chance he felt the same way about her.

"Why don't you drive and I'll watch," Nick suggested.

"Would you take snapshots of him?" She moved to the driver's seat. Hand on the throttle, she said, "Clay will get a kick out of showing pictures of his daredevil stunts to his buddies.''

''Take out the slack, Mom!'' Lying facedown on the slide with the rope handle extended over the board's bow, Clay could feel the steady flow of adrenaline pumping through him. Nick has to be the nicest guy in Winter Park, Clay thought, proud of himself for having the guts to be a man and apologize.

Slowly Marianne idled the boat forward until the rope grew taut.

''Hit it,'' Clay shouted.

''Tell me when he's on his knees.'' She accelerated. ''Clay has to strap the safety belt across his thighs to stay on the board.''

Keeping his eyes on Clay, Nick nodded. In one fluid move Clay surged from the water and tightened the belt. ''He's up and ready,'' Nick yelled. ''Thumbs up.''

Marianne swept her hand in a wide circle over her head to signal she was about to make a wide turn and point the boat in the opposite direction. They were getting too close to where the lake narrowed into the St. John's River.

Glancing over her shoulder, she saw Clay hunched low to get the least wind resistance. He popped five feet in the air as the rope whipped him across the wake. Clay barely touched the lake's surface when he turned the board to recross the wake. A rooster tail of water sprayed high as the side of the board dipped below the water's surface.

''He's good!'' Nick said. ''Damned good. I got a fantastic picture of him in the air.''

Clay landed in the churning vee of water behind the boat caused by the motor. He raised his thumb. ''Watch this!''

Laughing, Nick watched Clay hydroslide backward, then make circles by agilely shifting the rope from the front to his back. "Wish I'd brought the movie camera along. This would make a terrific television commercial."

"What?" Marianne shouted, leaning toward Nick.

"Later! I'll tell you later!"

His eyes left Clay and he turned the camera's lens toward Marianne. They were going fast, much faster than when Marianne had been on the board. She was standing on one leg with her other knee on the seat, her head higher than the boat's windshield. Her long braid with a red ribbon tied at the end reminded Nick of the graceful tail of a kite, whipping from side to side as though laughing at the wind.

Just before he pressed the button to take the picture, Marianne turned and smiled at him.

The perfect picture of the woman he loved.

I love you, Marianne Clark, he thought silently. Unable to contain his feelings, he shouted, "I love you, Marianne!"

"What?" She thought she heard him say he loved her, but she wasn't certain. "What did you say?"

Before he could answer, a honk from up ahead jerked her attention totally back to driving the boat. Ignoring the boating safety rules, a thirty-foot cruiser was crossing dangerously close in front of them. With a muttered imprecation at careless boaters, Marianne concentrated on steering their own boat safely out of the way.

Seeing Marianne start to turn the boat, Nick looked to see what was happening. The wake of the cruiser was heading straight for their bow. Nick turned to warn Clay, and saw that the boy had plenty of time to drop the rope and get off the board before it hit the wake. Nick opened his mouth to yell "Jump!"

And watched helplessly as Clay sent the board skimming off the surface of the water.

The world seemed to slow on its axis, putting everything in slow motion.

The boat slammed into the wake.

Nick pitched against the back of the seat.

Clay started the somersault he had chosen as his next stunt.

The engine raced as the boat rose out of the water. Marianne felt the steering wheel jar against her rib cage as the bow careened back into the lake.

The ski rope went slack, then made a loud snap as it instantly went taut.

Upside down, Clay felt the surge of power as his arms were yanked forward at precisely the wrong moment to complete the rotation. The hydroslide jetted out from under his knees. He screamed.

Nick watched in horror as Clay's body, resembling a limp rag doll, bounced on the surface of the water. The board flipped, end over end, and landed on Clay.

What seemed to Nick like an eternity was in reality only a matter of seconds.

"Cut the throttle!" he yelled, lunging to the back of the boat. Fifty yards away he could see the orange life jacket, but not Clay's head. He reached over the back, pulling in the ski rope hand over hand to keep it from jamming the propeller blade. "Circle back. He's down!"

Shaken by the panic in Nick's voice, Marianne cut the throttle back to low immediately. Her hands fumbled as she began turning the steering wheel. She scanned the water's surface looking for Clay, expecting to hear him give a hoot of laughter.

Clay saw the wake coming, she told herself. He knows to throw the rope. He's okay. He has to be okay!

And then the front of the boat came around. The flotation device held Clay's face out of the water. His limp body bobbed slightly, but otherwise he made no movement.

"Oh, my God!" she screamed, one hand flying to her mouth. "Clay!"

"Don't panic," Nick shouted, his heart pounding hard in his chest. "Steer the boat as close to him as you can!"

For one heart-stopping moment, it wasn't Clay that Nick saw floating in the water. It was Crissy. Shards of pain splintered through him.

Cutting the engine completely, Marianne rushed to the right side of the boat. She couldn't see any blood. Maybe the wind had just been knocked out of him.

"Help me, Nick!" she pleaded, nearly hysterical. "Help me get Clay into the boat!"

The sound of Marianne's voice pierced through Nick's nightmare. His reflexes took control of his body. He dived into the lake, surfacing beside Clay. Be alive, he chanted silently. Dammit, don't you dare die!

His fingers clamped on the cushion supporting Clay's head, holding it up. Numb with fear, he couldn't tell if Clay was breathing or not. He touched the pulse point on the child's neck, and tears spurted from his eyes as he felt a steady throb.

"He's unconscious, but he's..." His surge of relief faded when he saw the blood on Clay's head. He circled his arm over the vest, holding the boy protectively against his body. Sidestroking, he towed him to the ladder.

How was he going to get Clay into the boat?

Marianne saw Nick's dilemma. Knowing she lacked the strength to pull Clay to safety, she jumped into the water. When she surfaced, Nick had climbed the first rungs while holding Clay around the waist.

Wordlessly, swiftly, they worked together. Nick pulled; Marianne lifted.

She could hear small whimpering cries, but couldn't comprehend who made them. Nick? She? Clay? It could have been one, or all three of them.

"Cover him with the towels. We've got to keep him from going into shock," Nick ordered, once Marianne had pulled herself into the boat. "I'm going to get us back to the marina."

Crouched beside Clay, Marianne obediently followed Nick's command, then wrapped her arms around her son, hugging him tightly against her. "I'm sorry, Clay. It was my fault! Oh, God, I'm so sorry. Please, please, please be okay."

She felt so damned helpless. She didn't know whether she should try to stop the steady flow of blood oozing from Clay's scalp, or let the flow cleanse the wound. His skin was pale, ash white. The tiny freckles across his cheeks and nose were the only color other than the trickle of crimson.

"Call 911," Nick shouted as he neared the dock and saw three men with fishing rods in their hands. "Get an ambulance out here. My boy has been injured."

Chapter Fourteen

"Wait in here, please," the nurse said, pointing toward a small room where chairs lined the walls. "As soon as the results from X-Ray are available the doctor will be with you."

Marianne glanced at the chairs, but couldn't collapse into one of them. The past hour had been a muddled whirlwind of sensations, sights and sounds that had left her so emotionally keyed up, all she could do was pace back and forth.

She'd been the only one allowed to ride in the ambulance with Clay. Nick had no way of knowing that Clay had regained consciousness and spoken to her.

"Didn't make the somersault, huh?" were the first words out of his mouth. "Sorry, Mom. I shouldn't have been showing off."

Clay was sorry? That was utterly ludicrous. The sobs she held inside had prevented her from doing anything other than shaking her head.

As a parent, she was the one responsible for her child's safety. Who knew Clay better than she did? She should have realized he'd take daredevil risks. She should have made certain that he'd be careful.

Clay had lain on the stretcher being brave, while she sat beside him, holding his hand, feeling stupid and cowardly. She'd been scared, unbelievably frightened, that he would die before they reached the hospital.

The medic had stanched the bleeding and assured her that scalp wounds always bled profusely and looked worse than they were. Marianne hadn't believed him. She'd had to clench her teeth to stop from screaming at the medic to get busy.

When Clay chuckled and told the medic to help him up because his mother looked as if she were going to faint, her sobs had strangled her.

How could Clay have been kidding around when his own mother had almost killed him? she wondered. She should have reacted more quickly. She should have signaled Clay and gradually slowed the boat down. Her negligence had landed her son flat on his back under an X-ray machine.

She didn't think she'd ever be able to forgive herself or forget what had happened. Bits and pieces kept assailing her with memories of the near tragedy.

She stopped. Her hands covered her ears as she heard the roar of the engine and the twang of the rope. The coppery taste of fear still lingered in her mouth. She couldn't get the memory out of her head.

And Nick, she thought, remembering the utterly forlorn expression on his face as the ambulance had pulled away from the dock, leaving him behind. Poor Nick had been beside himself with anguish. He'd completely lost his patience and self-control.

She'd heard one of the bystanders say, "Don't go near the big guy. I asked the boy's mother what happened and he growled at me like he wanted to tear off my head with his bare hands!"

Without actually having heard what Nick had muttered, she knew he felt as much to blame as she did. But it wasn't Nick's fault. She'd been the one driving the boat.

The blame for Clay's injuries rested squarely on her shoulders, which sagged under her feelings of guilt.

Engrossed in berating herself, she was unaware that Nick had entered the waiting room until he spoke her name. She heard the tremor in his voice and saw how deathly pale his face appeared.

"Nick, thank goodness. I'm so glad you're here."

He looked stunned for a moment, then he opened his arms and she flew into them.

"Clay spoke to me in the ambulance." She leaned heavily on Nick, feeling as though she'd entered a safe haven when his arms held her tightly against his chest. His hands moved across her back to assuage her misery. "He's up in X-Ray. The doctor will come here when he has the results."

"Concussion?"

"The doctor in the emergency room who examined him didn't think so, but they want to make certain." She felt Nick shudder with relief. "I'd never have forgiven myself if Clay had died because of my carelessness," she said.

Nick's hands moved to her shoulders. When she looked up at him, she couldn't comprehend his expression of disbelief. She felt him sway.

"I have to sit down before I fall down," he said hoarsely.

His knees threatened to buckle. Without her support he wouldn't have made it to a chair. He felt weak, drained, nauseated. Knees spread, his elbows propped on them, he lowered his head and raked his fingers through his hair as the heels of his hands dug into his eyes.

"You should be blaming me," he said hoarsely.

"She did."

"She? Who?"

"Crissy's mother... Velma. She divorced me because Crissy's death was my fault." Nick slammed his fist into his open palm. "Dammit, why didn't I hear her? She must have screamed. Why didn't I check to make certain she wasn't alone in the backyard?"

"Stop it, Nick." She pulled his head against her shoulder. "Crissy's death wasn't your fault. Neither was Clay's accident."

"I can't stop. I can still hear Velma screaming, 'You killed my daughter,' over and over."

"Shh, Nick. She was hysterical. She probably didn't know what she was saying."

"She did," Nick contradicted. "She repeated it from the day of the funeral to the day we appeared in the divorce court. It's the only thing she did say to me. It's what you'd be saying if Clay had died."

"I'm not Velma. Don't compare me with her or Clay with Crissy."

"Why not? You're both mothers who love their children."

''That's where the similarity ends. I know you'd never let anything happen to Clay if it was humanly possible to prevent it. I'd never blame you. If today's accident can be blamed on any one person, blame me. I was driving the boat.''

''I was the lookout.''

''Then blame the person who cut in front of us. The people in that cruiser were so oblivious to what was going on, they didn't even realize they caused the accident.''

Nick shook his head. ''I should have seen them in time to warn Clay.''

''It wasn't your fault!'' Her voice trembled with intensity. ''Do you hear me?''

''Mrs. Clark?'' The doctor from the emergency room crossed to where Marianne held Nick locked in her comforting arms. ''Good news. Your son has a nasty bump on the head, but no concussion, no internal damage. I would prefer for him to stay overnight, though, just as a precautionary measure.''

''Can we see him?'' Marianne asked, anxiously rising to her feet, but holding on to Nick's hand.

''Give us five minutes and we'll have Clay in a room. The nurse at the desk will be able to give you the number.''

It was difficult for her to believe her good fortune. ''Can I spend the night here with him? Just in case he needs me?''

''That isn't necessary. Clay is young and rugged. A few stitches, a bandage on his head and a mild sedative for his headache aren't going to hold him down for long.'' The doctor grinned. ''He's making jokes with the nurses. His biggest concern is missing baseball practice on Monday.''

"Thank you, doctor." She held out her hand. "I appreciate all you've done for Clay."

"You're welcome." He shook her hand. "And stop worrying. Clay looks healthier than both of you. Maybe I ought to request two more rooms?"

"No, that won't be necessary. Seeing Clay will cure both of us."

Marianne managed a stiff polite smile, but her heart still ached for Nick. Intuitively, she knew the guilt he still carried over his daughter's death was forcing him to shoulder the blame for Clay's accident as well.

"You'd better go alone," Nick said, his eyes following the doctor.

"No. I won't. You have to see for yourself that Clay is going to survive." She tugged on his hand. "This accident wasn't your fault, Nicholas King. I was the one driving the boat and I should have seen the wake coming at us."

He shook his head, which caused a ringing sensation in his ears. "You aren't to blame."

"Are you afraid Clay is going to blame you?" She must have been right on target because Nick clenched his hand on hers. "Clay isn't going to shout accusations at you. He thinks it's his fault for showing off."

"That's ridiculous," Nick muttered, unable to fathom why neither of them blamed him.

He could have prevented Clay's accident just as he could have prevented his daughter's drowning. Once both of them thought about it, they'd put the blame where it belonged, on him.

Marianne had been gradually regaining her mental equilibrium since she talked to the doctor. She said firmly, "I'm not going to stand here and argue with you. Clay will think you're still angry with him. He doesn't need to be worried. We're going to go to Clay's room, together. Period."

Shortly after Marianne acquired Clay's room number from the nurse, she and Nick entered his room.

Clay grinned sheepishly and lightly touched the square bandage on his head. "You're going to have to clean my fish, Mom. The doc says I get to sleep over."

"I'll just throw it in the freezer whole," she quipped, trying to match Clay's lightheartedness. Tears filled her eyes. She blinked to keep them from spilling from the corners. It upset Clay to see her cry.

"I'll clean it," Nick volunteered, bracing himself for Clay's accusations.

Marianne crossed the room to the side of Clay's hospital bed. She needed to touch him to feel absolutely certain he'd survived. His pasty pallor had changed to a rosy flush. She had to look closely to see his freckles. His green eyes were as wet as her own.

"I think I need a hug, son," she entreated softly.

"Me, too," he whispered. "I was kind of scared."

Marianne lowered the hospital bed's railing and sat down. "Yeah. Me, too."

Nick had to avert his eyes. He could taste salty tears dripping down the back of his throat. He'd nearly cost Marianne the life of her precious son. The life of a child who had become precious to him, too.

"Nick?" Clay stretched one arm to the man he hoped was still his friend. "I could use a hug from you, too."

Unable to refuse Clay's request, Nick bent over the rail and wrapped his arms around Marianne's son. "I'm sorry," he murmured. "I should have taken better care of you."

"I should have taken better care of myself," Clay corrected, giving Nick a light tap on the arm with his fist. "I nearly broke my neck the last time I tried that stunt at Brad's lake house."

Nick straightened as Clay yawned.

"I'm real sleepy. Must be the shot they gave me in the you-know-where," Clay said, growing drowsy. His eyelids closed. "Don't forget about my fish."

"Get well...Clay," Nick whispered, almost slipping and calling him son.

With a trace of a smile, Clay answered, "See you."

Reluctant to leave, Marianne lightly kissed his forehead, then moved off the bed and lifted the railing back into place.

"He's asleep." Nick motioned for her to go out into the hall with him. "Do you want to stay? I'll go get a change of clothes for you."

She glanced at her stained cover-up and the smear of dried mud on her leg, then back at Clay. "I'll go get cleaned up. Later I'll call the nurses' station. If Clay is awake or sleeping restlessly, I'll come back."

Refreshed from her shower, Marianne slipped into a pair of cotton shorts and a plain blue top. Concerned for Nick, she went toward the kitchen. He'd been exceptionally quiet on the drive home. The minute he stepped from the car, he'd retrieved Clay's fish. Other than saying he'd fillet the bass while she cleaned up, he'd been completely silent.

He wasn't in the kitchen where she'd thought he'd be. A chill of apprehension shivered across her skin. "Nick?"

"In here," he answered from the family room.

She noticed he'd changed from his swimsuit into a pair of shorts and a clean pullover shirt. His clothing had changed, but his melancholy mood lingered. He sat in Clay's favorite leather chair, staring up at the ceiling.

"What are you thinking about?" she asked, sinking to the floor beside his legs and looking up at him.

"Clay. You. Me." Crissy. Velma. He could see his life's history repeating itself. It scared the hell out of him.

Resting the side of her face on his knee, Marianne said, "Start with what you're feeling about Clay."

"I had this mixed-up idea in my head that if I stopped myself from caring for Clay, I wouldn't be torn apart if anything happened to him." He dropped his head back on the chair. His hand listlessly stroked her hair as though touching the silky texture gave him succor. "That's a crazy notion, isn't it? Like lifting a ton of weights over my head and being surprised when I can't hold them up forever."

"Impossible?"

"Yeah. Clay reminds me of myself when I was his age. I thought I was invincible, too. Nothing could hurt me."

"Accidents happen, Nick." She addressed her own feelings of guilt as she spoke. "It's not as though we deliberately planned to take the boat out so Clay would be hurt. No one could have foreseen that Clay would try a somersault just as a wake came out of nowhere. It was an unfortunate set of circumstances that resulted in an accident. What we have to keep uppermost in our minds is that Clay is going to be fine."

This time he'll recover, Nick thought. But what about the next time?

"Clay was lucky this time," he said. When it came to the children he loved, his luck had all been bad. How could Marianne trust him to share in the responsibility for Clay's safety? He didn't trust himself!

"You aren't the only one who distrusts luck, Nick. Don't you think I'd like to wrap Clay in cotton and put him on a shelf where I'd know he was safe? Do you think he'd allow that?"

"No."

"So what else can I do? Worry myself sick every time he walks out the door? Clay gripes about me being overly protective now. Do you think he'll allow you to watch his every footstep so he won't step into one of life's potholes?"

"No."

"Nick, look at me." She waited until their eyes met. His dark eyes were haunted by shadows from the past and filled with pain over what had happened that afternoon. "I'm as afraid of something happening to Clay as you are. But I can't let fear dominate the future. Do you know what Clay would say to you? Get real, man. Yeah, that's the expression the kids use. And it fits this situation."

She placed his hand against the base of her neck. "What do you feel?"

"Your heartbeat." His thumb felt the steady pulsation of blood pumping from her heart.

"You can't make my heart keep beating." Her hands moved to the sides of his face as she rose to her knees. "You have limitations. I have limitations. Regardless of how well we control other facets of our lives, we don't have control over life and death. That's one limitation we must accept."

Nick dropped to his knees and crushed her against his chest. She could feel the tremors that shook him.

"I know," he whispered. "My head hears what you are saying and I know what you've said is true, but my heart denies the truth. I'm scared, Marianne. Scared something will happen to Clay. Scared you'll point the finger of guilt at me. Scared you'll stop caring for me."

"I love you, Nick." She locked her arms around his neck, bonding them together. "I didn't want to fall in love with you. I didn't plan it. It was an accident. All accidents aren't fatal though...unless you don't... love...me." With each pause she kissed his neck, jaw and brow.

"I do love you, so much the thought of losing you..."

Marianne stopped his fear the only way she knew how. She kissed him with all the love and faith and trust that she felt for him. His lips frantically devoured what she gave, as though her kisses would restore his faith in himself.

"What am I going to do?" he groaned, tormented by self-doubt and frustration. His hands scoured her bare skin where her top had separated from her shorts. "I don't want to lose you, but what happens when...?"

"Shhh." She nipped the bow of his lower lip. "I trust you. As long as we're together the future will take care of itself. Love me, Nick. Please."

He wanted to believe her. God, he wanted to believe her. He wanted to forget the horrors of the past and build a future whose foundation was made of only the good memories Marianne had compelled him to remember. Maybe...?

Marianne stopped his frenzied thoughts with her delicate hands and the sweet honeyed taste of her mouth. She touched him with a mastery born from her love. With hot, wet kisses she attempted to wash away his heartache and grief. Not because the death of his child had been unimportant, only because the weight of his worries barred him from attaining happiness.

She tugged his shirt over his head and cast it aside, along with her top. He neither assisted or resisted her efforts. He seemed content just to hold her.

No, her heart rebelled. She had to shake him up, shock him out of his complacency. She wanted him whole-hearted, unwilling to settle for less than being his best.

"Nick, what you said earlier—at the lake... Is it true? Do you love me?"

"You know I do," he whispered, overwhelmed by the feel of her soft body next to his.

"I don't believe you."

His eyes jerked open. "What?"

"You heard me." She pushed against his shoulders. "You're lying to me and you're lying to yourself."

"I am not a liar. I told you the day you chased me down at the park that I was falling for you."

Marianne glared at him. He'd denied her accusation, but she could still hear a note of resignation in his voice. She wanted emotion, be it cold anger or hot passion or heartwarming laughter. She didn't give a damn how hot or how cold, but lukewarm was not acceptable.

"*I* chased *you?*" she goaded. "Don't let the billboard go to your head. I turned you down so many times you should have felt like a quilt."

A muscle in his cheek quivered. Was it the beginning of a grimace or a smile? She couldn't tell which.

"Are you deliberately trying to pick a fight with me?" Nick asked, uncertain as to why she'd changed from kitten to tigress. His hand swept from her shoulder to her thigh. "I'd rather make love."

"Passively?" she inquired, raising her eyebrow. "When lovemaking is one-sided, the correct terminology is passive sex for you and lousy sex for me."

"Shut up, Marianne." His eyes blazed. "You don't know the first thing above passive sex. I do. It's when a woman's body is more rigid than her lover's. It's when a thin sheet provides more warmth than a naked body. It's when the air is so thick with anguish the taste of ashes clings to your tongue. Velma made me an expert on passive sex." He lowered her hand until she intimately touched him. "I get hot and hard just looking at you. Your sweetness lingers on my tongue long after the lovemaking. I love you, woman. We may both regret it, soon, but I do love you."

"Regret it?" Marianne searched his face anxiously. "Clay apologized, on his own. Clay won't cause regrets."

"Clay isn't the problem. I'm the problem. I've carried this grief so long I don't know how to put it down. And with the grief comes fear. I'm not certain I'll ever be able to get over my fear of something happening to Clay because I love him."

"Will you regret making love to me, too?"

He didn't answer, but he took possession of her lips as though he could solve his insurmountable problems by loving her, by making them inseparable. He became a part of her quickly to affirm his love in a way she could never doubt or question. Buried deep inside of her, feeling her pulsate around him, he made love to her at a feverish pace that swirled them both beyond the boundaries of regret.

Chapter Fifteen

Nick felt the weight of the world rest on his shoulders as he waited in his car while Marianne checked Clay out of the hospital. He'd planned on being with her, but the closer they came to the hospital the faster his heart had started to pound. Beads of cold sweat dampened his brow. Beneath his jacket his shirt clung to the contours of his muscular body, which was drenched with perspiration. His stomach felt hollow, as though he'd fasted for weeks.

Anxiety attack, Nick self-diagnosed silently, as he rocked his forehead against arms folded on the rim of the steering wheel. Sports figures often had them before important competitions. He'd never experienced one.

The excuse he'd given Marianne for not accompanying her was lame. She had to have known there was nothing wrong with his car. But how could he tell her the truth? The thought of going into the hospital and seeing Clay with a white bandage on his head sent quivers of panic through his mind.

Last night after they made love, while Marianne was on the phone talking to the nurse at the hospital, he'd relived the accident. In vivid detail he imagined Clay grotesquely ricocheting across the water, his arms and legs askew, with the hydroslide jetting up from the water, then crashing down on Clay.

"Clay could easily have broken his neck," Nick had agonized quietly.

Then he would have felt the pain of the death of two children. That would have driven him over the brink of sanity. Someone would have had to lock him up and throw away the key.

He rolled his head to one side as he heard the sound of Marianne's high heels striking the concrete. He avoided looking at her and Clay by staring at the key as he started the engine.

"Hi, Nick," Clay chirped. He opened the passenger's door for his mother, then jumped into the back seat. "Guess what? I get to play hooky from school today!"

Nick tightened his facial muscles into what he hoped would serve as a smile. "How are you feeling?"

"Super." He glanced at his mother, wondering if he'd given the wrong answer for a kid who wasn't going to school. What the heck! He could hardly wait to tell Brad and Peanut about riding in an ambulance with the horn blaring and the lights blinking just like in those shows on television. They'd think it was cool, real cool. "Maybe I ought to go to school, huh?"

"Not today," Marianne said decisively. "The doctor said to give you a day to get over the soreness in your muscles."

"Don't you have to go to work?" Clay buckled his seat belt. "It's Monday."

"Jayne is filling in for me." She twisted her shoulders and neck until she could get another good look at Clay. His green eyes were bright; his cheeks were rosy. The size of his bandage had been reduced to a one-inch square. He looked terrific, especially with that impish face he'd made at her.

As she straightened in her seat, she noticed that Nick looked ghastly, as though he were the one who'd gotten out of the hospital. Or on his way there, she amended silently.

"Clay, did you eat breakfast?" Nick asked, breaking the brief silence.

"Yeah." Clay groaned comically. "It was early and awful. Soupy eggs and soggy toast."

"I'll fix pancakes when we get home, son. Nick, would you like to stay for breakfast?"

Nick glanced in the rearview mirror, quickly returning his eyes to the road. The stark whiteness of the bandage taped on Clay's reddish hair made him feel nauseated.

"I have to go straight to work," he replied, his lips barely able to move.

"You're sure you can't play hooky, too?" Clay piped up from the back seat. "You might be able to beat me at Ping-Pong . . . if you're lucky."

Lucky? Nick mused. He'd used his quota of good luck yesterday when Clay hadn't broken his neck. "Not today, Clay. There's a big shipment arriving at the loading docks. I have to be there." Nick turned right on Marianne's street. "Maybe later. We'll see."

Marianne stared at Nick. Her son wasn't the only one who knew the meaning of "we'll see"—it meant no, Nick wouldn't be coming to their house. She wanted to ask him why not, but couldn't in front of Clay.

A strong sense of foreboding assailed her. She wasn't certain she wanted to know. He'd been aloof, taciturn, uncommunicative, speaking only when spoken to, since she'd provoked him into making passionate love with her. It didn't take a mental giant to realize Nick was still struggling with his reaction to Clay's accident.

From her own experiences she knew mental wars were the most difficult wars waged. No one could help. They had to be fought alone.

Watching Nick struggle made her feel helpless. But what else could she do? She'd reasoned with him, told him he wasn't to blame and shown him how much she loved him. There was nothing else she could do, was there?

Marianne touched Nick's sleeve. Softly she said, "Come over when you can, okay?" Her heart skipped a beat then slowed when she saw him shake his head.

"I can't," he whispered. "Not until I work through my problems."

"Hey, stop!" Clay said. "You're going to miss our driveway." As Nick swerved the car and Clay swayed to the side, he added, "Good thing I had my seat belt on, huh, Mom?"

Clay was out of the car before Marianne could formulate a reply. She'd watched Nick's face turn deathly pale.

"Nothing happened, Nick."

"It could have."

"It didn't."

"Dammit, Marianne. I can't live with the fear of causing another accident. You'd hate me if something happened to Clay." Like Velma does, he added silently. "We went through this last night. This isn't Clay's problem or your problem. It's mine. I have to cope with it."

Her fingers clenched on his arm. "Do you expect me to sit passively by and watch you don a hair shirt? Haven't you suffered and grieved enough?"

Nick inhaled deeply, held his breath, then expelled it. "No."

Recoiling as though he'd knocked the wind from her, she leaned back against the door. Don't shut me out, she cried silently, feeling as though a coffin lid were slamming shut on their love.

She was going to cry. Dammit, she wouldn't. He'd only feel sorry for her. She had too much pride to let that happen. Hurt turned to anger, the kind of anger only a redhead could understand.

"Then go ahead and run, Nick. Run hard and fast. It's a race you'll never win. There will be no trophy at the finish line."

Nick clenched the wheel to keep from reaching for his last hope of salvation. He backed from her driveway. Let her hate me now, he thought, hearing the door slam. At least she has Clay.

Inside the kitchen Clay set the box of pancake mix and bottle of syrup on the counter next to the milk and egg he'd taken from the refrigerator. He heard the door slam and glanced toward it, surprised. His mother never slammed doors.

"I'm in the kitchen, Mom. Did Nick...?" He stopped in the middle of his question when he saw the expression on his mother's face. "Did you two have a fight or somethin'?"

"Yeah, or something." She braced her arms on the counter and took a deep breath. She glanced up at the ceiling to keep from crying. "He won't be back, Clay."

"Because of me?" he asked, putting his arm around his mother's waist.

"No, sweetheart," she lied. No, it isn't a lie, she silently corrected. It wasn't Clay's fault or hers. This time the blame and guilt did belong to Nick. "Nick's little girl accidentally drowned. He's still grieving for her. His problems don't have anything to do with you or me."

"Does that mean he won't be coming to see us?" Clay asked, realizing he was truly saddened by the likelihood.

"We'll see." She hugged Clay. "We'll see."

Time passed, with only Clay's baseball games marking the passing weeks. At Marianne's office, Mondays and Fridays remained constant, hectic. Beach flu struck with regularity. But for Marianne, work had become...*work*. Every day without Nick seemed like eternity.

Standing in front of her full-length mirror, Marianne changed hats, deciding not to wear the one she'd worn the night she met Nick, even though it was the perfect match for her dress.

She tightened the wide belt another notch. She'd lost pounds she could ill afford. Even Clay had commented on her picking at her food. She'd become the featherweight he'd once jokingly called her. Nothing tasted good. She'd think of Nick and only taste the hurting words she'd hurled at him. Then she'd push her plate aside.

"Mom, we're going to be late for church if you don't hurry!"

Dressed in his Sunday best—navy-blue suit, white shirt, red-striped tie—Clay paced beside the car. Nervously, he slicked back his hair to make certain his rooster tail wasn't sticking up.

Staring at the weight equipment he'd used religiously ever since he'd last seen Nick, he silently declared, today is NK Day. As he'd gone about planning his strategy for a sneak attack on Nick King's flanks, he'd nicknamed the eventful day after the events he'd studied at school—D day, V-J Day and NK Day.

Like it or not, Nick was going to see him if Clay had to drop bombs on this front porch to get the door open. He wanted his mother to stop going around looking like a refugee from a concentration camp.

He made a noise that sounded like a bomb being dropped.

"Bombing the garage won't get it clean," Marianne teased, reminding him of the promise he'd made to clean it. "How about that being the first thing on the agenda when we get home?"

"Can't." Clay studied his mother's face, looking for hints of suspicion. He'd be a war prisoner around here if she found out what he was up to this afternoon. She looked tired, but not suspicious. He ducked inside the car and said, "You said I could go with Jennifer and her parents to the one o'clock movie."

"I forgot." She searched in her purse for her keys. "I'll be right back. I forgot my keys, too."

Clay groaned impatiently. He had a lot of praying to do before he went to Nick's house. He was going to need all the help from up above that he could get!

"Who the hell is that?" Nick growled, wanting to be left alone. Did they have to keep ringing the doorbell? "I'm coming!"

Straightening his shoulders to military erectness, Clay considered saluting Nick. When the door was flung inward so fast it almost sucked him inside, he considered rapid retreat!

"Clay?" Nick's face turned white. "Did something happen to your mother?"

"No. She's fine." Clay looked Nick up and down. He had thought his mother looked bad, but Nick looked terrible. "You look like hell," he blurted, then blushed.

Nick chuckled for the first time in weeks. He raked his fingers across the stubble of whiskers on his chin. "I need a shave."

You need more than a shave, mister, Clay thought silently, managing to keep his mouth shut. He shifted from one foot to the other. Oh God, he prayed, don't make me say what I gotta say out here on the porch!

"Come in, Clay." Nick took him by the forearm and ushered him into the house, giving the boy's muscle a squeeze when he felt it flex beneath his fingers. "You're looking great. You must be wearing out that weight-lifting machine. Can I get you something? A soft drink? Iced tea? Water?"

Clay's mouth was dry. "A soda if it's no bother." His eyes grew big as he glanced around and followed Nick into the kitchen. "Your house is big, real big, huh?"

"Too big for one person." Nick opened the pickled-oak-finished cabinet for a glass. "Ice?"

"Do you mind if I drink it straight from the can? It's fizzier that way."

Nick returned the glass and moved to the refrigerator. If Marianne is okay, what's Clay doing here? he thought. He's so nervous he'd jump out of his suit if I shouted "Boo."

"What will it be? Orange? Grape? Cola?"

Clay wasn't up to making choices. His strategy hadn't gone beyond bombing the front door. Now that he was inside he felt tongue-tied. "Anything."

Remembering that he'd been partial to grape soda as a kid, Nick removed two grape drinks from the refrigerator. "Here you go...uh, Clay." He'd almost slipped again. Gesturing toward the pool area, he said, "Why don't we go outside? There's a breeze coming in off the lake."

Clay was beginning to feel like a puppy dog's tail following along after Nick. He pulled out a chair from the wrought-iron table and glanced toward the lake. The tab on top of the can popped loudly. He poured the contents down his throat.

"Grape is my favorite." He grinned shyly at Nick. "I can almost feel it fizzing in my ears."

"It's one of my favorites, too."

Dropping his eyes, Clay said in a voice barely above a whisper, "I've missed you, Nick. Mom does, too."

"Has she...? Is she...?" Nick didn't know what question to ask first. He had to clear his throat of emotions. "I miss both of you."

"Mom is going to be home this afternoon. Maybe..."

Nick shook his head, unable to speak.

"Is it because of me?" Clay squashed the aluminum can between his hands. "Because I got jealous and ordered you out of the garage?"

"No, Clay." The boy looked miserable, unhappy. Nick felt guilty as hell. He should have called him. He'd wanted to, but hadn't been able to. "You apologized and I accepted your apology. I'm not angry with you or your mother."

"It's your kid, isn't it? Mom told me she died and you were grieving." Clay put the bent can on the table. "I've been doing a lot of thinking about that."

"So have I, Clay, so have I." When Nick wasn't thinking about Marianne and Clay, it was all he thought of. The good memories were the only thing that kept him functioning.

"Well, you know how they say you can't really understand how another person feels until you've walked in their shoes? I put myself in your kid's shoes, and do you know what I thought?" Clay paused, but Nick didn't respond. "I thought if I was your little girl and I was up in heaven looking down at you . . . I'd be sad. I'd think you blamed me for drowning."

Nick stared at him as though he were completely nuts, but Clay kept talking. "I'd think you were unhappy because I'd been bad. That's what I'd think."

Clay watched Nick knot his fingers together. "And I know you say that it isn't my fault you and Mom can't be together and be happy, but Mom probably sees me and how reckless I am—" Clay swallowed hard "—and how that scares you and makes you unhappy . . . and she probably thinks I should try to be more careful."

He waited and waited for Nick to say something, anything, but Nick just keep staring at him. "I'd feel lousy if something happened to me and I knew my mother would always be alone and lonely because of an accident. How do you think your daughter would feel right now if she knew you were afraid to risk loving us because of her?''

In the thousands of hours Nick had thought about Crissy, he'd never seen the situation from her angle. Crissy had been so full of love and life. She would be unhappy if she saw him. She wouldn't want him to grieve forever... to be alone and lonely.

Self-consciously Clay rubbed his damp palms on his thighs. He'd said everything he had to say. Nick still sat there like a stone. Clay wanted to reach over and feel his heart to see if it was still ticking, but he didn't.

"I guess I'd better go." He jumped to his feet and strode toward the kitchen. Nick still hadn't moved a muscle when he turned to say goodbye. "I don't suppose you want to see me play catcher at the all-star baseball game next Saturday, do you?"

Nick climbed the wooden bleachers during the bottom of the second inning. He was in the midst of another anxiety attack, but this time it stemmed from a totally different cause. Squeezing between two sets of parents and sitting down, he glanced heavenward.

Somehow Nick knew that if Crissy was watching over him, she'd be smiling because he was doing the right thing.

"Strike two!" the umpire shouted, sticking up two fingers on his right hand.

Clay gave the signal to the pitcher—low on the inside corner. He'd played ball against this kid before today. He was a sucker for a golfer's pitch.

Squatting so low that his you-know-what was getting sandy, he waited for the windup, the pitch. The ball whizzed across the plate. The batter swung and missed.

The ump called, "Strike three! You're out!"

Springing up, Clay tossed his mask off his face and wheeled around to see if Nick was in the bleachers. His face broke into a sunshine smile as he located him. But why was he in the visitors' section? he wondered. Why wasn't he sitting with his mother on the home team's side?

As he walked back to the dugout, Clay gestured from Nick to where his mother sat.

Uh-oh, he thought silently when he noticed that his mother's eyes had followed where he pointed, and that her smile had faded.

Marianne leaned against the bleachers bench back of her. What was Nick doing at the all-star game? Why hadn't he called and at least warned her that he was going to attend the game?

She glanced toward the dugout. Whatever was going on, her son was in on it, that was for certain. Clay hadn't been antsy until he saw Nick.

She lifted the wide brim of her straw hat far enough to fill her eyes with Nick without his knowing he was being visually devoured. He looks good enough to be on a billboard or a television commercial, she thought as she self-consciously ran one hand over her hips.

The mother sitting next to her said, "Isn't that your son coming up to bat?"

"Yes, it is," Marianne replied with pride in her voice. "He's the cleanup batter."

She grinned when she heard Nick shout, "Knock it out of the ballpark, slugger." One glance told her that the people seated around Nick were not appreciative of his enthusiasm.

Seeing the worried expression on Clay's face as he glanced up at her, she gave him the thumbs-up signal.

Whatever arrangement her son had made with Nick, she was happy to see him. She didn't mind in the least that Clay had swapped his baseball uniform for Cupid's wings!

At the bottom of the ninth inning with the score 5–4 in favor of the home team, all Clay's team had to do was keep the other team from scoring. There was a runner on third, but the team batting had two out.

One more out, Marianne thought, and Clay will be an all-star trophy winner.

Tension was high. In the top of the inning, when Clay had rounded third base and made a beeline for home plate, Marianne had thought the parents sitting around Nick would turn violent as he stood and cheered at the top of his lungs for Clay to "slide, slide, slide."

Excited by Clay's scoring what could be the winning run and by the prospect of talking to Nick, Marianne had flung her hat high into the air as the umpire yelled, "Safe!"

Clay beamed a triumphant smile at his mother while he dusted off the back of his uniform. He laughed when he saw the killing stares being shot at Nick. "You'd better move over to the winning side, Nick!" he shouted, which turned the glares toward him.

Realizing Clay was right, Nick quickly moved to the end of the row of seats and vaulted to the ground.

He considered going boldly over and sitting next to Marianne, but he wasn't certain what her reaction would be. He'd almost started a riot already. He didn't need to stir up Marianne's redheaded temper. He moved to the high fence that protected the bleachers from stray balls and stood there watching the second half of the inning.

From this angle he could see Clay hugging the plate, glove in position to catch the pitch. One more strike, he chanted. One more strike. He noticed Clay fidgeting up and down. Keep your head down, Nick wanted to yell.

The pitcher delivered the ball low. Nick saw the batter dip his bat and start to swing. At the same moment Clay bobbed his head.

Nick feared Clay would get clobbered with the bat. He inhaled sharply.

The batter swung and missed, his bat missing Clay's helmet by a tiny fraction of an inch.

Nick exhaled, and felt a sudden flare of joy.

Yeah, he thought, I was scared for a second, but that's natural. I wasn't petrified. I don't feel faint and my knees are still locked, holding me upright.

"Strike three!" the umpire roared. "You're out. The game is over!"

The players went wild, as did the parents on the home side of the bleachers.

Nick turned toward the place where Marianne had been sitting. She was no longer there. Now he did feel a bit dizzy and his legs did feel watery.

But that's normal, too, he thought. He had every right to be scared to death that Marianne wouldn't take him back, that she no longer loved him.

"C'mon, Mom! I've got somebody I want you to meet!" Clay practically had to get behind his mother and push her once she spotted Nick. When she was less than three feet away from Nick, but still on the opposite side of the chain link fence, Clay stopped. "Mom, this is Nick King. Nick, this is my mother, Marianne Clark."

Each of them stared at the other without moving or speaking.

"Now listen, guys," Clay scolded. "I went to a lot of trouble to get my two favorite people together. Look at his shoes, Mom."

Marianne lowered her eyes from Nick's intense gaze. He was wearing his lucky shoes—with new shoestrings that had pink hearts on them.

"You gotta be in love to wear something like that. Don't blow it," Clay preached. "I'm going to the refreshment stand to be with the other guys. Brad's offered to take me home after the ice cream party at Brittle's house. By the time I get home...in a couple of hours or so, I expect you two to have made up. Got it?"

Marianne grinned. Clay's lecture sounded very much like ones she'd given him when he quarreled with Brad. "Got it."

"Got it," Nick said, returning her smile, feeling as though he'd swallowed the sun.

He raised his hand and flattened it against the fence. Slowly, Marianne raised her hand to touch him. She curled her fingers around his.

"Whooooopeee!" Clay took of leaping, skipping, jumping into the air.

Unwilling to break contact, both of them dragged their fingers across the fence as they walked to the edge of it. Nick held his arms open. Marianne walked into them as though she were coming home after a long arduous trip.

"I've been in hell these past few months, but I'm back, thanks to your son," he said softly. "He made me see things through Crissy's eyes. She wouldn't want me to grieve forever."

"What would she want?" Marianne asked, a bit hesitant, a bit shy.

"She'd want me to be family friendly. She'd want you and me and Clay to be a happy family."

Holding Marianne tightly in his arms, he knew he was finally a whole man again. The weight of his grief had lifted shortly after Clay talked to him. Now, as Marianne wrapped her arms around him, hugging him, he felt as though he were weightless, as though he could fly.

"Would you like to go home for a while?" She smiled up at Nick. "A long while."

"How long?" No longer able to resist, he brushed his mouth across her lips. "Until death do us part?"

Certain that any man who'd gone to hell and back had the strength and endurance to love both her and Clay for eternity, she wrapped her arms around his neck and asked, "Is that a proposal, Mr. King?"

Although his head nodded yes, he said, "Me? Propose while we're standing on the baseball field? How unromantic! Shame on you, sweetheart."

"What could be more romantic than having the man I love proposing to me in front of a grandstand filled with cheering baseball fans?"

"The stands have emptied, love. Everyone must be at the concession stand or have left for home."

"Oh," she sighed, oblivious to anyone other than Nick.

He lifted her hand to his lips, then started walking toward his car. "We'll come back for your car later. Right now I don't want to let you out of my sight."

Grinning, she matched his stride until they were both jogging, laughing as they ran to the parking lot.

In spite of his romantic intentions, once they were in the privacy of his car Nick couldn't wait any longer. He felt as though he'd waited for aeons as it was.

The key he should have used to start the engine unlocked the glove compartment. He removed a small blue velvet box. Slowly, he opened it for her to see.

"It's beautiful," she whispered. Her eyes widened in awe of the beautiful diamond solitaire winking up at her. She looked at Nick, searching his face for any trace of doubts. The love shining from his eyes was far more dazzling than the diamond. They held a promise of the happily-ever-after he'd spoken of the night they met.

"Will you marry me, love?" His voice was husky with emotion. "Let me be part of your family? I love both you and Clay."

"Yes! Yes! Yes!" She was in his arms, kissing him before the final "yes" had passed her lips.

*   *   *   *   *

Silhouette Special Edition®

COMING NEXT MONTH

#697 NAVY BABY—Debbie Macomber
Hard-living sailor Riley never thought he'd settle down with a preacher's daughter. But he couldn't steer clear of Hannah and their navy baby, though it meant riding out the storm of his life.

#698 SLOW LARKIN'S REVENGE—Christine Rimmer
Local bad boy Winslow Larkin, was back in town...and out to seduce the one woman who'd almost tamed his heart years ago. But loving Violet Windemere proved much sweeter than revenge!

#699 TOP OF THE MOUNTAIN—Mary Curtis
The memory of Lili Jamison's high school passion lived on in her love child. Reuniting with Brad Hollingsworth rekindled the actual fire...and the guilt of her eleven-year-old secret.

#700 ROMANCING RACHEL—Natalie Bishop
Rachel Stone had her hands full raising her stepson on her own. When strong, stern Tyrrell Rafferty III entered the picture, he completed the family portrait...better than she knew!

#701 THE MAN SHE MARRIED—Tracy Sinclair
Teenager Dorian Merrill had fled her hometown and broken marriage to find her fortune. Now the *woman* was back, a penthouse success—but lured to the other side of town by the man she married.

#702 CHILD OF THE STORM—Diana Whitney
When Megan O'Connor lost her beloved sister, she vowed not to lose her seven-year-old nephew. Not even to his father, who resurfaced to claim him...and Megan's heart.

AVAILABLE THIS MONTH:

#691 OBSESSION
Lisa Jackson

#692 FAMILY FRIENDLY
Jo Ann Algermissen

#693 THE HEALING TOUCH
Christine Flynn

#694 A REAL CHARMER
Jennifer Mikels

#695 ANNIE IN THE MORNING
Curtiss Ann Matlock

#696 LONGER THAN...
Erica Spindler

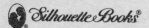

Take 4 bestselling love stories FREE

Plus get a FREE surprise gift!

SILHOUETTE®
OFFICIAL SWEEPSTAKES
RULES

NO PURCHASE NECESSARY

1. To enter, complete an Official Entry Form or 3"× 5" index card by hand-printing, in plain block letters, your complete name, address, phone number and age, and mailing it to: Silhouette Fashion A Whole New You Sweepstakes, P.O. Box 9056, Buffalo, NY 14269-9056.

   No responsibility is assumed for lost, late or misdirected mail. Entries must be sent separately with first class postage affixed, and be received no later than December 31, 1991 for eligibility.

2. Winners will be selected by D.L. Blair, Inc., an independent judging organization whose decisions are final, in random drawings to be held on January 30, 1992 in Blair, NE at 10:00 a.m. from among all eligible entries received.

3. The prizes to be awarded and their approximate retail values are as follows: Grand Prize — A brand-new Ford Explorer 4×4 plus a trip for two (2) to Hawaii, including round-trip air transportation, six (6) nights hotel accommodation, a $1,400 meal/spending money stipend and $2,000 cash toward a new fashion wardrobe (approximate value: $28,000) or $15,000 cash; two (2) Second Prizes — A trip to Hawaii, including round-trip air transportation, six (6) nights hotel accommodation, a $1,400 meal/spending money stipend and $2,000 cash toward a new fashion wardrobe (approximate value: $11,000) or $5,000 cash; three (3) Third Prizes — $2,000 cash toward a new fashion wardrobe. All prizes are valued in U.S. currency. Travel award air transportation is from the commercial airport nearest winner's home. Travel is subject to space and accommodation availability, and must be completed by June 30, 1993. Sweepstakes offer is open to residents of the U.S. and Canada who are 21 years of age or older as of December 31, 1991, except residents of Puerto Rico, employees and immediate family members of Torstar Corp., its affiliates, subsidiaries, and all agencies, entities and persons connected with the use, marketing, or conduct of this sweepstakes. All federal, state, provincial, municipal and local laws apply. Offer void wherever prohibited by law. Taxes and/or duties, applicable registration and licensing fees, are the sole responsibility of the winners. Any litigation within the province of Quebec respecting the conduct and awarding of a prize may be submitted to the Régie des loteries et courses du Québec. All prizes will be awarded; winners will be notified by mail. No substitution of prizes is permitted.

4. Potential winners must sign and return any required Affidavit of Eligibility/Release of Liability within 30 days of notification. In the event of noncompliance within this time period, the prize may be awarded to an alternate winner. Any prize or prize notification returned as undeliverable may result in the awarding of that prize to an alternate winner. By acceptance of their prize, winners consent to use of their names, photographs or their likenesses for purposes of advertising, trade and promotion on behalf of Torstar Corp. without further compensation. Canadian winners must correctly answer a time-limited arithmetical question in order to be awarded a prize.

5. For a list of winners (available after 3/31/92), send a separate stamped, self-addressed envelope to: Silhouette Fashion A Whole New You Sweepstakes, P.O. Box 4665, Blair, NE 68009.

PREMIUM OFFER TERMS

To receive your gift, complete the Offer Certificate according to directions. Be certain to enclose the required number of "Fashion A Whole New You" proofs of product purchase (which are found on the last page of every specially marked "Fashion A Whole New You" Silhouette or Harlequin romance novel). Requests must be received no later than December 31, 1991. Limit: four (4) gifts per name, family, group, organization or address. Items depicted are for illustrative purposes only and may not be exactly as shown. Please allow 6 to 8 weeks for receipt of order. Offer good while quantities of gifts last. In the event an ordered gift is no longer available, you will receive a free, previously unpublished Silhouette or Harlequin book for every proof of purchase you have submitted with your request, plus a refund of the postage and handling charge you have included. Offer good in the U.S. and Canada only.   SLFW · SWPR

SILHOUETTE® OFFICIAL SWEEPSTAKES ENTRY FORM

4-FWSES-2

Complete and return this Entry Form immediately – the more entries you submit, the better your chances of winning!

- Entries must be received by **December 31, 1991.**
- A Random draw will take place on **January 30, 1992.**
- No purchase necessary.

Yes, I want to win a FASHION A WHOLE NEW YOU Sensuous and Adventurous prize from Silhouette:

Name _____ Telephone _____ Age _____

Address _____

City _____ State _____ Zip _____

Return Entries to: **Silhouette FASHION A WHOLE NEW YOU,**
P.O. Box 9056, Buffalo, NY 14269-9056   © 1991 Harlequin Enterprises Limited

PREMIUM OFFER

To receive your free gift, send us the required number of proofs-of-purchase from any specially marked FASHION A WHOLE NEW YOU Silhouette or Harlequin Book with the Offer Certificate properly completed, plus a check or money order (do not send cash) to cover postage and handling payable to Silhouette FASHION A WHOLE NEW YOU Offer. We will send you the specified gift.

OFFER CERTIFICATE

Item	A. SENSUAL DESIGNER VANITY BOX COLLECTION (set of 4) (Suggested Retail Price $60.00)	B. ADVENTUROUS TRAVEL COSMETIC CASE SET (set of 3) (Suggested Retail Price $25.00)
# of proofs-of-purchase	18	12
Postage and Handling	$3.50	$2.95
Check one	☐	☐

Name _____

Address _____

City _____ State _____ Zip _____

Mail this certificate, designated number of proofs-of-purchase and check or money order for postage and handling to: **Silhouette FASHION A WHOLE NEW YOU Gift Offer,** P.O. Box 9057, Buffalo, NY 14269-9057. Requests must be received by December 31, 1991.

ONE PROOF-OF-PURCHASE

4-FWSEP-2

To collect your fabulous free gift you must include the necessary number of proofs-of-purchase with a properly completed Offer Certificate.

© 1991 Harlequin Enterprises Limited

See previous page for details.